THE OCTOPUS MURDERS

Jennet Clyde

CHAPTER ONE

I opened the door of our meeting room to find Annabel's body slumped across the desk. Her throat had been cut, and her bright red blood gathered in a pool on the floor underneath.

I'd never seen a dead body before, and for just a second it didn't look real. One of Annabel's jokes, surely. She wrote plays. One had been staged at *Òran Mór* in Glasgow. She'd also had a few radio scripts commissioned by Radio 4. They always had a touch of the macabre. This was her acting out a scene to see if it was convincing. That thick red blood oozing out of her neck was too theatrical to be authentic. As for the neck wound, that had to be some kind of make-up. Latex, maybe. Any moment now, Annabel would stand up and laugh.

But she didn't. Her face was white and lifeless, and her eyes were staring up at the ceiling, pale, dead eyes, which brought me swiftly and brutally to the realisation that Annabel would never laugh again.

"Will you let me in, dear? My feet are killing me." Vee Kirk tried to push past me, but I held her back roughly. "Why, Mirren, what are you doing?"

"You can't come in here, Vee."

"I can't what?" Vee was the oldest member of the Port Gowrie writers' group and wasn't used to be being told what she couldn't do. Seventy-five and still writing, mainly short stories for magazines like *People's Friend*. "Mirren, what's wrong? You've gone pale?"

Billie May came running up the stairs, her pale blond hair

flecked with ash highlights, her green eyes wide. I watched her face go out of focus for a moment, and I knew if I didn't hold on to something I was going to faint. I grasped hold of the door frame and took a deep breath, still barring Vee, and anyone else, from getting in.

"Billie, your phone..." Suddenly I was breathless. I made a phone pressing motion with my thumb. "Phone the police, quick."

"But, what?" came Billie.

"Accident... Been an accident," I gasped. No wonder I concentrated on writing comedy. An accident? Like anybody cuts their own throat.

"But who?"

"Billie just call the police!" I snarled. Billie practically jumped back down the stairs. She'd never seen me snap. I was the funny one, but there was nothing funny in this.

Vee was determined to push past me. "Get out of my way, Mirren. Let me see."

So I did. What right did I have, after all, to hold back a grown woman, no matter how hideous the sight that awaited her. Horrific death, after all, should hold no terrors for her. Her last piece, published in *Scots Magazine*, was a history of hanging in Scotland, '*Death by the Rope.*'

I leaned against the wall and waited. Seconds later, I heard a thud. Vee had fainted, as I knew she would.

One by one, the rest of the group arrived for our usual Tuesday evening meeting. Doctor Bonnar came first. He was our treasurer. Professionally, he'd written for medical journals, and for top newspapers, but the work he was most proud of was *PanzerKommander*, a pulp war novel that had been published a few years back. The doctor immediately took matters in hand. He helped me carry Vee's unconscious body into the hall, then he examined Annabel and pronounced her dead. He tutted when I muttered, "On what evidence do you base that?" Then he posted himself at the door to turn away the rest of our group as they arrived.

"I'm afraid," he told one and all. "That Mrs DeVere, our President, has suffered an incident." Definitive medical articles he might excel in, but when it came to real life there was no one like a doctor for hedging round the truth.

Only certain members of our group were entrusted with the facts. Elsa Fordyce, our secretary and self-published romantasy sensation, was one. Thanks to her newfound fame, and the Amazon cash that kept rolling in, she'd started flaunting increasing amounts of flashy clothes and jewellery. And it suited her. She was definitely the prettiest of us all, with her slim build and her short slick brown hair, always curled neatly to the side to frame her heart-shaped face. Now with added style, the books were pouring out of Elsa. She'd published five this year already. Pouring like... it would be cruel of me to say, diarrhoea. But the thought does come to mind. I thought the books were awful, as romances, that is, and fantasies, though as unintentional comedies they were priceless.

Lisette Bonvieux was another. She was as Scottish as I was, but her father was French, and had left her a more exotic name than mine: Mary Mirren Murdoch. Lisette was our youngest member, but was just coming into her own with some cracking short stories, one of which had been published in a prestigious US mystery magazine. Immediately she whipped out her notebook and started jotting down every sensational detail. If that's what makes a born writer, I plead not guilty to being one. The last thing I could think of, as I sat on the top step cradling Vee's head in my lap waiting for the cops, was my writing. All I could think of was who would have done such a thing to Annabel? She'd never achieved what you would call fame, but she'd earned some money from her writing, which was more than could be said for most. She'd written the local Panto three years in a row, and some of her plays were well used in community drama groups across the country. She'd been our President for two years. A little arty, a bit of a snob, and pretentious, sometimes in the extreme. Sometimes, or maybe often a bit fuddled with gin martinis, but she was generous to all with her advice and her time. I liked Annabel. Or, *had* liked her.

"Was anything stolen?" I asked the doctor, trying to find a motive.

"Yes," he said.

I think I almost breathed a sigh of relief. Here, at least, was a motive, yet I wondered why he was hesitating. "Well, what?"

"Two of her fingers," he answered.

Vee was still unconscious when the police arrived, sprawled across the landing at the top of the stairs. They had to step past us, as I didn't want to move her. On their heels came a young detective. He hesitated in front of me, his dour, unsmiling blue eyes shifting between me and Vee. I was almost about to say cheerily, 'Don't worry, she's not the dead one'. The fact I even thought that shows what a warped sense of humour I have. Fortunately, I was able to hold my tongue.

I was the first to be questioned and was led into another of the many rooms in the community centre. This one held the art club on a Tuesday, and the evidence of their presence was strewn all around. I lifted a couple of canvases from a chair so I could sit down.

"You were the first to arrive?" asked the detective.

I nodded.

He looked too young to be in charge of a murder. I always thought it would be a Morse or a Barnaby; middle aged men with world-weary faces, greying round the temples and lined round the eyes, but this man was like one of their assistants. I guessed he was about thirty-something, with a thatch of brown hair and a strong Highlands accent. He introduced himself as D.S. James Morrish.

"D.S.? I thought you'd be a D.I.?"I said.

"You've been watching too much TV," he replied simply, gazing round at the art, before settling his eyes on me. "So you discovered the body?"

"Yes."

"Did Ms DeVere always arrive early for your meetings?"

"No, in fact…" I stopped, as I realised the significance of that.

"In fact?"

"In fact, it was a regular joke that our meetings always started ten minutes late because she, our President, was never on time."

He wrote that down. "Yet tonight she was early. You don't know why?"

"I haven't a clue. It wasn't a special meeting or anything."

"Could she perhaps have been meeting someone here?"

"You'd better ask Elsa. Actually, I'm surprised she wasn't here first. She usually is." I regretted saying that almost immediately. DS Morrish's eyebrow shot up.

"Who's Elsa?" I had a feeling he already knew.

"Elsa Fordyce, our secretary."

"Elsa Fordyce," he nodded. "My mother reads her books."

He'd be treating Elsa with kid gloves then, or there would be no chance of an autographed copy for mummy.

"And where was Muzz Fordyce tonight?"

I didn't know whether he was pronouncing Ms or Miss, or it was just a happy Highland amalgam of the two. "You'd better ask Elsa herself."

"Were they on good terms, these two women?"

"As far as I know, yes."

That was actually a lie. Only a week ago they'd had a terrible argument, but let him find that out for himself. I'd said too much already. "Anyway, why ask us? Whoever did that to Annabel had to be out of their mind, an escaped loonie or something."

He frowned. "We don't use that term, Muzz."

"Well I'm not in the police, I'm the general public and I'll call them what I want. What are you doing asking me questions? Shouldn't you be putting out an A.P.B or something?"

He looked at me strangely and wrote something down in his notebook, probably marking me down as a chief suspect.

"Can I go now?" I asked.

I was already at the door when he spoke again. "By the way, Muzz Murdoch, you won't say anything about the missing fingers to anyone, will you? In fact, no phone, no texts, nothing. So far, apart from the police, only yourself and the doctor know about them... and the murderer of course."

"Do you think I could take Mrs Kirk home now?" Billie asked as soon as I stepped out of the art club room. "She isn't feeling well at all."

Someone had brought out a chair for Vee. She was flaked across it, with Lisette wafting her face with her notebook. "Sorry, Billie, but I think the detective wants to speak to everyone."

Billie's pretty face pinched in alarm. "But I didn't even see the body. What could I possibly tell him?"

"He wants to know if Annabel had any enemies."

I'd never seen anyone's face drain of colour so fast. "What? He surely can't think anyone here... anyone who knew... could do..." She pointed at the door of the meeting room where Annabel's blood-drained body still lay alone. A policeman was guarding the door, but there was no one inside. They were waiting for the forensics team to show up. "It was a lunatic, Mirren, it had to be."

I mimicked the detective's frown. "We don't use that word anymore, Billie."

"Oh, sorry." She thought I was being serious. I suppose any normal person would be at a time like this.

"I suppose they think so too. They've just got to check out all the possibilities." I noticed that Lisette had stopped fanning Vee, and was now sitting cross-legged on the floor scribbling in her notebook. Billie followed my glance.

"Sickening, isn't it?" she whispered. "Our great writer has so much compassion. You know she was desperate to see the body. She followed one of the policemen in and had to be asked to leave."

I was annoyed at Lisette, and I showed it, though why? I was every bit as tasteless.

Billie went on. "She's already tried to ask Mrs Kirk what her feelings were on seeing the body. If she asks again I might just punch her."

"I'll hold your coat."

Lisette was the newest member of our little eightsome group, and certainly the most promising since Billie joined. Lisette's enthusiasm and ability attracted the attention of our self-appointed Fuhrer, Victoria Ashe, who had suggested she join us. Octopus, we called ourselves. We were a splinter group of Port Gowrie writers, though that made us sound like some kind of terrorist faction. As far as some of the other writers' group, we may as well have been. The eight members of Octopus were the people who, in Victoria's opinion, took their writing seriously enough to be included. The whole thing was really unpopular. The others viewed us as elitist. I wasn't sure that I didn't share their disapproval. At this point in my writing career, I didn't feel too elite. Apart from a couple of stories in a new writing magazine, and a commission for a comedy script from the BBC that seemed to be going nowhere fast, my writing was going nowhere. Everything I sent out seemed to disappear into a black hole. One of these days, Victoria was going to blackball me into the backbenches once more.

Lisette, however, seemed like she was heading for something great.

The undoubted star of Octopus, much to Lisette's annoyance, was Billie. She'd become Victoria's darling. Billie had quietly joined Port Gowrie Writers one autumn evening a few years back, shyly clutching a well-worn manuscript. I remember her reading it aloud, her voice breaking nervously. I remember how we had all sat in stunned silence at the sheer beauty of the prose. Billie's face had gone red, then chalk white, not quite knowing how to interpret that silence.

"It's probably just rubbish I suppose," she'd stuttered at last, almost in tears.

Rubbish, indeed? That manuscript had been the first chapter of a novel, one that went on to get published and then get shortlisted for several big literary awards. Victoria had been right about her from the beginning. She'd told her on that first night that she was destined for great things.

Victoria. It suddenly seemed she was significant by her absence. "Where's our Miss Ashe, by the way?"

"I wondered that," said Billie. "I've never known her to miss a group meeting. And today of all days. That's strange."

Vee, having recovered somewhat, was called in next to see the dour detective. I thought she was going to faint again on the way into the room, but Billie caught her arm just in time and helped her in. Lisette followed on, while still scribbling notes. She'd written so much she'd literally run out of space in her notebook and was using the back of an envelope. I 'accidentally' knocked against her, and her pen flew from her fingers. It rolled through the staircase railings and clattered onto the steps down below.

"Shite!" she hissed, proving she was about as French as I was.

"Sorry, Lisette."

Poor Lisette, I'd interrupted her flow, and it would take her a few minutes, at least, of precious lost notes to retrieve it. Lisette was not the easiest of people to get on with. Too little patience, especially with other people's literary efforts, too greedy for success to be likeable. The trouble was that her writing sparked right off the page. It crackled with energy and pace, and her stories were hard to put down. She was good at murder. It struck me that I'd better not mention that to the detective. "Let me get it for you, I'll throw it up. I'm going now anyway."

I hurried down the steps, and there was Lisette's pen, lying beside a grating in the floor. I can be rotten when I want to. I tapped it gently through with the toe of my shoe. "Ack, sorry," I said, and Lisette's head appeared over the banister, her blond ponytail dangling down behind her ear. "It's fallen down through here."

"Has it?" Her steely eyes never left my face, accusing eyes, annoyed, and finally cynically amused. "Never mind, I'll borrow Vee's." I was sure she would. As writers, we all carried pens, much like the ancient Highlanders who all carried dirks about with them in their socks.

At the bottom of the staircase, I bumped into the rest of our writers' group, all standing impatiently with folded arms and looks of disapproval.

"Oh dear, one of the clique has finally deigned to come down and speak to us plebs." It was Maya Brodie, who'd from the beginning been the chief rabble rouser against Octopus. I don't know why she joined a writing group in the first place, for she'd never produced anything in the way of writing, except for once; as a practical joke, her son sent a three-line poem she'd written into *The Viz*, which they only went and published on their letters page. No one had the heart to tell her it was a satirical magazine. Mind you, she wouldn't have cared if they did, because this achievement gave her the right, in her opinion, to call herself a published writer.

"What are you all doing down here anyway?" I asked. "Why don't you just go home, or go up?"

"OH!" came Maya in mock astonishment. "We're allowed, are we? I thought only the hallowed few were allowed to climb the sacred steps."

I glanced around me. "I don't see any barriers, If I felt that strongly about it, I'd probably just go up."

That was all the encouragement Maya needed to push past me.

Lexie Starr grasped my elbow, speaking in a hushed tone. "Is it true you found her, Mirren?" I liked Lexie. She tried hard with her writing and I did my best to encourage her. At the moment, though, my writing needed more help than hers.

"I'm afraid so."

She gave a small gasp. "That must have been terrible." Her grasp on my elbow tightened and she leaned in, speaking in an even more hushed tone. "Is it true about the fingers? Two of her fingers missing?"

"How the hell did you know?"

She waggled her phone about. "It's already on WhatsApp."

I almost laughed out loud. So much for DS Morrish and his big secret.

I left the community centre, standing for a moment in the street to savour the cool night air, catching the scent of the pines wafting over from the dense woods across the bay and the seaweed from the shore. I became aware of my phone pinging in my bag. That would be the WhatsApp group. I decided to ignore it. Mind you, if it hadn't been me who found her then I'd probably be on the chat myself, desperate to find out what was going on.

The community centre was a sprawling sandstone Victorian building in the nicest part of Port Gowrie, which we locals call *the Splash*. It had a promenade and an ice cream shop and even a few brightly-coloured buildings that made it look a bit like a Highland fishing village. We often all walked home together, enjoying the quiet stroll and the chat about the evening's session. Only last week, Annabel had turned down my offer of a lift, commenting how lucky we were to hold our meetings in such lovely surroundings.

Only last week, and now she was dead. Annabel, with her throat sliced open, her blood drained and her two fingers cut off. It had to be a maniac – was that a better word than loonie? Who else could do such a thing?

A maniac, it suddenly occurred to me, who might well still be around.

My little Volkswagen was parked in a dimly-lit car park behind the halls. It never bothered me before how dark and secluded it was. Here in this part of Port Gowrie, the *nice* part, you were always safe.

Now I was afraid. There were police milling around the front of the building. Police cars were parked right up the street. A blacked-out van had arrived and forensic officers in their white suits were getting ready to enter the murder scene. As I turned round the rear of the building, I left it all behind. All was quiet.

I reached into my bag and rested my fingers around my can of pepper spray, then I hurried to my car. The only sound was the clip-clipping of my boots on the tarmac.

A movement caught my eye, silent, furtive. It was a car, its engine off, free-wheeling silently out of the car park by the rear exit. There was something familiar about that car, but for the moment I couldn't remember what it was. The roadway around the rear exit was in a bad state, with pot holes and rubbish strewn about. No one ever used that exit. You had to drive round the block to get out anyway, so they just used the front. Why, I wondered, would someone be using it tonight?

CHAPTER TWO

Victoria Ashe called an extraordinary meeting of Octopus in her house the following weekend. That made me laugh. Every meeting with Victoria was extraordinary. She'd written two historical novels for a small Scottish press, as well as non-fiction books on the craft of writing. She also had a blog. She was hard and quick to criticize, intolerant of incompetent writing but generous in her praise of hard work and talent. She was the heart and soul of Octopus.

I could remember our first meeting when she had invited some of us to her house for afternoon tea.

Midway between the shortbread and the home-made marble cake she stood up and pounded the table with a paperweight. She waited until she had our full attention before she spoke.

"Too many of our writers' group only come for a coffee and a blether. It's a mere social gathering. The real writers in the group, the people like us, need a forum to fire them with enthusiasm. I intend that we should create that forum ourselves."

So, Octopus had been formed, the eight of us that Victoria considered the real writers. I thought the name more than appropriate. An octopus, according to the dictionary, wasn't just a sea creature with the right number of tentacles. It was also an organised power of influence, often a harmful one. That was certainly the meaning that the rest of the group took from it, the excluded ones. Far from firing anyone up, it had immediately sown division, jealousy and discord.

I'd been flattered and more than a bit surprised that I should be included among the real writers. Victoria invited me to join on account of my inclusion in the short story anthologies.

Victoria was, perhaps, the only one of us who'd never been bothered by any criticism. Nothing, in fact, seemed to bother the indomitable Victoria. She was always above such things. Her reaction to Annabel's murder was more one of anger that anyone should dare to harm a friend of hers, than that poor Annabel was actually dead.

"I wish I'd been there," she said, standing as she liked to do, in order to make her speech. "It would never have happened.

She was sixty-eight, tall and regal even at those times when arthritis crippled her. So sure she was of her own resolution, she took it for granted no maniac would have dared to strike with her in the vicinity. I had a feeling she might be right.

"Why weren't you there?"

It was Billie who asked the question, and I wondered why she hadn't asked before now. She was usually asked along to these meetings earlier than anyone else. She was Victoria's darling protégé. They were like a clique within a clique.

"I had a very bad headache." We all looked at her funny, as if being paralyzed from the neck down wouldn't have been a good enough excuse for her to miss one of our meetings. "It was, after all, only going to be a discussion of some of the regular members' work. I felt I just couldn't take the mediocrity, not with my head." She could be cruel, Victoria.

Vee Kirk stood, solemnly, hands folded in front of her like she was at a funeral. "I would like to suggest a moment's silence in respect for Annabel."

"Here, here." Doctor Bonnar applauded heartily, that is until he realised he was the only one doing it, and his clapping died away.

"I disagree." On principle, Victoria usually disagreed with anything Vee did suggest. They had long been rivals. That rivalry had increased only recently when Victoria had written a blog entry on Vee's hatpins. Vee was obsessed with hatpins and had been researching just such a piece herself. Victoria assured everyone she had no idea, but Vee never believed her. Relations between the two of them had been even more strained since then. Outwardly, Victoria was the more successful of the two, but there was a rumour going about that Vee's husband, Gordon, had passed up Victoria many years before for Vee's more sensual charms. Looking at Vee now, with her pudgy face, and her grey hair sticking out from under her hat, along with the dangerous-looking hatpin, it was difficult to imagine her young and sensuous and stealing anything from Victoria. If she had, then she was the only one who ever dared.

"And why not, may I ask?" Vee's nose twitched with indignation.

"Footballers get a minute's silence, or deceased monarchs." Victoria stated this as if they were far below writers in the order of things. "Writers, on the other hand, should have their work read out. That is a far more fitting tribute."

I had to agree with that. I thought a minute's silence was a silly idea, and a bit on the pretentious side. I would probably have burst into giggles before the minute was up.

"If only we had one of her stories or plays we could read," said Elsa breathlessly. She said most things breathlessly.

"Oh, but we do… don't we, Victoria?" this was Lisette. "I put it in with your notes before tea." She said that last bit pointedly, and we all knew why. She was broadcasting to us all that it was she, instead of Billie, who'd been invited early to Victoria's tonight.

Victoria beamed at her new protégé. She held up a manuscript. "Yes, Annabel gave it to me last week. She'd just finished, and wanted the group to be the first to read it. Lisette…" Again, she beamed. "Kindly made some copies so that we can all take part. Fortunately, there are seven characters, and, well, there's only seven of us now. A part for each of us."

Fortunately? Wasn't it lucky that Annabel had the foresight to get murdered so that no one would have to sit it out. I almost said this aloud, but my sense of humour often didn't go down well with the rest of Octopus.

Victoria went on, handing each of us a copy. "I think this should be most exciting. I did suggest to Annabel that she really should consider one of her most atmospheric plays as a vehicle for radio. Instead, she wrote a completely new play. She told me she was delighted with the result. If we give this the thumbs up tonight, I intend to submit it, on her behalf, to the BBC at the next Writers Room." Her critical gaze landed on Vee Kirk. "Now that would be a fitting tribute."

Victoria turned to me. "Perhaps you'll play the maid, Mirren. She's a..." She gave a short, dismissive cough. "Humorous character, I believe, with a rather common accent. You'd fit the bill marvellously."

She said it innocently, never expecting that I would take offence. And neither I did. I was the token working class element in Octopus, and as such any time they needed a working-class voice to read something, or, like now, when maids or cleaners were needed for plays. I glanced at Billie, whose lips were pursed with suppressed laughter. We were used to Victoria.

"Perhaps Lisette would like to pour us all a G and T before we start," said Victoria, sweeping her arm towards her drinks cabinet.

Lisette stood up, lithesome in her sleek, skin tight jeans. She was tiny, like a china doll, with her playful blonde hair tied up in its pony tail and her baby blue eyes.

I glanced at Billie, thinking she must be hurt, confused, and perhaps even angry. If she was, she didn't show it. Anyway, I'd decided to tell her later that she didn't need Victoria's help any longer, or her advice. Lisette had a talent, certainly, and the promise of one day becoming a best-selling novelist. With her drive and her energy, I had no doubt that she would make it one day, but Billie? She had true greatness in her writing. Depth, honesty, magic. She had already won national recognition from her debut. She didn't need Victoria's patronage any more. She'd outgrown it, and had moved on to more fertile pastures.

Soon, we were sitting around Victoria's cosy fireside with Annabel's script on our laps. It gave me a funny feeling looking at the title and the list of characters. She hadn't known when she wrote about them that they would be her epitaph.

"Is it scary?" I asked. Annabel had been good at spreading fear and trembling. The macabre was her speciality.

"I couldn't say," Victoria answered. "I never read it. Annabel put a resume of the characters on the front page. That was all she told me to read."

"I didn't read it either," added Lisette. "I was under strict orders not to." She smiled, as if she would always do as instructed by the master.

Watch out, Victoria, I almost blurted out. Lisette wasn't the type to do anyone's bidding for long.

"She wanted us all to read it for the first time together so she could judge if her ending had sufficient frisson to put the fear of death into us all." Victoria paused for a moment, smiling to herself, as did others. We all saw a glimpse of dear Annabel in that. That such a gentle, delicate lady could write such horrific stuff genuinely amazed me. It was funny what depths people had, and how those depths only came up to the surface in their writing. "Anyway," Victoria went on. "Even with her death I felt it was appropriate that we all read it together, a tribute to Annabel's commitment to Octopus."

"I still think a minute's silence would be more respectful," chipped in Vee.

"May I suggest something before we begin?" Elsa stood up a

little shakily.

"Yes." Victoria's tone was a little tart. She only tolerated Elsa in the group because of her success, even though, in her view, it was 'only self-publishing', or 'only romantasy'. According to our great leader, Elsa was wasting her talent. "She should try writing a real book," she would often say.

Elsa was well aware of these sentiments and consequently, and completely out of character, she suffered greatly from an inferiority complex in Victoria's presence. "Perhaps this is the wrong time to bring it up..."

"Oh, go on..." Victoria was impatient with any kind of reticence.

"Since Annabel has..." Elsa swallowed. "Well, she isn't here anymore. That means there's one less of us in the group. We are seven instead of eight."

"I think it's entirely the wrong time to bring that up, Elsa," snapped Vee. Elsa half sat down, chastened.

"No, go on, Elsa, the floor is yours..." said Victoria, determined at every point to contradict Vee.

Elsa stood up again and continued. "We are Octopus. That means there has to be eight of us in the group. I just feel I'd like to put a word in for someone... well, perhaps not to fill Annabel's shoes, of course, no one could do that... but to... become the missing tentacle, so to speak."

"And what someone had you in mind?"

Elsa hesitated, then stammered, keeping her eyes on the floor. "Patrick Myer."

Why did I already know it would be him? Patrick Myer, he of the intense dark eyes and brooding sensuality. I was pretty sure she'd already written him in as the hero of her next romantasy. Added to the good looks, he had actual talent. He had shown that in the months since he'd joined the club. His writing had intensity. Yet Patrick Myer was an enigma. He tended to leave the meeting room as soon as the meeting was over. He hardly spoke to anyone, except Billie. I'd thought I had seen the beginnings of a romance there, and I was glad. Which was rather big of me, because I fancied him myself. I'm only human.

"Patrick Myer..." Victoria repeated thoughtfully. "Mmmm."

"I think it's gruesome talking about this so soon," said Vee Kirk. "Gruesome and unfeeling. Annabel's just died. Anyway, I don't even like him. There's evil in those eyes. I vote no."

Poor Vee, would she ever learn? The die was cast. Victoria had already made up her mind. Patrick Myer would be asked to join Octopus, if, for no better reason, so that Victoria could spite Vee.

"It would also mean another man in the group. We're sadly lacking men." Elsa smiled at Dr Bonnar.

He laughed. "Not that it isn't delightful being the only male." He leaned towards Billie jovially. She noticeably flinched. He looked embarrassed and laughed even louder. "Yes, I'll certainly miss being the only man for you to spoil."

Victoria tapped her pencil against the arm of her chair. "I think that's settled then, if there are no other objections to him joining." She had a way of looking around the room and completely missing Vee, who tutted loudly, but otherwise said nothing. "Well, in that case, let's begin Annabel's play."

In true Annabel fashion, by page two we were already embroiled in Satanic ritual. On page four the first murder occurred and we all stopped reading.

The victim's throat had been cut, and two of her fingers were missing.

We called the police at once of course. Well, not quite at once. Billie threw up all over Victoria's new Indian rug, and Vee fainted again. She was still unconscious and lying across the couch when DS Morrish arrived. One of his eyebrows furrowed slightly as he took her in. It was the second time he'd turned up and she was horizontal.

"And you're sure no one read this play before tonight?" he asked, after we had explained.

"Annabel insisted on it," said Victoria. "She wanted us to read it all together for the first time so that she could judge how well the surprise ending worked."

"Well, we were surprised," I muttered, and Victoria glared at me. She didn't approve of my sense of humour.

"And you didn't read it, Miss Ashe?"

Victoria drew herself up. "Young man, haven't I just told you that?"

Morrish gazed back at her, unperturbed. "But why did she give her manuscript to you? Why not just bring it along on the night?"

She looked down her nose at him as if he had just asked some damn stupid question. "To make copies of course. We have a photocopier that we use. When we're doing crits, everyone needs to get a hard copy."

"Right," said Morrish. "But you didn't?"

"Didn't what?"

"You gave the script to Muzz Bonvieux."

He turned his attention to Lisette, who smiled angelically. "Victoria's photocopier, the one we normally use, was on the blink, so she asked me if I could help. I can just do it at work."

His eyes never left her face. "And you didn't read the play either?"

"Of course I didn't. Victoria asked me specifically not to."

And Lisette lied. I could tell as plain as if someone had stamped 'LIE' across her forehead. Her voice never wavered. She didn't blink, but I knew that she had lied. I wondered if Morrish could tell too.

He didn't, however, follow that up. He turned back to Victoria. "So it's you who normally handles the photocopying?"

"Actually, no."

The detective gave a short gasp, with perhaps a hint of exasperation. "Right, so, who normally does it, then?"

Elsa coughed and stepped forward. "Usually me. I'm the secretary."

"So, why didn't Mrs DeVere ask you this time, Mrs Fordyce?"

Her lip quivered. I could almost see inside her mind as it flicked over all the possible answers. She'd been too busy. She'd run out of paper. Her copier had run out of ink. Finally, in typical Elsa style, she resorted to attack. "What on earth does it matter now anyway? I most certainly never read the damn play, so it couldn't have been me who carried out any copycat murder."

"You mean, there are only two people in this room who could have read it and have done so?"

"Yes! I mean… no!" She looked helplessly at Victoria. "No, of course not… no…" She slumped into a chair.

"Is it true, Mrs Fordyce, that you and Mrs DeVere had an argument recently?"

"Maybe," I suggested tactfully. "Elsa could speak more freely if the two of you were alone."

Elsa managed a half-smile in my direction. "Yes, if we could be alone."

"Would you like to come down to the station?"

Poor Elsa went chalk white. "My God, I'm not being arrested, am I?"

"Of course not. I tell you what, why don't we go back to your own house? You can talk there."

Elsa suddenly perked up. "Yes. And I can give you that

autograph for your mother."

DS Morrish's ears tinged with pink and his glance darted at me. I pretended to look surprised.

After Morrish and Elsa left, we all stayed for a cup of tea.

"You do realise the murderer must have been someone who read that play," said Victoria, dramatically.

Sitting in a circle, our eyes shifted around each other's faces. Suddenly it was like being in one of those reality game shows where someone in the house is a traitor and no one knows who. "It would seem so," I agreed reluctantly.

"The maniac is among us," said Victoria, eyeing us in turn.

Lisette whipped out her notebook, and her pen zipped into action. "What a great title for a book. I might use that."

Billie sat pale and sickly and staring into the fire in the log burner, so while the others were clearing up, I went over and sat with her. "I can't believe this is happening, Mirren," she said. "Just as I was getting over Caroline's death." Caroline was Billie's sister, who'd suffered for years with a terrible progressive illness. Billie had cared for her right until the end. "Just as I was beginning to think things were getting better... this..."

Billie's sister had passed away less than a year ago. I'd never seen anyone so devastated by a death. I had only met Caroline once, and she was almost totally paralyzed, with only a slight movement in her hands. I would have thought death would have been a blessing, both for her and for Billie, who did everything for her. Instead, she seemed to be living in some kind of half-life.

"This has nothing to do with you, and you can't let it interfere with this new book of yours." I already knew she found it hard to concentrate since her sister's death, and the second book had been slow coming. She'd allowed me to read the first draft of her first chapter, and as soon as I did, I cried. I wished desperately that I was able to write like that. I'd never be able to.

"I know," Billie said, blowing on some Kleenex.

"Feeling better?"

"It was the shock. Who could have done it, Mirren?"

"I don't know. Let's just hope it's finished."

"Of course it is!" She almost snapped at me. "Annabel didn't have any enemies. It must have been one of those opportunist crimes. You know, you read about them all the time. A complete stranger passing by finds Annabel alone and..." She shuddered.

A homicidal stranger who just happens to be passing our committee rooms after reading Annabel's play? Yes, Billie, of course. "I'm sure you're right," I said. My reluctant agreement seemed to assure her. God knows why. I didn't believe a word of it myself. Something deep down told me this wasn't over.

I paid my first visit to Annabel's husband, Robin, the next evening. He was more than a little drunk.

"I'm the prime suspect, did you know?" he slurred, leading me into their untidy living room. The glass in his hand was overflowing with white wine and soda. He swayed to a chair and sat down on a pile of newspapers. This meant that when I sat down on the sofa opposite, he was a foot higher on his seat.

"Me...." He went on, "Cutting Annabel's throat... doing that..." He stared down at his hands, imagining. "What sick mentality could think up such a horrible thing?"

Annabel herself, I almost reminded him. Her books were full of it, some of it worse. I was suddenly reminded of a time at the club when someone scolded her, saying, "You wouldn't like to die like that yourself, would you?" And then Annabel's flippant reply: "If you have to go, why not go in style?" Now who was it who said that? I had almost caught the answer when Robin, still talking, interrupted my train of thought.

"She was my wife, Mirren. And I didn't even read the play, I swear. I never read any of her stuff. She was always telling me off for not being interested in her career." He was right. Annabel had told me that often enough.

"She wasn't planning to meet anyone at the committee room before the meeting started, was she?" I asked. She was always late. I couldn't help wondering why she might have been early.

He downed the rest of his spritzer in one go. "I don't know. She was upset about something. I told the Inspector that. She'd been to Glasgow that day, and when she came back, she had a phone call. I don't know who it was, but that upset her too. She wouldn't say why, but she was in a hurry to get to the club that night. The last words she ever said to me were, 'There's something very strange going on.'

He looked down at me from his perch. I looked up at him. I was trying hard not to giggle. How could you not see the funny side of it? He was a man I'd always felt was quite supercilious, and a little chauvinistic towards Annabel. That rankled with me. Here now, I saw a man shattered, his eyes filling with tears. "What am I going to do without her, Mirren?"

And he burst into tears.

I stayed with him until his daughter, a large, capable woman who bred dalmatians, arrived. "Some people need valium at a time like this. Gin does the same job for Daddy," she said at once. "Mummy liked her gin too. But they weren't drunks, neither of them."

"I know." I liked the way she defended them. "Your mother was a fine woman. I liked her very much."

"She liked you too. She always said you were going places."

Going places? I thought about that as I drove home. Everything had gone quiet on so many fronts. The BBC producer, an agent I'd been corresponding with, and the editor of the story magazine had all started ghosting me, and I couldn't work out why. People said it happens. At the moment the only place I was going was nowhere fast.

CHAPTER THREE

"Surely that club of yours isn't holding a meetin' the night?"

My mother disapproved strongly of our acting president's decision, our acting president being Victoria, to hold the usual Tuesday meeting. "Yon poor wumman no' even cauld yet," she croaked.

"Victoria thinks this is what Annabel would have wanted."

"That wumman talks a lot of shite." Mother never minced her words. "Well seein' she's no' got a family. All she's got is yon club." She folded her arms under her ample bosom and drew it up. "Wouldn't be surprised if she murdered Annabel herself just so she could be president. I've always had my doubts about Johnson as well."

My mother was a master at the art of leapfrogging from one subject to another.

"Johnson, who?"

She looked at me as if I was half-witted. "Yon Lyndon B. Johnson. I think he murdered Kennedy so he could be president an 'all." She gestured up at her framed photo of John F Kennedy, which was hanging on the wall next to the Pope. It had hung there for decades, an heirloom from my Grandmother.

"Point taken, dear," I told her. "But Victoria stepped down only last year so Annabel could take over. She insisted on it. So, there's your theory in smithereens, Sherlock."

"Don't you be too sure what you see is what you've got. Appearances can be helluva deceivin'."

I mused on that piece of wisdom. "Anyway, I agree with you. I don't think the meeting should be going on."

So why was I going? Because Victoria expected us all to be there? Or was there another, more macabre motive? Did I want to be in that room again? The picture jumped into my mind: Annabel slumped across the table, her throat sliced open, the blood pooling on the floor. It still seemed too theatrical to be real. And wasn't that the idea? The murderer had used the method that Annabel herself had dreamed up for her play. Or, there was another possibility? Perhaps she hadn't dreamed it up. Perhaps it was a genuine thing among Satanists, an actual ritual. It was Morrish who put the thought into my head, asking in his quiet Highland way, "Do you know of anyone else interested in the occult?" And I knew no one except Annabel. "Was this something she was seriously interested in?" he'd asked.

I shrugged. "I guess. She was interested in the macabre, and she always did her research thoroughly."

I remembered too Annabel whispering to me one night, "If you read into it seriously, it would frighten you. The play I'm researching at the moment..." And she had shuddered. "Quite terrifying, the rituals they practice. Had she been researching this play at the time? Maybe there was a black magic coven right here in Port Gowrie. Maybe through her research she'd got involved with them in some way. Maybe she'd asked one too many questions, or poked her nose in where it was not welcome. D.S. Morrish had told us all to keep quiet about the play. I hoped he would have more success with this than he had with his other little secret. Certainly, nobody had put it on the WhatsApp group yet. I for one, didn't want to talk about it anyway. It was difficult enough to imagine a murderer in our quiet little town, but a black magic coven in Port Gowrie too?

I sat in the committee room that night, watching them all assemble one by one. I tried to imagine each of them dancing around a cloven-hoofed figure, semi-naked and dripping with sensual lust. Vee Kirk seemed the most likely. She was steeped in Tam O'Shanter. I could picture her with her cutty sark flying behind her in the breeze, her grey hair hanging as long as her pendulous breasts, chasing people about with one of her lethal-looking hatpins. She would be chasing Victoria, however, not Annabel, and as soon as she saw blood she would undoubtedly faint again.

Then there was Elsa. As a witch she would wear diaphanous black, with diamond stars hiding her interesting bits, flimsy enough to be ripped to shreds by the wizard of the coven, who'd naturally take her on the altar in front of everyone. Elsa's romantasies always included at least one rape, though she bridled at the idea of them being rapes. Passionate encounters, she called them, where the reluctant heroine finally succumbs to the forceful charms of the satanic hero. Usually there was a dragon or a wizard involved. Everyone else called it rape.

Victoria...? Not Victoria. She dismissed any kind of belief in the supernatural. You only had yourself to rely on, according to her, no one else. There was no God, no higher power. I admired her tremendously, strove to be like her in so many ways, and yet... I couldn't be an atheist, not least because my mother would kill me.

Lisette? Could Lisette be involved in the occult, I wondered? If it would get her a good story, I was pretty sure she would sell her soul. But I couldn't believe she would take anything like that seriously.

Doctor Bonnar filed in, his briefcase tucked under his arm. A jolly, kindly gentleman, helpful to everyone, who positively adored his wife. I had never seen a man so attentive and loving, which was especially surprising given the woman's looks. Perhaps he was under the spell of a love potion, that would account for a lot of things. I couldn't imagine him as a wizard, though I could certainly imagine his wife as a witch. She looked not unlike the wicked witch in the Wizard of Oz, barring the green skin.

And yet, when I thought about it, this same kindly man had some very funny ideas about stuff like genetics and animal testing. "All for the future of mankind, my dear," he would assure me in a superior fashion whenever these subjects came up. And then there was his book, PanzerKommander, which was set on the Russian front in World War Two. Empathy was important in a writer, the ability to put yourself in someone else's shoes, but somehow this jolly middle-aged Doctor had managed to put himself in the shoes of a hardened Nazi tank commander. Where did that come from? I was often amazed by the stuff that came out of people's heads when writing. It spoke of depths and mysteries under the surface.

Billie didn't come. She'd put a message on the Octopus WhatsApp group to say she didn't think it was decent. She was probably right. But what was she doing instead? Sitting in that mausoleum of a house, of course, grieving over a dead sister, and now, her friend. Billie, burning incense and chanting prayers to Satan? Maybe that explained how she achieved her astonishing success.

Maybe I should give it a try.

Billie was fascinated by anything strange and new. I could remember her once asking Annabel if there were any magic remedies that might help her sister. She had already tried everything, from acupuncture to reiki therapy. Had she tried black magic too?

"You're not listening to a word I'm saying, Mirren. Mirren!" I jumped in my seat. I was being scolded by Victoria. The group laughed.

"In a dream world, as usual," someone said.

"Penny for your thoughts," said another.

"I bet they were funny."

"Hilarious," I assured them all.

"She's probably thinking we have no right to be here. It's unfeeling." This was from Vee. She was promptly silenced by Victoria.

"Then why did you come? No one frog-marched you up the stairs?"

"I came to register my protest that this meeting was held at all. And now that I have, I intend to go." She stood up and looked around the room. "If any of you have any decency at all, you'll join me."

She was looking for a majority to overthrow Victoria. Unfortunately, no one else stood up with her. It struck me that I should probably say something to support her at least. "I agree with Mrs Kirk. I think tonight's meeting should have been cancelled. Or, at least, not held here, in this room." I wasn't the only ghoul glancing around, looking for signs of blood stains on the floor. The conference table and the chairs had at least had been replaced. "But now that we're here, we might as well stay. We've both registered our protest."

Vee smiled at me, glad of my support.

"Take a note of their protest, Elsa," Victoria snapped. "Then maybe they'll both shut up and we can get on with the meeting."

Vee glared at her, but she nevertheless sat down, and Victoria continued.

"And I am not being unfeeling, as some people put it, by holding the meeting tonight. In case you'd forgotten, tonight was the adjudication of the crime story, and I didn't think it fair to let those who had entered down."

"If there's a murder in one of them, and one of them has her throat cut, I'll die," said Maya Brodie. I don't even think she was joking. I glanced at Vee. She looked ready to faint again. We, in Octopus, who knew the significance of those words all glanced guiltily at one another.

"I adjudicated them and there isn't," Victoria said curtly. "But I felt it was necessary to keep to our syllabus. Annabel would have wanted it that way. Getting on with the job."

I twiddled my pen. If Victoria said, 'The show must go on,' I'd throw it at her.

She didn't. It was Elsa who said it instead. I didn't throw the pen, I giggled instead. Everyone looked at me, as usual, the group's giggling wreck, and scowled.

"Sorry," I said.

It was at that moment that Patrick Myer came into the room and slid unobtrusively into a seat. Or, as unobtrusively as a six-foot tall, exceptionally good-looking Irishman can slip into a room predominantly made up of females.

"Patrick, how nice to see you." Victoria was all smiles. "I'd like to talk to you later."

He only nodded. He hardly ever spoke, but when he did it was in the softest Irish tones that reminded me of black velvet. I made a point of not looking at him. It's rude to stare, and once I started looking at him, I knew I couldn't stop. Elsa stared openly, delighted as ever at the embodiment of all her heroes actually joining our group. She was pushing forty, but she was an attractive pushing-forty, with two grown-up kids who'd fled for Uni, leaving her with a podgy, garrulous husband who had definitely not weathered as well as she. I had the feeling that if Patrick Myer pulled back the bedclothes, she'd be in the bed beside him before you could utter the words 'bodice ripper'.

It was Patrick's story which won the competition. All the rest were rubbish, according to Victoria, which criticism brought rumblings of discontent from the body of the kirk.

"I know the next one who's going to be found lying across that table with her throat cut," Lexie Starr whispered at me. Victoria had been particularly scathing about her story.

"If you like, I'll look at it later. I know it won't be as bad as she says."

"She doesn't believe in boosting your ego, does she?"

No, but to be fair, she could be lavish in her praise when she thought you did well. Criticism, she said, was all part and parcel of being a writer. If you couldn't take it, you didn't believe in yourself enough. You didn't deserve success. In fact, you weren't a writer at all.

Patrick, she had long ago decided, was born to be a writer. His story, she assured us all, was head and shoulders above the rest, and when Patrick read it aloud, we could all see why.

In his seductive Irish lilt, he told the story of a man on the run, accused of horrific murder. The thing of it was, the thing that made it so good, was that you didn't know whether he was guilty of innocent until the final sentence. Your sympathies were with him, then against him, then with him again, until that final telling sentence revealed all. We didn't even applaud politely as we usually did when someone finished reading out a story. It was much too good for that.

"I should perhaps tell you," he added. "It's been accepted for publication. I got word only today."

That was when everyone applauded. Despite our petty rivalries, we all genuinely loved success. Even a letter in the local paper warranted applause. Even Maya Brodie got applause when her piece got in *The Viz*.

Victoria asked Patrick to wait behind at the end. I noticed at the close of the meeting that Elsa was trying to hang back, but Victoria was having none of it. "I am quite capable of handling this myself," she said.

As I passed Patrick, I caught his attention by touching his arm. "Congratulations, it was a wonderful story."

He had the most beautiful sea green eyes I had ever seen. "Thank you, Mirren. I appreciate that from you."

"I don't know why, you're a much better writer than I could ever hope to be."

"Is that why you write humour, so you don't have to take yourself seriously?" And suddenly, those eyes seemed able to fathom deep inside me. "Why does her ladyship want to see me?"

Why should I not tell him? I had as much right as anyone else. "They're going to ask you to join Octopus."

His brow furrowed slightly. "I don't know whether I approve of Octopus or not."

"I don't either, but at the moment we're a tentacle short."

"Will you wait for me?"

What for? Why? His request came as such a surprise that before an answer could form itself in my stupid brain, Elsa was grabbing his arm, congratulating him, pulling him away from me. I would wait anyway.

Or I would have. Still holding on to Patrick, Elsa turned to me. "Will you run me home, Mirren? Mike took the car, but he'll be late. Business."

Patrick glanced at me for a moment, then he shrugged and moved towards Victoria, who was standing imperiously at the desk.

At that moment, I swear Elsa almost became the second murder. She seemed oblivious to my glare, linking arms with me as I made my reluctant way downstairs. "I hope you don't mind. That was all subterfuge. Mike could have easily come for me."

Why did Elsa always have to talk like one of her romances? "What are you talking about, Elsa?"

She glanced around, suspiciously. "Not here." And she refused to say another word until we were outside, in the darkened street. She pulled me into one of the doorways, talking in an urgent, hushed tone. "I need to talk to someone, someone I can trust."

Her face looked green, although that could have been the streetlights. But in that moment, I saw fear in her eyes. "What are you afraid of, Elsa?"

"Someone's been following me," she said, and she burst into tears.

"Have you told the police?" I had managed to get her into my car, and we sat there in the gloomy interior of my 10-year-old Polo. Her face was streaked with tears, and for once she'd lost all her glamour.

"No, do you think I should?"

"Of course I do. There's been a murder. You've got to tell the police if you think you're being followed. When did this start?"

"Before Annabel's death." She blew into a dainty lace handkerchief. "I felt a couple of times there was someone following me. Once, when I put the car in the garage I could have sworn someone was in there with me. I could feel them. It was dark, but I could sense someone standing in the shadows. I ran inside the house and told Mike. He went down and had a look. There was no one there. He said it was a product of my overactive sexual imaginings. That's what really frightens me now, after reading Annabel's play. In almost every one of my books the heroine is threatened by some villainous piece in the shadows."

Life copying art, I thought with a chill. Annabel's death, Elsa's shadowy threat.

"We'll go to the police right now. I'll take you."

I didn't see the point of wasting time by waiting till tomorrow. DS Morrish obviously never had a wife or a girlfriend, or else his relationship was in a very dicey state. Here it was, 10pm, and he was still in the incident room which had been set up at the local station, his fair head bent over some files on his desk.

He listened without a word as Elsa told him her story, all the time fingering her lace handkerchief on her lap.

"And when did the last incident occur?" he asked finally.

"There's been nothing since Annabel..." Was anyone ever as reluctant to say the words, *was murdered*? "But the last time was just over a week ago, I was in the house by myself and someone was outside watching. I could hear the bushes rustling, footsteps crunching on the gravel, feel the threatening presence of someone there..."

I could see Morrish wondering if she was writing another book on the spot. "When Mike came home, I almost crowned him with a poker."

"Why didn't you call us then?"

"I knew you'd say exactly what Mike said. It was my nerves. I was imagining things. Well, it wasn't and I didn't. Someone's watching me. What frightens me more than anything is that... I believe I was the intended victim, not Annabel."

"You?" Morrish and I said at once.

"Yes, me. I'm always the first one to arrive at our meetings to set things up, never Annabel. It was me they were waiting for. And now, they realise their mistake... they'll come back." She gasped as if the thought was too terrifying to bear. God, I wished I'd never brought her.

"Did you see whoever it was? Can you give us a description?" he asked.

In a typically dramatic gesture, Elsa threw her arms up. "How the hell should I know? I didn't actually see him." I noticed the tiny lift of Morrish's eyebrow when she said this. "But he was there," she insisted. "I tell you he was there, and he'll be back."

"How do you know it's a he?" asked Morrish.

Elsa lifted her head regally. "A woman knows when a threat is sexual, Inspector."

Well, a romantasy novelist like Elsa certainly knows. "You don't believe me, do you?"

I didn't see any reason why he should. Elsa was overacting like mad. Like some actress in a third-rate soap opera. If I was him, I wouldn't believe her either.

He looked at me. "You know Mrs Fordyce. Do you think she's telling the truth?"

My estimation of the man's intelligence rose a notch or two. "Surprisingly, I do. I think Elsa's afraid of something."

"What do you mean, *surprisingly*?" Elsa snapped.

Both the Inspector and I ignored that.

"So what are you going to do about it?" I asked him.

He sat back, rolling his pen around in his fingers. "I'm going to put a man on to keep his eye on Mrs Fordyce. He'll be discreet, but you'll know he's there. We've had a murder here. We can't afford to dismiss anything."

Even, his tone seemed to suggest, the sexual imaginings of a crackpot like you.

Billie called me the next day. Her voice was hardly audible. "Sorry to disturb you, Mirren. Have you got a moment?"

If she thought she was interrupting some great inspirational writing binge she was wrong. I hadn't written anything in days. Ideas tumbled around my mind as fast as they ever did. Normally, I took great joy in sifting through them, sorting them, like I was going through a laundry basket. Lately, I'd begun to feel it was hardly worthwhile. Every idea, every story seemed only to be sent into oblivion. "No, I'm not busy. Anything important?"

"I don't know," she said. "Will you come?" Then, just as I was about to end the call she added. "I've had a parcel. I don't know what's in it. Please hurry."

Billie's house was in the west end of Port Gowrie, the nice bit, not far from the community centre. It was a sprawling Victorian mansion where Billie's grandfather and then her father had once presided as magistrates. The extensive gardens had always been kept beautifully. They were Billie's pride and joy. She had tended them, she had once told me, for her sister, who loved sitting out in the sun. "Her only pleasure," Billie had said, and added quickly in case I thought she was being too totally unselfish. "But it's wonderful for me too. That's when I get my best inspiration."

As I drove up towards the house, I could see that those gardens were for once neglected. There was no sister now to give pleasure to, and for the moment, no inspiration. Poor Billie. She had editors queuing up for her work, and no fire to write. I was on fire all day, and all editors were willing to do was throw cold water over me.

Billie was waiting by the front door. She looked agitated. So pale I leapt from my car and ran to her.

"Oh, Mirren..." she mumbled, then she fell in a crumpled heap at my feet.

I tried to lift her inside but she was heavier than she looked, so I ran into the house to telephone her doctor. There was a small parcel lying by the phone, it's wrappings ripped open, the top half lying off. Billie obviously couldn't wait for my arrival to see what was inside. No wonder she had fainted on me.

Annabel's missing fingers had turned up at last.

"You always seem to be there or thereabouts when anything happens, Muzz," DS Morrish said accusingly when he arrived.

"Billie asked me to come."

"As did Mrs Fordyce."

"Yes."

"Mirren is someone you can depend on in a crisis, Inspector. She's the first person I thought on when the parcel came."

I looked at Billie, recovering now on the sofa, and was pleased by what I knew was meant to be a compliment, no matter how it was worded.

"Am I? Did you?"

"You're a true friend, Mirren."

"What was it about the parcel that aroused your suspicions, Muzz May?" said Morrish. It struck me that I could listen to D.S. Morrish arousing his RRRs forever.

"Nothing really, except... I don't get much personal mail in the post. I get e-mails, of course, but that's all. So I did wonder who would send a parcel to me. But I never thought..." She grew pale again, clearly remembering the opening of the box. "Oh, but there was something about it that frightened me as soon as I saw it... I don't know if I've mentioned this, Inspector, but I'm supposed to be rather psychic."

Oh God, *I see dead people.* D.S. Morrish was going to think we were all a bunch of freaks.

"Who on earth told you that, Billie?" I asked, exaggerating a laugh.

"The woman at the séance," she answered calmly.

"When did you go to a séance?"

"Didn't I tell you?"

"No!"

"When was this, Muzz?" asked

"A couple of months ago. Annabel took me."

Morrish and I said at once, "Annabel?!"

"Why didn't you say anything?" I asked. "You know the police want to know everything about Annabel. Where was this, and what happened?"

D.S Morrish turned on me. "Do you mind? I'm supposed to be the one asking the questions."

I sat back, rebuked. "Sorry."

He turned back to Billie and asked the very same questions I had.

"I didn't consider it black magic. Anyway, I only went once. To be honest, I think the woman was a charlatan, saying she could contact my sister. Annabel wanted me to go again. Said she knew another woman, even better."

"But you didn't go back?"

"I was going to. I told Annabel I'd give it another try, but she said, forget it. Maybe it was a mistake to get involved in these things. She seemed worried about something."

Frightened, upset, worried. All these words had been used to describe Annabel's state of mind before her death. Words that usually would never be associated with her. "I only wanted to contact my sister," Billie added. "You can understand that, can't you, Mirren? The woman said she couldn't get through. She said I was too psychic or something, and I was blocking the way with my own vibes."

"Well, at least that's an original excuse for being a phoney," I said.

"Do you think there's something in that black magic stuff, Inspector?" I asked him as we left Billie's house.

"I'm not dismissing anything."

I put on a poor impression of Inspector Clouseau. "I suspect everyone… and I suspect no one…"

Morrish just stared at me. He clearly wasn't a film buff. "Aye," he said. "I suppose I do. Do you make a joke of everything, Muzz?"

"I wish you would call me Mirren," I said. "After all, we seem to be seeing a lot of each other. And I wish I didn't have to keep calling you Inspector. It's an awful moothful."

"I keep telling you, I'm a D.S, a detective sergeant, not an Inspector."

"I can't call you that, it's an even bigger moothful."

There was a small smile in his eyes that he couldn't hide. I bet I could make that dour Scotsman laugh, given the chance. "All right, Mirren it is."

I noticed, however, that he didn't clarify what I should call him.

He left a police constable with Billie. At this rate, Octopus would be using up all the manpower of the Port Gowrie police force.

CHAPTER FOUR

Sadly, I wasn't a full-time writer. I wasn't even a part-time writer. The only money I'd earned came intermittently. Yet I was still hopeful. For a while, I'd started getting more e-mails. I'd had a few conversations with a producer at the BBC. I even had a few Zoom calls with interested editors. Lately, that had all dropped off, and the post brought nothing but bills. One day, I hoped, I would still make it. For the moment though, it seemed like I had it all to do.

Most of my income came from driving a taxi. My mother didn't like it one bit. She couldn't understand why I opted for that rather than the cosy little job in the control office that they had offered me.

"But can't you see the fund of stories a taxi driver collects?"

"Stories?" she said. "You're head's full of stories. You could get it bashed in driving a taxi."

It was true that I'd faced my fair share of dangers. One bloke tried to fondle me. He soon found out when he met my friend, *torchy*, a high-powered torch made out of 10-inches of solid metal. Another man had tried to rob me. He slammed the door shut on his jacket as he tried to make his escape. I had him running backwards all the way to the police station. And the most obnoxious man I'd ever met had thrown up on the back seat and then refused to give me a tip.

None of that had really worried me, because those incidents were few and far between, and you could usually see them coming. Now I was worried. There was a killer on the loose. Port

Gowrie was a seafaring town. There was a container terminal, with ships coming in and out, and sailors from all countries, creeds and colours mixing among us. I comforted myself with the notion that perhaps the killer was one of those seafarers. He'd be well on his way now, far across the sea. I hoped so, and yet, had this seafarer read Annabel's play, or known Billie's address?

Thursday nights were usually quiet around Port Gowrie, except when it rained. When it rains everybody wants a taxi.

The sky was clear, the stars sparkling like diamonds on velvet. I had plenty of time to sit and look at them as I sat in my solitary post in a dark street down near the docks.

Suddenly, someone pulled open the passenger door and jumped in. "Why on earth do you sit here on your own? Anyone could come in." The soft Irish lilt, the sea green eyes, it was Patrick.

I tried not to sound delighted. "Anyone's supposed to, I'm a taxi."

"You shouldn't be driving around at night like this, not now."

He slipped in beside me, wearing his black polo neck sweater. A lock of his coal black hair hung over his forehead. My mother had always warned me about black-haired Irishmen. She said they'd been spawned from the shipwrecked Spanish sailors of the armada who never made it home.

"Surely it must have been someone who was specifically after Annabel. Something to do with the…" I almost said the occult, then I remembered I wasn't supposed to know anything about that.

"I think," he said softly. "That's what we're supposed to think."

"Why? What's your theory?"

"I don't have one," he said. "But Mrs DeVere was a very nice woman. Why would anyone want to kill her?"

"Maybe she had a secret. Lots of people do."

He just stared at me when I said that, and didn't say a word. It was quite disconcerting. "Anyway, where can I take you?"

"I was hoping to take you somewhere, if you're finished."

"It's so quiet tonight. I was about to finish up anyway." That was a lie. I wondered if he guessed.

"Would you like to eat somewhere?"

"Thanks. I am quite hungry."

Hungry? With a mother like mine? She hardly let me set foot outside the door without a four-course meal inside me. It was a miracle I wasn't twenty stone. I might not have Lisette's blonde hair, but my figure was every bit as good as hers. "I'll have to take the taxi back to the depot and pick up my own car, okay?"

We went to a quiet Italian restaurant which had just recently opened down by the river, Rocco's. It was secluded and cosy and the windows looked out over the sparkling river. Patrick ordered two courses, so I did too; pate to start, and then a simple spaghetti *aglio e olio*. Lovely though it was, I was struggling to finish. "How are you enjoying the club?" I asked.

He shrugged. "Seems to be a ladies' coffee evening for the most part. I was honestly thinking of not going back."

"Oh!" Did I really sound that disappointed?

"But now..." he added.

"Now that you've been summoned to join Octopus?"

"That's actually what I wanted to talk to you about."

So, that was it. Nothing personal, only Octopus. I might have known.

"Victoria thought the same as you, that it was more like a ladies' coffee evening. That's why she formed Octopus. It's quite an honour to be asked."

"Even if you don't approve?"

"You're thinking of joining us anyway?"

"I'll come. See what it's like. I'll give it a try."

I almost spluttered out my pasta.

"What's so funny?" he asked.

"You're giving us a trial period. Victoria would be affronted. It's supposed to be the other way about."

"Is that so? Has anyone ever failed, been drummed out?"

"As a matter of fact, yes." I recalled shamefully the poetry lady who Victoria decided would have to go when it was discovered that her volume of poetry was self-published, and it was shoddily self-published at that.

"We could all claim to be published writers if we did that," she'd said. Elsa of course, being self-published too, had stood up for the woman. There was a difference, Victoria had told her, launching into a lecture about how Elsa had done it successfully, and she'd done it professionally. Hadn't Amazon had picked her up for one of their own imprints? After all that, Elsa could hardly sustain her objection. So, the lady in question was blackballed. My shameful part had been to sit and keep quiet. Silent approval. I had always been ashamed of that. Annabel, I remembered now, had seconded the proposal.

"You're off in a dream again."

"I know. I always am."

"I watch you sometimes in the club. You can cut yourself off completely. I often wonder what's going on in your head when you do that."

He'd been watching me, and I'd never been aware of it. For once in my life, I didn't know what to say. Patrick had his phone out, his features reflecting the light from his screen. "There," he said.

My phone pinged, and I pulled it out to check. Patrick was now a member of the Octopus WhatsApp group.

"I guess that makes it official," he said. "There's a meeting on Monday night, I hear."

"Yes, at Victoria's house. But Annabel's funeral is the same day. Will you be going?"

"Not to the funeral, but I will see you at Victoria's."

I drove him back to where we had met. His own car, he assured me, was parked a little way off.

"See you Monday then," he said as he got out.

"By the way, how did you know where to find me?"

He leaned into the car, and for a split second I thought he was going to kiss me, which was horrifying, because my spaghetti had been extremely garlicky. I should have thought that one through. But he didn't. he touched the tip of my nose with his finger as if I was a child. "I know a lot about you, Mary Mirren Murdoch."

I was flattered. More than flattered. I watched him in the rear-view mirror as he climbed into his own car and drove away with a wave of his hand.

It was only as he disappeared into the distance that I realised with a chill that it was the same car I had seen on the night of the murder, inching silently out of the rear exit of the car park.

I determined to ask Patrick about his car on Monday night at the meeting. But first there was Annabel's funeral to get through.

The tiny chapel of rest in the middle of Port Gowrie's cemetery was packed. Annabel's husband, Robin, had to be helped in between his daughter and son-in-law. I had never seen a man so devastated. The stiff and dour minister spoke a eulogy. All I could do, while staring at the coffin, was wonder if the police had given back her fingers to be buried with her. Weren't there tribes somewhere in the darkest jungle who believed you couldn't reach your happy hunting ground unless you were intact? Maybe someone was trying to stop Annabel from reaching her happy hunting ground in much the same way, then remorse overtook them, so they sent the fingers back. As a theory, it was pretty flimsy, and not nearly as good as my black magic theory. Though it was certainly in keeping with my warped imagination.

Patrick didn't come, as he said, but the rest of the Port Gowrie writers' group were out in force. Lexie was sniffling into a hankie. Maya Brodie, beside her, was stiff and formal. She would be clamouring for a committee meeting soon. She was always trying to break the stranglehold that Octopus had on the club committee. I wondered too if I wouldn't back her if she attempted to become the new president. I didn't really like Maya, but I did, in my heart of hearts, fundamentally agree with her. The elitism within Port Gowrie writers was destroying our club.

Seated along one row, way out in front, was the remainder of our group. Victoria sat straight and strong. She wouldn't cry. I didn't think she ever had. Beside her, Elsa, trying to be just as strong... for the moment. Undoubtedly, at some critical point during the service, she would break down and cry uncontrollably. She always did at funerals. Dr Bonnar sat with his wife, his hand tucked in hers, as always. I had never known such a devoted couple. Yet she wasn't a pleasant woman. Her face was etched into solid unsmiling lines. Once, Dr Bonnar had told me proudly, she'd been the matron of a nursing home. "The old dears had loved her, Mirren," he assured me proudly. "She has such a way with the elderly."

To me, however, she always looked like she would have been more at home in a concentration camp.

Billie sat next to her. I could see her shoulders shake with her every sob. Vee had her arm around her and Billie's head was on her shoulder. The last funeral we had attended here had been for Billie's sister. Then, Billie hadn't cried. She held up beautifully, and I had been proud of her. A newspaper photographer had been there, bulbs flashing heartlessly, but

Billie had carried herself with dignity. It had been Elsa who'd given the press copy that day, dressed in a chic outfit with wide-brimmed hat: ROMANTASY NOVELIST COLLAPSES AT FRIEND'S FUNERAL, LOCAL WRITER GRIEF-STRICKEN OVER COFFIN OF DEAD FRIEND.

It had been nauseating. I had no doubts that the grief Billie was showing today was compensating for the grief she refused to show at her sister's funeral.

At the end of the row sat Lisette, almost with a smile on her face. Yes, no mistake, almost smiling. She was taking everything in, every sensation, every nuance, filling her mental notebook. If she had just a little more nerve her pencil would be out just now, and she'd be scribbling.

"You aren't sitting with your friends, then?"

I was startled by the whispered Highland tones of D.S. Morrish sliding in beside me in the back row.

"As long as I'm here, that's all that matters."

"Miss Ashe won't be offended? I thought perhaps she wanted you all to show a united front."

"And do you think I'm afraid of Victoria Ashe?"

"If you're not, you're the only one who isn't," he replied.

"Ssshh!" One of Annabel's relatives turned round and silenced us, and for the rest of the service we didn't dare speak.

We never spoke, but Morrish sang, and what a voice he had. He boomed out Morning Has Broken and By Cool Siloam like a professional, and I congratulated him on his fine singing as we filed out of the chapel into the sunlit cemetery.

"I sing in the church choir," he told me with more than a touch of pride. "Been on television too. Songs of Praise."

"Doesn't surprise me," I said honestly.

We had to stand back as Elsa was practically carried out in

tears, supported between two cohorts.

"She's taking it very badly," he observed.

"Think so?"

"Genuine, do you think?"

I glanced at him. "What do you think?"

He watched her for a long moment.

"Do you ask everyone all these questions, Inspector?" I asked.

"Only the ones who answer me with another question."

I think it was then I decided I liked James Morrish.

He offered me a lift home, which I declined. "I get very little chance to walk," I told him.

"Aye, a taxi driver. Strange job for a bit of a girl like you."

"You've made my day, D.S Morrish. A bit of a girl. I'm twenty-seven."

"You're not one of those women who refuse to divulge their age, then?"

"Never seen the point of it," I told him honestly. "Except that when people find out your age they usually expect you to behave in a certain way... I don't like that."

"I can't see you ever behaving in a way people expect, somehow."

We smiled at each other. D.S. Morrish grew more attractive every time I saw him.

"Are you any further ahead in your investigations?" I asked.

He shrugged. "The parcel was posted in a busy shopping area of Glasgow. No one remembers it, and the post office doesn't have CCTV. And there are no distinguishing marks, no fingerprints on anything."

"Including, I suppose, the fingers themselves?"

"Exactly."

"And have you found anyone following Elsa?"

"Not a soul."

"She was genuinely afraid. I'm sure of that."

"Aye," he said. "Just as she was genuinely upset today. She likes the emotion, that one, being the centre of attention."

"You're getting to know our Elsa."

He shuffled a bit beside me. "There's one thing I'd like you to do for me, Muzz..."

"Mirren."

"He seemed to be finding that difficult. "Don't go out in that taxi alone. Whoever we're looking for knows you all, I'm sure of that. It's foolish to take any chances."

Suddenly, there in the cemetery, despite the sun filtering through the monkey puzzle trees, I felt chilled.

"Do you honestly think the rest of us are in danger?"

"I think until we've caught the person responsible it would be foolish not to take that possibility into account."

That night at Victoria's, I told them all about D.S. Morrish's fears.

Typically, Victoria dismissed it. "Nonsense. Some maniac followed Annabel into the committee room. She was the first to arrive. He sees the halls are in darkness. He goes in after her, kills her..."

"For what reason?" I asked.

She ignored that. "He must have heard someone coming up the stairs, panicked, and ran off before he could steal anything..."

"Except two of her fingers."

For once, she was lost for words.

"The way I see it," Dr Bonnar coughed to get our full attention. "Annabel was embroiled in something beyond her control. Her research had taken her further than she'd ever been before. When someone saw her script, they realised they would have to silence her, which they did."

"But we were the only ones to see her script," Victoria reminded him. "And she asked us specifically not to read it."

"Tell me," I said as a thought came to my mind. "If someone had asked Annabel not to read a script specifically... what would she have done?"

Lisette and Billie both answered me. "She'd have read it, of course."

"She couldn't have resisted a peek. We all know that." In my mind, it corroborated the doctor's theory. "You see, we can't be sure no one else read it. Annabel probably had shown her script to someone before us."

"And don't forget this person who was helping her with her research," added the doctor.

"I never heard her talk of anyone," said Vee. "Did you, Mirren?"

"I suppose I did, but don't ask me who it was. I remember her telling me she had a source, a very special source."

"She told me that too," said Billie. "She said she would acknowledge that help if and when the play was produced."

Dr Bonnar took that as all the justification he needed for his theory. "Well, there you are then. That's why she was killed. She got herself involved in some secret cult and was about to expose them."

"Just one small point," I said. "Why send Billie her missing fingers?"

"To warn the rest of us off," he said with assurance.

Elsa turned quite pale. It was amazing how she could do that to order. "She prophesised her own death... I always told her that she would."

And I remembered then that it had been Elsa that night at the meeting who had said: "You wouldn't like to die so horribly yourself, would you?"

"What nonsense you talk, Elsa!" Victoria had even less time for Elsa than usual.

But Elsa would not be silenced so easily. "We are all in danger. I know we are."

"Maybe I should think twice about joining this group. I don't know whether I could take all the excitement."

This was Patrick.

"You're not in any danger. You hardly knew Annabel." Lisette had seated herself next to him as soon as he'd arrived. I had hoped he might sit next to me, but he had only nodded and smiled, then taken the empty chair in the corner. Lisette seemed to pause for a long time, before repeating, "You hardly knew her, did you?"

Patrick answered without looking at her, "Hardly."

Victoria took charge then, tapping the top of her Adam fireplace with a Parker pen. "This is all speculation. Anyway, I doubt if the police in Port Gowrie know what they're doing, especially that young Inspector, but they're all we've got. And I think we should let them get on with it. Annabel's dead. It was tragic, but it had nothing to do with the rest of us."

"Don't forget, Victoria, the fingers were sent to Billie," I interrupted.

She frowned at me. "I'm not forgetting that, Mirren. Nor am I minimising the shock that it must have caused Billie. But it's over now, and we should forget it."

"It's alright for you, no one's following you," came Elsa.

Victoria dismissed that with a casual wave. "Following you, Elsa? Quite frankly, I don't think anyone is following you.

Wishful thinking, that's what you're suffering from."

Elsa was on her feet in an instant, her face shot red. "You bitch! You're jealous of me, of my success. That's what's wrong with you. Always trying to bring me down, making out I'm nothing compared to the rest of you because I'm self-published. Well, let me tell you, my next book is going to surprise you." She looked around our faces. "The lot of you. Then we'll see who can't write."

She made for the door, but I was up and after her. I grabbed her arm and managed to pull her back to her seat again. "We're all a bit wound up about this business."

I glared at Victoria. "You had no right to say what you did." Victoria looked totally stunned. So was I. Had I really just scolded Victoria Ashe? So, I turned round and scolded Elsa too. "And you had no right to say the things you did to Victoria. She's only ever helped and encouraged you, no matter what her personal feelings are about self-published romantasy novels."

Elsa pouted her lips, genuinely upset. Her eyes went to Patrick, and he was watching her. True to type, I saw the change myself, the flickering eyelids, the smile, the breathless acceptance.

"You're so right, Mirren. I apologise." Her apology took in the whole room, Patrick in particular, although her glance did not encompass Victoria. "We are rather a happy little group, you must believe that. We never quarrel."

"Seldom," quibbled Victoria. "When we do, it's usually in a constructive way, about our writing." She smiled. Our venerable leader in control once again. "Well, Patrick, have you brought anything to read to us."

He had a story about a tortured individual who had, through omission, caused the death of his child. It was powerful stuff and left even Victoria with nothing to criticise.

"Are all your stories about guilt and death?" I asked him as we helped each other to our coats in Victoria's hallway.

"And punishment. How people punish themselves whether they're guilty or not."

"You were at the community centre that Tuesday, the night Annabel was murdered."

If my sudden statement took him by surprise, he didn't show it.

"You saw me?"

"Why did you leave so quietly?"

"Why not? I couldn't help the police. I knew nothing. Why? Did you think I had an ulterior motive?" There was a sadness in him when he asked that. As if I'd disappointed him. Before I could say another word, Lisette was at his elbow.

"Remember you offered me a lift, Patrick?"

Obviously when they had been cosily sipping tea together side. How good they looked, she so blonde and petite, a striking contrast to his tall, dark good looks.

"I've not forgotten," he replied.

"Wasn't his story wonderful?" she said to me.

"Wonderful," I agreed, my eyes holding his. Lisette seemed to pull him away, her arm linked in his possessively.

I tried not to watch them go down the path from Victoria's cottage. Nor to watch as Lisette leaned close and whispered something in his ear, probably sweet nothings. Nor to hear her giggle, or see his slow smile.

There was something about Patrick Myer that made my insides churn, and yet... He frightened me. He was hiding something. I was sure of it. And that something had been the reason for his leaving so furtively on the night of Annabel's murder.

CHAPTER FIVE

As I suspected she would, Maya Brodie caused quite a storm by insisting we vote for a new president.

"I shall be more than happy to hold the position until the next AGM," Victoria said, at her most charming. There was a veiled threat in those words. She was determined to hold the position until then.

"Yes, you'd like that, wouldn't you?" Maya stood up. "Well, I say we need an election. A president that is the choice of the people."

I had a feeling from the confident way she spoke that she had already registered her eagerness to stand for the post – and had counted her votes.

"Do you have a candidate in mind?" Victoria asked.

She said nothing, but her glance flickered to Lexie by her side.

Lexie's voice was shaky as she got to her feet. "I'd… I'd like to propose… Maya Brodie."

There was a murmur of assent from round the room.

"I think perhaps we should take a vote," said Victoria.

"I'll second Maya Brodie," another voice said.

There was half-hearted applause.

Victoria delivered her coup de grace. "I think the president of the writers' group should be a published writer at least. I mean properly published."

"Why?" I asked.

Victoria positively glared at me, but the question to my mind was valid. "Why do we need a published writer? What we need is someone who cares about the club. Who can take control, make decisions. Someone who cares about the future of Port Gowrie writers."

Maya looked triumphant. "Does that mean I can rely on your support?"

"I didn't say that."

"Mirren, I'm surprised at you. I thought I could depend on you," said Victoria.

"I didn't say you couldn't."

"I think we should take a vote," said Maya.

Elsa stood up. "Can we have a show of hands for Maya Brodie?"

I watched as both Maya and Victoria counted along with Elsa, neither of them trusting her arithmetical skills.

"And those in favour of Victoria Ashe?"

Again, the hands went up, Patrick, I noticed, among them.

"It seems we have an equal count for both," said Elsa.

"Wait a minute." Victoria was staring at me. "You, Mirren, didn't vote."

"Didn't she? Didn't you?" Elsa was flustered. "Really, I didn't notice. I was just counting the hands."

"You must vote, Mirren," came Vee Kirk.

"Must I?" I didn't want to.

"You must vote for one of us," said Victoria.

I knew that, but which one? Both of them were looking at me, willing me to raise my hand in their favour. Who would it be, Victoria with her authoritarian manner, or Maya, who would engage the club in so much trivia I couldn't bear it.

I looked from one to the other, and finally, my eyes rested on

Patrick. He was sitting almost directly opposite me, watching as if he could see directly into my soul.

"Madame acting president." His voice was rich and resonant. "Since there's a balance of opinion between the candidates, can I propose another?"

His eyes didn't leave mine.

"Another candidate?" Victoria said with some surprise. "Who?"

"Mirren Murdoch," he answered.

And that was how I became president of Port Gowrie Writers Group. It seemed I was much more acceptable to the main body of the club and totally acceptable to Octopus. Even Victoria agreed to back me, mainly because I'm sure she thought I'd be easily moulded to her way of thinking.

"I ought to be angry with you for this," I told Patrick later. "I didn't want to be president."

"You surely didn't want Maya Brodie to be president?"

"Heaven forbid."

"I think you'll make a very fine president."

"Will I?"

"You sound as if you're going through some kind of crisis of confidence."

"I am." Suddenly, I wanted to tell someone. No, not someone, only him. But not here.

"Come on, I'll take you for a drink. You can tell me about it."

Who could refuse an offer like that?

Vee Kirk called me over to congratulate me. She had seconded me almost immediately, glad of anyone who wasn't Victoria or Maya. "You'll be very good for the club, dear. I know it." She took my hand in hers, holding it tightly. "Don't let any lack of success at the moment make you downhearted. It will come. I do like you, Mirren. You've been a breath of fresh air since you joined us. We were all getting a bit stale until you came along." Her eyes darted to where Patrick stood waiting for me, and her smile became a frown. "You're not going home with him, are you?"

Before I could answer she was shaking her head so violently I thought her swans head hat pin was going to spin off and impale someone. "Do be careful, Mirren. There's something wrong with Patrick Myer. I don't know what it is, but just... just be careful, won't you?"

I would have asked her what she meant, but at that moment Dr Bonnar broke in on us. "Excuse me, Mirren. Mrs Kirk, you wanted to see me about something?"

"Yes, Dr Bonnar, I did. It was about..." she smiled again, squeezing my hand even tighter. "You won't forget what I told you, will you?"

"I'll be careful." If Elsa had been writing the scene, then this is when I would have kissed her tenderly on the cheek, before scooting off to ride some dragons, but I'm not Elsa and this was real life. So I only squeezed back, and left her with Dr Bonnar.

"What did Mrs Kirk want?" Patrick asked as I came to him.

To warn me against wicked Irishmen, like you, I wanted to say, but I didn't know how he might take that, so I only answered, "She wanted to congratulate me, that's all."

I had a distinct feeling that he knew I was only telling part of the truth, but he didn't pursue it. Instead he took my elbow to lead me outside. I saw Lisette's questioning eyes following us.

Halfway down the stairs, Elsa came hurrying after us. "Do you think anyone could give me a lift home?"

I couldn't believe this was happening again. "What happened to your police escort?"

"They've called him off, can you believe it? Mike insisted. Said I was imagining everything, and that he would take care of me. So what happens? First night, and he has to go away on business."

"Look," Patrick said. "Why don't you take Elsa home? I'll meet you at Rocco's."

The romantic novelist in Elsa came bursting out at that point. "Actually, Patrick, I'd feel much safer if you took me home."

Patrick looked at me, amusement in his eyes. I helped him out of his dilemma.

"Why don't I go along to Rocco's and get us a table?"

Elsa linked her arm through his. "You don't mind, Mirren?" She fluttered her eyelashes at Patrick. "Mirren knows I'm the kind of woman who needs a man. Not like Mirren." That was me dismissed as a rival in those three words. "Driving a taxi around town till all hours in the morning. I wouldn't dare."

Patrick's eyebrows went up and I felt safe again. He didn't take Elsa seriously. He preferred women who drove taxis at night to those who went weak at the sight of him. I did both, but maybe I didn't show it. I wondered if that made a difference.

"I won't be long. Fifteen minutes."

As they walked off towards Patrick's car, I distinctly heard Elsa saying, "You must let me help you with your writing."

It would never occur to Elsa that Patrick didn't need her help.

I was on my second coffee, and on the point of ordering my third. I checked my phone, but there was nothing from Patrick. On WhatsApp he was showing as inactive since earlier that day. I wondered about calling him, but did that seem needy? I'd almost given up on him, torturing myself with visions of him carrying Elsa up her stairs with her lace negligee trailing behind them.

Elsa was still an attractive woman, and her newfound income from self-publishing only made her more attractive. She was also ripe for some real-life research into her novels. I was sure, though she denied it, that she'd had a face-lift last year. It would be a nose job next. Not that I blamed her. If I'd had the money, I might consider having my nose changed too.

Suddenly Patrick appeared at the door, whipping off his green scarf, which, I noticed, matched his eyes. "Sorry, sorry, sorry." He looked flushed, like he'd been hurrying to meet me, or fighting off Elsa's advances. I decided not to ask which.

"I didn't think you were coming." I tried to sound unconcerned. "You've been over an hour. We could have made it another night."

"No, I wanted to come, you know that."

I wanted to ask why. I wanted to know why he wanted to see me. Was it more personal this time? Instead, I handed him a menu. "Fancy sharing a pizza?"

After we ordered, the conversation naturally moved back to writing, and he asked me once again why I had lost my confidence.

"I've always had oodles of confidence. I'm a born writer, Victoria says. Since the first night I came to the club she told me that. I started just a few weeks after Billie. Of course Billie is a great writer, with a capital G. That was obvious from the very beginning. I could never match her for talent, but I didn't care. I never wanted to be a great writer. Taking three years to write a novel would bore me. I just wanted to write, anything and everything. It poured out of me. Last year, it seemed it was coming together. I had a producer interested in one of my scripts at the BBC. I even had an agent interested in a funny kids book I wrote." My voice trailed off. I'd never told anyone this before, not these innermost fears and inadequacies. Not my mother, not anyone. And here I was telling Patrick Myer. I had a strange feeling he had known it all along.

"So what happened?" His hand strayed over the table to cover mine. How good it felt.

"All in the space of a few weeks, it was like the shutters had come down. Bang, bang, bang. Positions closed. It felt like being blacklisted. I keep telling myself that's how it goes sometimes. Things go quiet, people ghost you, and it will get better some time, but it hasn't. If I wrote Bleak Expectations and sent it out, I'm pretty sure it would just disappear into oblivion."

"So what have you been doing then?"

"All the right things. I keep sending things out as if nothing's changed. Then I wait."

"You always look so confident. You give everyone at the club confidence that they can do it too."

"I know," I said. "I always say, if I can do it, anybody can. Somebody up there must have heard me and decided to rub my face in it."

"Haven't you got to learn to handle that kind of thing if you want to be a writer?"

"I always have before. In all the rejections, there was always a nugget of hope somewhere. But now, I can't seem to please anyone. Oh, I'm sorry, Patrick. I must sound so self-pitying. I don't mean to be. You shouldn't have got me started."

"So…" he said. "What are you going to do about it?"

I shrugged. "I don't know. Keep trying? What's your advice?"

He paused for a moment. "Give up. Stop writing. Stop sending things out altogether. It's not worth it."

I pulled my hand free of his. "What! Are you serious? Give up writing? It's never even crossed my mind to do that. I couldn't. If I stop writing, stop sending things out, the hope is gone. I wouldn't even be trying anymore."

"So what's the alternative?"

"Just keep trying, as I said. Keep writing the best I can. Keep sending stuff out. And I will."

He smiled, as if I'd just fallen into a trap he'd laid. "I knew you would." And he leaned across the table and kissed me.

He kissed me again as we stood by my car outside the restaurant. A long, lingering kiss. If I didn't have my mother waiting I would have invited him home. Yet even as he kissed me something struck me as strange. Strange and suspicious.

The smell of Elsa's perfume was on his shirt.

For the first time in weeks when I woke up the next morning, my first thought wasn't writing. It was Patrick Myer. I could still taste him, hear his soft voice. He was right. I could never give up. I had the solution all the time in myself. He had only helped me put it into words. Hadn't I already started another novel? This one would be even better. Now I jumped from the bed ready to carry on, fired with enthusiasm... and Patrick Myer.

I bounced into the kitchen, humming. My mother was already there, making up the sandwiches for her dinner. She was a nursing auxiliary at the hospital, though she insisted on calling herself a nurse's helper. She also insisted she was 'buttering her chits' rather than making up sandwiches. "Don't you put on the posh talk wi' me, lassie," she would say whenever I corrected her. "Don't think you're going to do an Elsa Fordyce."

It rankled with my mother that she had grown up with Elsa's mother and her family. "And they didnae have a pair o' knickers between them." Now, Elsa refused to acknowledge her humble beginnings. She had come, as she would say in interviews, from an impoverished background. However, she would infer strongly that her father had lost the family fortune through unwise speculation. "Aye, on the horses, more like," my mother insisted. But, in spite of the poverty, Elsa would say, they had never lost their elegance, that inner quality only the well-bred have. "Whit horseshit!"

It was always a mistake to get my mother started on Elsa Fordyce.

"You're helluva happy this mornin'," she went on. "Anything' happen last night that I should know about?"

"I'm twenty-seven years old, dear. There's absolutely nothing that happened to me last night that you'll ever know about."

"I see the mooth is workin' again. You must be in love."

Actually, I knew she'd be pleased no matter what the reason for my good humour. She preferred it when I answered her back. I was still singing as I chewed on some toast and switched on the radio. A nasal voice was reading the Scottish news.

I hardly listened. I saw my mother off at the door to wait for her lift at the corner, and I sat down at the table and poured myself some tea.

"A woman's body was found in the early hours of this morning in Port Gowrie. She has not yet been named but it is thought she was a member of the Port Gowrie writers' group, whose president was murdered only two weeks ago."

I spat out my tea. My first thought was Elsa. Elsa was dead.

My phone rang almost immediately. I got such a fright I dropped my cup and scalding tea saturated my pyjamas.

It was Victoria, making sure I was still alive.

"I can't get hold of Billie, or Elsa, or Vee. Lisette's the only other one I was able to contact." Nice to know I was last on the list.

"It could be Maya Brodie, or Lexie. Maybe we should put out a WhatsApp to the whole group…"

She dismissed them as if they didn't matter. "We both know it isn't any of them. It's one of us: Octopus. I can't sit here not knowing."

Neither could I. "I'll be over for you in ten minutes."

I was with her in five. No shower, clothes pulled on hurriedly, my hair hardly combed. Victoria was her usual glamorous self, her hair coiffured neatly, her fingernails freshly painted. Even in times of crisis, like an impending asteroid strike, she would go to her doom like a lady.

Dr Bonnar was already at the police station when we arrived. As soon as we ran to meet him, Lisette appeared from the ladies with a pale Billie on her arm. Another one struck off the list.

"Do you know who it is yet?"

"Have they named her?"

"I don't know," said Lisette. "I can't get hold of Elsa. I've been trying to phone. It's just going straight to voicemail. WhatsApp shows she's been inactive since last night. Same with Vee. And the police aren't saying anything until the next-of-kin are informed."

"Stupid policemen," Victoria snapped, as if she had more right to know than any of the relatives.

"How did they both get home last night?"

I hadn't wanted anyone to ask that question, least of all Lisette.

"Vee walked, I know that," Billie said, tears rolling down her cheeks.

"Oh pull yourself together, Billie. I never thought you'd fall apart like this," said Victoria. If only she could hear herself. She didn't sound too in charge of her feelings either.

"I can't help it, Victoria!" Billie snapped so loudly the policeman at the desk looked up at her and stared. "I'm frightened, and I don't understand what's happening."

"Mrs Kirk walked home?" Dr Bonnar asked. "Why on earth did she do that? I was the last to speak to her when she left the club and she didn't mention walking. I took it for granted she was getting a lift. Even Elsa's policeman could have dropped her off on the way to Elsa's."

"Elsa's policeman wasn't there. She moaned about that to me during coffee," said Billie. "I offered her a lift home but she said she'd made other arrangements."

"That's funny, she told me she wanted to walk home," Lisette told us. "Because it was such a lovely night."

"So did she walk?"

I'd been dreading that inevitable question. But I'd have to answer it.

Like a saving grace, right at that moment D.S Morrish came out of his office. "Ah, you're all here. Would you come into the office?"

We all filed in obediently.

"Which of us has been murdered?" Not a question, a demand, in typical Victoria fashion.

James Morrish ignored her. I had to admire him for that. He, for one, would not be browbeaten by her. "Would you all like to take a seat? I'm sorry to have kept you waiting, but we had to inform the next of kin first, you understand."

"Who was it, inspector?" asked Dr Bonnar.

He sat down behind his desk, eyeing us all carefully. "It was... Mrs Kirk."

He paused, scanning our faces. "She was found this morning in a little side street in the west end of town, Laburnum Grove. A man walking his dog found her. She's been strangled."

Vee, dear Vee. I closed my eyes. When I opened them again, D.S Morrish was watching me closely.

"I knew she shouldn't have walked home alone." Billie burst out crying. "What was she thinking of?"

"Who did she usually go home with?" asked Morrish.

"She used to have her own car, but it's been off the road for a while. So she's been getting lifts. Her house is on the way to Elsa's, so Elsa's husband often dropped her off," I said.

"But she didn't last night?"

Suddenly, Billie stood up and shouted at him. "If you hadn't taken off Elsa's policeman, none of this would have happened."

D.S Morrish raised an eyebrow. "Is that what she told you? That we took her policeman off? It was Elsa herself who insisted he didn't come last night. She said her husband was taking her and picking her up."

I interrupted. "But she told me it was her husband who insisted the policeman be taken off."

"Did she now? As it happens, I've discovered that her husband is away on business. She'd informed him that she was going to stay with friends. He's been on the phone to us, distraught, thinking his wife had been found dead. The friends she was supposed to be staying with knew nothing about her coming, and she's not at the house. In fact, we can't reach her at all. Do any of you know how Mrs Fordyce got home?

I felt his gaze fall on me. "She asked me for a lift."

"So you took her home?"

"Well, no actually… I was with Patrick Myer, and Elsa decided she'd feel safer getting a lift from a man."

"And you never saw either of them again?"

"Yes. Patrick met me in Rocco's later."

He leaned forward. "How much later?"

"About…" I considered lying. Considered against it. "Nearly 11, I think."

He said nothing. Common sense alone would have told him it's a long time to take running someone three miles home.

"And none of you saw Mrs Kirk again after she left the meeting?"

We all shook our heads. After a few more questions we all rose to leave.

"Just one more thing before you go."

We stopped and turned back to Morrish. "Mrs Kirk seems to have been strangled with a rope. There were rope burns on her neck. Would that have any connection to her writing?"

He could tell by the gasps and moans that it had. It was Dr Bonnar who answered. "'*Death by the Rope.*'"

I glanced around them, all of them reacting exactly as they should be; shock, horror, sadness, all of these showed on their faces. Except for Lisette. Her eyes flashed. All this was sending her adrenalin soaring. She didn't care enough about any of us to worry about a little thing like murder. She was in the middle of a real-life drama, and she was savouring every second.

"What does it all mean, Inspector?"

"It means a whole new theory has opened up."

"And what could that possibly be?" asked Billie.

"That someone is out to pick you all off one by one, using the methods you yourselves write about."

CHAPTER SIX

"Would you wait behind, Muzz Murdoch?" D.S Morrish asked as we were filing out in shocked silence.

I'm sure none of the others liked this singling out of me for special attention. I, however, felt quite flattered. I closed the door and sat down.

"Did you mean that? You really think someone's out to destroy Octopus?"

"Now that Mrs Kirk has been murdered, and considering the method that has been used, then yes, it's a distinct possibility." He hesitated. "Has anyone else died recently in your group?"

"Why do you always ask questions you already know the answer to?"

"For the same reason you always answer a question with a question."

We both smiled.

"No," I said. "The last death to even touch our group was when Billie's sister died."

"Did that death come as a surprise?"

"Well, no, not really. She'd been gravely ill for a while, she took pneumonia. In her bedridden condition, that can kill. Why do you ask? You surely don't think Billie's sister's death could have anything to do with this?"

"In her book, the main character loses someone they love dearly. I just wondered."

This new idea stunned me. "But why? You think someone would kill someone we cared about, because we had written about it in a book?"

"Who knows, if it suits their own plot?"

"Please don't mention it to Billie. If she thought anyone killed her sister... I don't know what she would do."

"At the moment, it's just a vague possibility, that's all."

"I don't know why anyone would want to kill any of us."

Morrish shrugged. "Jealousy? There's a lot of bad feeling about your little clique."

"Jealous enough to kill? No, that's too far-fetched."

"The human mind, when it's warped, can justify killing for the slightest reason. That's why madness is so terrifying. A man can live with his wife, no arguments, they seem perfectly content. Then one day, he kills her with an axe because his tea was a little weak."

"You're telling me we have a madman in our midst?"

"Or madwoman."

"Yes, it's more likely, I suppose. We have a preponderance of women in the club. I'd say they're all slightly mad. Take your pick."

His eyes narrowed at me. "You looked relieved when I said it was Mrs Kirk who was dead. I wondered about that."

His way of changing the subject so suddenly was deliberate. He wanted to see my reaction. Unprepared for it, the ploy certainly worked on me. I knew that I looked guilty, and I could feel my face flush. "Did I? I'm sorry about that. I was very fond of Vee." I was ashamed. Some people complained that Vee could be nasty and rather small minded, but to me she had always been encouraging and kind.

"Tell me about Patrick Myer." He'd done it again. My face went even redder.

"There's not much to tell. He's only recently joined the club. He's a very good writer. He was asked to join Octopus after Annabel died." I paused. "In all honestly, when he hears about this he'll probably resign."

"And you were with him last night? Did he say anything about Mrs Fordyce when he joined you in Rocco's?"

"No. We hardly mentioned her."

"Did he take her directly home?"

"I took it for granted that he did."

"Did he offer to take her home, or did she ask him? She was quite definite to our man about getting a lift there and back."

I decided to be bluntly honest. "She singled him out. I offered to take her home, and she refused. She said she wanted a man." I thought about that for a moment. "She wanted Patrick."

"And was he pleased?"

"I don't know him well enough to answer that."

"He certainly took his time getting back to you."

I wondered when he would come to that. "You'd better ask Patrick about that?"

"I plan to. Do you know his address off hand?"

I suddenly realised I didn't. In fact, I knew very little about Patrick Myer. "No," I admitted.

"Then who would know?"

"Our secretary. She'd have the addresses of all the members."

"And your secretary is?"

He knew the answer as well as I. "Elsa Fordyce."

Lisette was waiting in the corridor for me when I emerged from the office. Her cheeks were flushed. Her eyes glimmered.

She was alive.

"I'm taking Victoria home." So, Lisette had indeed taken over Billie's mantle.

"Fine."

"What did the Inspector want?"

I lied. "He wanted to know if I could think of anyone who would want to kill us. Cut off our tentacles, one by one."

"Of course." I could see her jotting the line down in her mental notebook.

"And can you?"

"Not off hand."

"We must think. We must get together and go through everyone who might have a reason to hold a grudge against us." She didn't move. Finally, she said, "And didn't he want to know about Patrick?"

"I couldn't tell him anything about Patrick."

"Maybe he should have asked me."

If I was supposed to rise to that I didn't disappoint her. "Oh, and what could you tell him about Patrick?"

"Lots of things," she said, studying her pale pink nails.

"Like what?"

"Like... Patrick had already read Annabel's play."

"Did Annabel tell you this?"

"I saw them together. She was giving him her script. Very furtive, they looked."

Furtive, another word used often to describe Patrick.

"How do you know it was her play?"

"She told me so," she said triumphantly. "I confronted her later when I met her in town. She was on her way to Glasgow.

She hinted that Patrick had done so much to help her with the research. She asked me to keep it a secret. Patrick didn't want anyone to know."

Her very special source… Patrick.

"Have you told the police this?"

"No… and neither has he. Strange, eh?"

Victoria was at the door of the police station, her voice echoing along the corridors. "Lisette, you are coming, aren't you?"

Lisette made to move, but I held her back. "You have to tell the police now."

"If Elsa had been the victim I would have, but it was Vee. He must have some reason for keeping it dark. Why should I interfere?"

Yes, Lisette was a great one for letting her characters have their head and create the story for themselves. Choose your own adventure. This was her doing it right now.

Yet, he must have a reason. There was some strange secret about Patrick. I didn't know what it was, and it wasn't my romantic imagination. I was sure of that. Patrick was hiding something.

"That's it, lassie. You're no' going back to that club!"

My mother had come home early as soon as she'd heard about the murder to make sure I hadn't been the victim. Didn't matter a damn that she'd had breakfast with me. She had to be sure. Now she was giving me an ultimatum. "Don't know how you ever joined it anyway. Hoity toity lot, yon Victoria Ashe. Her books are rubbish, and yon Elsa…" Her eyes soared to the ceiling. "If you ever wrote stuff like that, I'd disown ye. Half the time she's on aboot dragons, the other half she's on aboot bits of the body I've never even heard o'" She'd read every one of Elsa's books anyway, I almost said. Maybe she was studying biology. "The only one that writes good stuff is yon Lisette. Right good murder stories, nice and gory. I don't know why ye don't try something like that."

The doorbell rang. "See if it's mair of them reporters..." she waddled to the door, pushing up her sleeves. Local and national reporters had been hounding us all day. I almost felt sorry for the one at the door now. Mother was well into her sixties, but I didn't fancy their chances.

"We've just about had enough of this... Away ye to hell!"

I could just see him through the open door, black hair falling over his brow, the green, amused eyes. Patrick.

I ran to the door. "It's okay." Not taking my eyes off him, him not taking his eyes off me. "This is my friend from the club."

"From yon club..." She stepped back from the door to let him in. "I'd search him for offensive weapons if I was you."

Patrick's eyes crinkled to a smile.

"We'll go into the front room, mother."

"Please yourself," she said, following us.

"We'll have some tea." I barred her way, and began to close the door firmly in her face.

"Think I'm a bloody home help or something?" she was muttering as she went off towards the kitchen.

I closed the door and turned to Patrick, not realising he was so close behind me. His arms went round my waist. His lips were on my neck, and when I turned it was for a full frontal assault. It was wonderful.

"Mirren, Mirren," he was whispering. "I came as soon as I heard."

The name of the victim still hadn't been announced. "It was Vee," I said.

I felt the relief flood through him.

"I thought… God, I thought…"

"You thought it was Elsa, why?"

He stopped kissing me for a minute. "I was probably the last person to see her. I took her home, remember?"

"To her own home?"

"Of course, to her own home. Where else?"

I ran my fingers along his face, and let him kiss me again for a long time before I answered that one. I had a feeling I knew what his reaction would be to my answer. "Elsa's missing, Patrick."

He sprang from me just as I expected, and held me away from him. "How can she be missing?"

"She's not at her house. They can't find her. Her husband was away on business. She told him she'd be staying with friends, but it wasn't true."

He nodded and moved to the window. He lifted back the curtain and stared out. "She'll turn up. She's been afraid to stay at the house herself."

"Perhaps she was hoping she wouldn't have to."

He seemed about to say something, then changed his mind. "Wait… no, I thought she said her husband was just away to a business meeting. Didn't he come home?"

"No, all lies. He was away for the night, and like I said, she told him she was staying with friends."

He glanced at me. "Perhaps she is."

I shrugged. "She's not been answering her phone, and she's been off WhatsApp. The police will want to speak to you, Patrick."

"I can't tell them anything."

"What about Annabel?"

This time the hesitation was more obvious. "What about

Annabel?"

"You read her play. You were her very special source of research."

He didn't deny it. Instead he said, "Do the police know?"

"Not yet, but you have to tell them, Patrick."

He was shaking his head. "No, I don't know anything about Annabel's death. We got talking one night at the club, and I told her I'd done a fair bit of research on the occult for a book I was writing. She was welcome to any information I could give her."

"Well then, why not tell the police that?"

"I can't get involved, Mirren."

"But you're already involved. And you'll make it worse if you don't tell them all you know."

He groaned. "I should have left after Annabel's murder."

"Why?"

"Because I'm getting drawn into this, deeper and deeper, like drowning in quicksand. And if I don't get out now, I have a feeling I never will."

"What are you afraid of, Patrick? What are you hiding?"

I crossed to the window and took his hands in mine. "You can tell me."

He pulled me close to him and his lips brushed my brow. "Can I do that? Can I really, Mirren?"

I felt as if he was talking to himself, debating whether he should confide in me or not. He was a long time deciding and I was so afraid my wee mother would bustle in with three mugs on a tray and spoil everything.

"My name's not really Patrick Myer," he said, finally.

"It's not?"

"My real name's Patrick O'Kane."

Patrick O'Kane, where had I heard that name before? Pat O'Kane, yes, five years ago, or was it more? In Aberdeen, oil rich city, Pat O'Kane, tried for premeditated murder of his mistress.

Pat O'Kane, verdict Not Proven.

In Scotland, the Not Proven verdict meant Innocent… but only because there's not enough evidence to prove your guilt.

CHAPTER SEVEN

That was when my mother burst in with her three mugs.

"Well, here we are, nice and cosy. Need the fire on?" She looked up, noticed Patrick's arms around me and the tray went down with a clatter. "Is everything okay?"

"Patrick has just heard about Mrs Kirk, mother."

She thought about this for a moment, wondering if it was enough justification for holding her daughter in the living room in the middle of the afternoon.

"I knew they'd found someone. I didn't know it was Mrs Kirk. She was always very kind to me," he said.

Well, that was it, as soon as my mother recognised the Irish in his voice she was a goner. After all, with an accent like that there was a good chance he was a Catholic too. I wondered what she'd do if she discovered he might also be a murderer. As long as he was a catholic, one, then she'd probably consider that the lesser of two evils.

Patrick, a murderer? A not proven one. As good as guilty, that had been the opinion of the day. There just hadn't been enough hard evidence to convict him. It had all been circumstantial. I remember reading about it, and I had thought so too. I'd been convinced of his guilt. A passionate relationship with a woman. He had wanted to break it off. She refused. She harassed him, followed him everywhere. It was fatal attraction. He'd been heard to threaten her if she didn't leave him alone. Then finally she'd been found, strangled, in her bedroom.

Strangled, just like Vee.

His eyes, looking at me from across the mugs of tea, were pleading. I wanted to talk to him, hear his side. I wanted to believe he was innocent. My mother, however, refused to shut up.

"Are you friends of the Myers from the East end? I remember a family that came from Arthur Street. Or was their name Meechan? You remember, Mirren, them that used to have the licensed grocer."

"That was the McMenemys, mother."

"Oh, aye, so it was. You're no' related to them, are you Patrick?"

"The McMenemys?" he said, confused. "No."

Was there ever a mother like mine? She was the mistress of irrelevant conversation. "You're awfy like the boy McMenemy. Maybe you went to school with him."

This was my mother's not-so-subtle way of finding out if he went to a Catholic school.

"I was born and brought up in Cork, Mrs Murdoch. I was taught by the nuns at St Davids."

Her face lit up with pleasure. "Ach, here, have a scone, son. I baked them myself." She looked on, satisfied, as Patrick bit into his scone, and pronounced it delicious. "By the nuns, eh? Well, in Cork, I'd never have guessed."

Patrick spluttered into his tea. For the first time, I heard him laugh… for the last time, too.

We were on our way to the police station before we had a chance to speak again. "I didn't do it, you know."

"Do what?"

"The murder I was tried for… why, what did you think I meant? Murder Vee? Of course, she was strangled. That was apparently my modus operandi, wasn't it?"

"I didn't mean that at all."

"Of course you didn't. As long as you believe in me, Mirren. I doubt anyone else will. Lightning striking twice and all that."

"What about the…" I shrugged, not knowing how to ask.

"The other murder? Rosa Boyle, that was her name. She of the lovely black hair and the Spanish look. I didn't kill her. I've always wondered who did, but it wasn't me."

I wanted to believe that, so much.

He went on, "I promised myself then I'd never let them put me in a cell again, and they never will, Mirren."

"Then you moved here and joined the writers group. Bit of bad luck, eh?"

He smiled at me. "I'm glad you're coming with me."

He squeezed my hand as we walked up the steps of the police station. It buzzed with even more activity than usual. A second murder, and the big guns from Glasgow had been sent for. I hoped that didn't mean James Morrish would be taken off the case. He was always at pains to point out he was a D.S, not a D.I. so maybe a D.I would be taking over.

I was relieved to find him still in his office, still in charge. I felt he was not surprised to see us. I could see him glancing at our linked hands. Was that disapproval, or something else?

"You're a hard man to get hold of, Patrick Myer."

Patrick waited until the door closed and we were sitting in his office before he corrected that. "It's Patrick O'Kane, Inspector."

"He knows that already," I said. "It's an old trick of D.S. Morrish's. Isn't it?"

Morrish just looked at me. Patrick went on.

"I took Elsa, um, Mrs Fordyce home last night. To her own house. When I left her, I was under the impression she was there for the night. If she's not, I don't know where she is."

"And how was she when you left her?" asked Morrish.

Patrick glanced at me before he answered. "She seemed... fine."

"Well, you just tell me what you know, Mr..." he hesitated. "Myer."

I was glad he used that name. It seemed to give Patrick more confidence to go on to tell him the events of last night.

"And what time was it when you left her?" Morrish asked when Patrick finished.

"Just after ten."

"It was near eleven when you got back to Mirren."

"Perhaps it was a little later. Mrs Fordyce insisted on giving me advice about my writing. It would have seemed rude to dash off." He laughed bitterly. "Of course, I didn't think I'd be needing an alibi, or to be quite honest good manners could have gone to hell."

"Did you go into the house with her?"

Another pause. "Yes. Her husband wasn't there and she asked me to come in and make sure it was safe. How could I refuse?"

"And you saw nothing of Mrs Kirk as you drove back into town?"

Patrick shouted his answer. "No, I didn't!" He turned to me. "See? They're going to pin the whole thing on me. I'm prime suspect, Patrick O'Kane. I shouldn't have come."

D.S. Morrish took no heed of this outburst. "What colour of car do you drive?"

"A black Ford estate, it's quite old."

He wrote that down. "Is there anything else I should know?" And he knew the answer to that one already too. God, I could read this man like one of Elsa's books.

"You'd better tell him about Annabel." I reached out and touched Patrick's hand, and he stroked my fingers gently before he spoke again. D.S. Morrish was watching that closely.

Patrick told him softly about his involvement in Annabel's research. "I met her on the day she died. She was on her way to Glasgow, but she wanted me to read the finished version."

"Did she seem upset or worried about anything?" I asked. I couldn't fail to hear Morrish's sigh. I was doing his job again.

"No," Patrick said. "She was in a fine mood. Pleased with her play. I would have said there was nothing worrying her at all."

"So it was whatever happened in Glasgow, or when she came back that upset her?"

"I'm so glad you're here to sort these things out for us." James Morrish's voice was scolding.

"Sorry."

"May I continue?" he asked me.

"Be my guest," I said.

His tone changed when he spoke to Patrick. "And that was the last you saw of Mrs DeVere?"

"It was."

"And did you read her play?"

"No, I didn't. I didn't have time that day… and with her death… I couldn't bring myself to."

"So, what were you doing for the rest of that day, Mr Myer?"

"Working on my book. Quite alone. Not much of an alibi, is it?"

Morrish shook his head. "No, it isn't."

"I told you, Mirren," said Patrick. "Deeper and deeper I sink. How can they help but suspect me now?"

"If you're ready to confess, we'll be glad go arrest you," said Morrish. "We're always glad to close a case. But for the moment you're free to go."

We stood up and made for the door. James Morrish called me back. "Muzz… can I speak to you for a moment alone?"

I smiled at Patrick. "Wait for me, I won't be long."

"I'll wait in the car, if you don't mind. I can't abide being in this place any longer than I have to."

I stepped back into the office and closed the door. "What is it?"

"You're going to say it's none of my business, but… in a case like this you should be very wary of placing your trust in anyone, especially him."

"It *is* none of your business," I said.

"I didn't realise you were that close to him, or to anyone, for that matter."

"Why, have you been investigating me?"

"You told me you hardly knew him."

"I didn't. I'm getting to know him better, that's all."

"If you want my advice, then you won't get to know him too well."

"He was right. You do suspect him."

"I suspect everybody."

"Even me?"

He paused. "Do you know anyone with a red Fiat car?"

"My car isn't a red Fiat."

"I know that, but do you know anyone who has one?"

"Well, of course I do. Billie has a red Fiat." Even he looked a little surprised.

"Billie?"

"Yes, why?"

"Because last night, a red Fiat car was seen cruising along the road that leads to Laburnum Grove."

What had Billie been up to? Why hadn't she said? I went outside to find Patrick in the street smoking a cigarette nervously.

"I didn't know you smoked," I said.

"I needed one after that." We were just getting into the car when suddenly flashbulbs started exploding around us, and reporters materialized from nowhere.

"Excuse me, aren't you from Octopus?"

"Yes." I tried to start the engine, but it wouldn't catch. My pesky ignition had been playing up all week.

One of them thrust a microphone inside the car, which meant I couldn't shut the door. "Could you tell us how you feel now that another of your members has been brutally murdered?"

Were they trained to ask stupid questions like that? "I'm just dandy, obviously! How the hell do you think I feel?"

The reporters jotted that down. God knows how it would look in tomorrow's paper.

"And is it true there's another member missing?"

"I think you'd better talk to the police about that."

The man with the microphone leaned further into the car, wafting the mike at Patrick. "And your name is, Sir?"

The engine roared into life. I pushed the reporter out before Patrick could answer, slammed the door and zoomed off.

"What did the Inspector want?" He didn't give me a chance to answer. "He has his eye on you, you know."

"He doesn't. Don't be silly."

"Oh, but he does. I could tell by the way he kept looking at me, with your hand in mine. And the way he kept calling you Mirren. Very unprofessional."

I ignored that. "Billie's car was seen last night, near where Vee's body was found. So, you're not the only suspect."

That made him smile, a slow languorous smile that was most attractive. "Billie, a suspect? I'd be more likely to squeeze the life out of a woman than Billie." His fingers, strong and cool, stroked my face. "Don't you agree?"

And D.S. Morrish's warning echoed in my head.

By evening, Elsa had still not surfaced, and still not answered her phone. I knew if she didn't soon then Patrick would be back down at police headquarters, and more questions would be asked.

Patrick had driven me home, kissed me quickly and left, and I still didn't know where he lived.

That evening, I was out in my taxi again. My mother had her jacket on ready to go out with me. My chaperone, five feet tall, and just as round but with a tongue that was so sharp it could be classed as an offensive weapon. I refused to let her come.

"I'll be careful, I promise."

"You don't know what kind of cutthroats you'll get in that cab. It's a daft job for a lassie."

Everyone thought the same. When I got to the office, John, my boss, asked if I was sure I should go out. "You can stay here and do control."

The last time I'd worked on control I had taxis whizzing about looking for passengers, and passengers standing for hours waiting on taxis. I was too dreamy to work on control, and John knew it. "I'm rubbish at it. Do you want to lose business that much?"

"I just don't like the idea of you going out tonight."

"I have my phone. It'll be on at all times."

While I'll admit to being a little scared, I had to work, and that was that.

My first call was to a party on the east side of town. Three raucous females, slightly drunk, going on to a club. They insisted on singing me a Taylor Swift, before finally alighting at their destination. Their high spirits cheered me up. Usually, it was a quiet night for fares, but I was kept busy with one call after another. A foreign boat had come in, and between sailors leaving the ship and furtive females boarding them, I was continually on the go.

After one such escapade, I received a call to go to Pier Thirteen and pick up some more.

Back I went, this time past the container terminal where boats were docked at Pier Eight and Pier Ten. Pier Thirteen wasn't lit up. No boat was tied up there. In fact, nobody had used Thirteen in years. It was outside the terminal's fence. Pier Thirteen was dark, deserted and derelict. There was an icy fog hanging around the few streetlamps in this part of town.

The silence was eerie as I cut off my engine and called control. "Who am I supposed to be picking up here?"

"Three passengers. You better wait a bit. You know what'll be keeping them."

"Who made the call?"

The girl on control was new. I hardly knew her. "I don't know. I can't remember. Does it matter?"

It doesn't usually, but somehow it did tonight.

There was no one here. To hell with it, I thought, I was going back. I swivelled the wheel, turned the car, and the headlights caught something, someone. A fleeting movement, someone ducking into the shadows. I wasn't going to hang about and find out who. I pressed hard on the accelerator and the car shot forward. Suddenly there was a screech and a bang and I felt both my front tyres explode.

Instinctively, I screamed.

Here I was, alone and stranded at Pier Thirteen. I grasped hold of my torch, refusing to feel threatened. I wouldn't be afraid, though my breath was hoarse and I could feel beads of sweat forming on my brow.

I called control again. "That call for Pier Thirteen. Are you sure you can't remember who made it?"

"Sorry, it's going crazy in here. Hundreds of calls. Gah... how the f... should I remember?" The new girl was stressed already, well she should try being in my shoes.

"There's nobody here."

"Just leave it then. There's a taxi needed at St Clair Street. You're nearest."

"I can't. I've run over something and both my tyres have blown."

"Aw, FUCK!" I heard her relay the call to another cab.

"Hey you!" I screamed into my phone. "There's somebody out here, and I can't move. Will you get a taxi to come for me?"

She swore again, as if I was asking for the impossible. "Oh, awright!"

In the silent darkness, I swung my torch around the shadows. No one. A couple of rusting capstans on the pier side, a dilapidated old pier house and a gangplank lying askew on the ground. No one. I was being silly.

But with two women already murdered, both from Octopus, I would be silly not to be careful.

With one more sweep around, I got out to survey the damage to my tyres. I'd gone over a large piece of planking with giant nails poking out of it. It was a disused pier. I was being paranoid, thinking that someone might have placed it here deliberately. Adventurous kids came here to play, teenagers to snog or take drugs, so even if they did, it was probably nothing more than a nasty prank. I flashed my torch around again. There were lots of pieces of wood lying about. Had they all been put there deliberately, just in case I missed this one? Stupid suggestion, but... two women dead.

I decided the safest thing for me to do was to get back in the taxi and lock all the doors. Then I could wait on the arrival of the other taxi. I checked my watch. Five minutes was my boss, John's much-trumpeted and advertised target time for getting a taxi out, but they wouldn't be in such a hurry with me, even in my unique circumstances. I climbed back into the car and locked myself in.

And suddenly, there came a noise. A loud crashing sound, vaguely familiar. So close. My hand trembled as I swung the torchlight round the pier. No one, nothing, except... the gangplank. I had played as a child on the abandoned gangplanks down here. Running backwards and forwards, tipping them this way and that. And that had been the sound, as it had crashed, see-saw fashion, to the ground. The sound I had heard just now.

Someone was on the pier side.

"Who's there?" I screamed out uselessly, from inside the car. Who the hell was going to answer? The murderer? *'Oh yeh, hi, it's me! Soz!'*

But someone was definitely there. I knew it as certainly as if I could feel their breath down my neck. What a bloody stupid fool I had been. Driving a taxi at night with a murderer on the loose. Perhaps my mother was right; women shouldn't be allowed to drive taxis, not unless they were six feet two and built like sumo wrestlers. I was five feet and couldn't arm wrestle a flea. I thought of phoning someone, but who? My mother was on night shift, so she wouldn't answer. Elsa had disappeared. Billie didn't have her car. What about Patrick? Of course. I dialled his number, but it went straight to voicemail. My heart pounded, and I waited.

I don't know how long I sat there, before lights began moving towards me. It was a car, the other taxi coming to pick me up. My fear drained away, replaced by relief. I jumped out of my own car and began running towards the lights, waving my arms frantically.

The car skidded to a halt just inches in front of me. And that's when I did begin to cry, as I rested my head on the bonnet. I heard the driver's door open, and footsteps. Someone cradled me in their arms, holding me.

"Mirren, are you alright?"

And I felt myself once more recoil in fear. Couldn't have stopped myself if I'd tried. The voice was Patrick. He felt me stiffen in his arms. "What is it?"

"What are you doing here?"

"I just called the taxi office looking for you. I thought you'd be there. I can't believe they let you go out. They said you were stranded down here. I told them I'd come and pick you up."

"Your phone was busy, I tried phoning you."

He shook his head. "Other than me calling your office, my phone's off."

"Why?" I asked.

He puffed his cheeks out. That was all he could offer by way of explanation.

"Someone was here, Patrick," I said, staring around warily. "Waiting for me. Somewhere on this pier."

He was slow in speaking again. "Did you see who it was?"

"No."

He reached out for me, and though every part of me ached to be held by him, I drew back.

"You don't think it was me?" he asked.

I hesitated, probably a moment too long. I was working out the possibilities in my head. Could he have been the someone?

Perhaps his car was parked somewhere back along the road by the container terminal. Perhaps he ran back to it in the dark – would he have had time? And then he drove in, posing as my rescuer? There was pain in his voice. "You don't trust me either."

I watched his shoulders slump and his hands reach into his pockets. I almost fainted when I saw what he took out. Cold metal, steel. I had never seen a real one before, a gun. "Here," he said, and he handed it to me. "You sit in the back with it. I'm hardly likely to attack you with that in my hand, am I?"

"I wouldn't even know how to use it." That's what I said, though I could tell what he really wanted to hear was me refusing it, telling him I had no need for it because I trusted him.

He shrugged. "Well, you can always bash me over the head with it, can't you?"

All the way home we were silent. Him driving, and me, sitting in the back, cradling a handgun. I knew I had spoiled something, perhaps ruined it forever. But I couldn't help it. I couldn't even say sorry. I was still too afraid it had been Patrick out there in the shadows of Pier Thirteen.

CHAPTER EIGHT

Next day, the papers were full of the story of Vee's grisly murder. TV reporters and journalists buzzed around the town. The quiet roads around the laburnum-lined lane in the west end where she had been found were crowded all day with sightseers and the media.

One paper, however, managed to scoop every other, and now I began to understand why Patrick's phone had been switched off when I tried to call him.

The astute photographer who had caught Patrick and I leaving the police station had realised what a story he had almost as soon as he took the photo. The man in the image with me was no anonymous writer. That man was Patrick O'Kane. THE Patrick O'Kane.

The inference of the front-page story was clear. If Patrick O'Kane, the so-called Not Proven murderer, was involved with Octopus, then police didn't have to look any further for their killer. One murder could be passed off as circumstantial. To be this close to two, and now three, well that was downright incriminating. Lightning never strikes twice, and all that.

As soon as I saw it, I wanted to speak to him, reassure him that we didn't all feel like that. But how could I? I had thought, feared, almost the same thing last night. When he'd left me, it was without so much as a kiss. When I had so needed him to kiss me.

When he eventually turned up, to give me a lift back down to the pier to await the RAC man, he was just as cool and tight-lipped as he was the night before.

"You should go to the police about last night," he said finally, as we reached the pier. My car was still there, its tyres burst. We both got out to take a look.

"I don't think that's a good idea," I said.

"Afraid I'll be incriminated, arrested on the spot?"

I shook my head. "They'd only say it was my imagination."

And they probably would. What had I seen, after all? A movement in the shadows. What had I heard? A single sound. Both could've been caused by any number of things, like a cat skulking around in the dark.

"We both know it wasn't your imagination," Patrick said. At the end of the road, the RAC van appeared. He got back into the car, and then he was gone, his car screeching off angrily.

The next morning, I phoned him. I just wanted to hear his voice. It went straight to voicemail. I let it play, listening to the sound, until my mother screamed. By this time, even she'd seen the news. She sprang out of the kitchen as fast as her legs would carry her. "Pat O'Kane, sitting in ma hoose as large as life, and you lettin' him kiss you. Well, that's it, my lassie. I forbid you to see him ever again. I don't care if he is a Catholic."

He'd never want to see me again anyway. I was sure of that. Yet, when my phone rang ten minutes later, I dived for it.

"That better no' be him," she growled.

To my disappointment, it was Billie, screaming hysterically. I mouthed her name at my mother.

"That yin's no' the full shillin' either," she said charitably.

I waited until mother had slunk back into the kitchen before I tried to make sense of what Billie was saying.

"I think they're going to arrest me, Mirren!"

"Arrest you? Billie, don't talk so daft."

"But you don't understand..." She began to sob and it took me a while to soothe her.

"Billie, what don't I understand?"

She didn't answer that. Instead she said, "I can't talk over the phone. Will you come down to the police station with me?"

Once, no matter what, Victoria would be the obvious person to accompany her anywhere. I wondered what I'd done to deserve the honour. Or what Victoria had done to relinquish it. Perhaps that could be summed up in one word: Lisette.

"Why do you want to go to the police station?"

Another long sob. "To confess."

If this had been Elsa, I wouldn't have taken her confession seriously. Elsa would have confessed just so she could be the centre of attention. But this was Billie, who didn't do things like that.

"Confess… to what?"

And suddenly, I remembered Billie's red Fiat cruising along the road near where Vee had been found. "Wait, they saw your car."

"I know." Another great sob. "Oh, Mirren… I lied. I lied to them. I said I'd gone straight home. It couldn't have been my car that was seen. I don't know why I said that. I was just so confused, so frightened."

"What exactly did you do, Billie?"

"I went after Vee," she said after a long pause. I was afraid to ask the next question.

"What for?"

"I began to get worried about her walking home on her own. I went after her to try and find her."

"Why on Earth didn't you tell the police that?"

"I don't know. Oh, I don't know."

"I'll be over in ten minutes."

D.S Morrish took Billie's 'confession' calmly and without changing his expression.

"We knew you were lying, Miss May. We can usually tell, you know. Unless the liar is an extremely accomplished one."

"Which I'm not," Billie said, as if that would be a stain on her character.

"Why were you afraid to tell us? It was a very logical thing to do, and a caring one."

"I don't know. I can't explain it. I heard myself saying, 'it couldn't have been my car,' and then I couldn't go back on it."

I put my arm around her. "We've never been involved in a murder investigation before. We're allowed to make mistakes."

"The innocent usually do. I just wish the guilty one would hurry up and make one too."

"No clues then?"

He glanced at Billie, which made me realise he wanted her away before speaking to me alone. I asked her to wait in the corridor. As I walked back into the office, he held up the front page of a newspaper, with Pat O'Kane's name emblazoned in headlines. "I'm sorry about this," he said sincerely. "But it was inevitable that it would come out."

"I know, thanks." Why I should be grateful for his concern only made me realise just how much Patrick was beginning to mean to me, in spite of last night, and my nagging doubts that he was still hiding something.

I wondered in that moment if I should tell him about last night, and decided almost immediately against it. Patrick would be the obvious suspect. I would check it out myself first. "Did you want me for something else?"

His right eyebrow crept up. "I did. I'd like you to get the rest of your group together as soon as possible."

"You mean, just Octopus?"

"Yes. And try to think if you've ever done anything together as a group that would justify a vendetta against you."

"Lisette has already suggested just that."

He rolled his eyes. "Oh, that one. She'd be running this case if I gave her half the chance."

I stared out the window, watching the water on the river, wondering about a vendetta. "Do you really think someone might hold a grudge that bad?"

He nodded. "People have murdered for less."

"You'd better arrest the whole of Port Gowrie writers' group then. I mean, many of them don't like Octopus, and even if they did, we've criticised a lot of work. Some writers don't like their work being criticised."

His eyes creased into a smile. "We have considered that possibility."

"All right. Anything else?"

"How did you get on driving your taxi last night?"

He must have seen by the flush on my cheeks that something had happened. I saw the question in his eyes. I shrugged. "Fine."

"You're still determined to do it then?"

I hated to admit, but last night had frightened me, but I was feeling braver in the cold light of day. "Of course I am. What part of 'I need to work' do people not get?" I wanted to change the subject, so I went on quickly. "Any news of Elsa?"

"None at all, I'm afraid. We're taking her disappearance very seriously indeed."

As I drove Billie back home, she asked about Elsa too. "Where can she be?"

"Oh, you know Elsa. She's not the centre of attention, and she always likes to be. She probably thinks this will put her back centre stage."

"You think that's all it is?"

"I hope so, Billie. I really do."

It was a different Billie May that I drove home from the station. Relaxed, almost happy. Confession really is good for the soul.

"If I can get everyone to come to a meeting tonight, will you come along?"

"Of course. Shall I phone Victoria and arrange it?"

You don't need Victoria's approval, I felt like yelling at her. You were her protégé, and you've blossomed and outgrown her. You don't need anyone, Billie, you've made it. Not like me... I didn't think now that I ever would.

"I was just going to send out a WhatsApp, but why don't you do it instead? I am driving, after all."

We met, for a change, at my house. Victoria said it wasn't convenient to meet at hers.

"I think she's in a bit of a huff that you called the meeting instead of her," Billie whispered as she came in.

Victoria was haughty as she arrived, with faithful Lisette following in her wake, like a tug boat after the Queen Mary.

"I really don't see what there is to talk about," she said, but I declined to enlighten her until everyone was present. Our everyone was getting smaller by the day.

"We're going to have to change our name soon," said Lisette. "To Hexapod, maybe."

"I'm supposed to be the funny one, remember?" I had a feeling dear Lisette knew I didn't even know what the word meant. I made a mental note to go and look it up.

"Who is coming?" she said.

"Elsa is hardly likely to appear, unless she arrives back unexpectedly." This was Victoria, sweeping past on her way to my mother's trolley for a second gin and tonic.

"Where can she be?" whispered Lisette, as if she knew the question might annoy Victoria. "She's not answering her phone or checking WhatsApp. Has she gone off like this before?"

"Yes, actually, she has," I said. "Perusing the muse, she likes to call it. If she has a thorny writing problem, she gets herself a remote Airbnb and scoots off there to work on it. Let's hope this time, that's what has happened."

"You don't think she might be dead, do you?" Lisette asked hesitantly, bringing silence to the group. No one had actually said it. No one had dared. Now it had been said, I was forced to really consider it. "I can't imagine her dead."

"Perhaps she's just in hiding. She knows something, and she's afraid something might happen to her, like it happened to Vee."

"Except she disappeared before Vee was found," I reminded her.

"Then perhaps she knew something about Annabel's murder?"

"Perhaps it was really Elsa who the killer was after. She evaded him the first time, and then he killed Vee instead."

Lisette was not to be beaten in coming up with ideas. "She knows who the killer is. She saw something important. She's run off because she's afraid."

"And who..." Victoria turned dramatically from the fireplace, her gin and tonic swilling in her glass. "Was the last person to see Patrick Myer. Or, should I say, Pat O'Kane. I can't believe we invited him in. Did you know, Mirren? Did you know who he really was?" Her eyes were accusing me of withholding vital information.

"No, I didn't. And I wouldn't have told you if I had."

"He was a murderer. With murders happening among us, we

had a right to know."

"A Not Proven verdict… so, not a murderer. Doesn't that count?"

"I say we still had a right to know.," she insisted.

"For all we know, Elsa might have had a secret lover she ran off with," I answered, tossing out a theory of my own.

Lisette raised an eyebrow theatrically. I'd heard she also did amateur dramatics, and now I could see why. "Is there any particular reason you're sticking up for him, Mirren?"

Victoria glanced at me while taking a gulp from her gin, which she attempted to disguise as a sip. I considered how to answer that question. "Really, I'm just playing devil's advocate."

As the last of our members arrived, Patrick was all the topic of conversation. Billie hadn't mentioned him earlier, but I took it that she knew but she already had too much on her own mind to think about. She was disappointed that Patrick hadn't responded to any of my calls, or checked his WhatsApp. He'd gone dark, like Elsa.

"We don't really need him," I said. "What I want to discuss doesn't really concern him."

"Can you be sure of that?" asked Dr Bonnar, who then went on to insist that he had always known about Patrick. The face had always been familiar, he said. He just couldn't place it.

"D.S Morrish thinks there might be something in our collective past that could be leading to all this."

"What do you mean?" said Victoria, her brows creasing down.

"I've never done anything that might make anyone want to murder me," said Billie. "At least, I don't think I have."

"No, Billie, I mean, we as a group."

"What about the black magic theory?" Lisette flipped open her notebook, and I saw the meeting, every word, every inflection, going into one of her stories.

"I think they just about dismissed that."

"But why?" Victoria asked. "It sounds perfectly feasible to me. The way Annabel was murdered. Her fingers, for goodness sake." She nervously twisted the gold chain round her neck. "Bizarre... just like her play. And Patrick... he was the one helping with her research, and now we find out that he is a murderer."

I lost my temper. "Christ, Victoria, the verdict was Not Proven! Does that mean nothing?"

Obviously not. "I don't believe in coincidence. Does murder just follow him about? What is he, the Angel of Death?"

"Of course, there could be another theory..." said Lisette, tapping her pen against her lips.

We all turned to listen. "If he is innocent..." she went on. "He says someone else murdered that woman in Aberdeen. What if the real murderer tracked him down, followed him, as it were, to try and prove he must have been the murderer in the first place?"

"What utter nonsense! said Victoria, which made Lisette blush.

Billie was shaking her head. "Killing poor Vee Kirk, and Annabel, total strangers, just to get back at Patrick... no."

"It's sheer jealousy, nothing else. Some warped member of the group who wanted to join Octopus, and wasn't good enough." This was Dr Bonnar's theory, and Victoria nodded as if it met with her approval. Lisette was suitably subdued.

"What about some warped member who was drummed out..." I began looking around them. I could see they all remembered who I was referring to. This was the hapless poet, Petronella Green.

"Surely, she must have seen she had no right to be in the group. The woman was an idiot!" said Victoria, who'd given up pretending and swilled her gin.

"Do you think so," I said. "I rather liked her, Victoria."

"You like everyone, Mirren. That's why you make such a god-awful critic. You never damn anyone's work. You always try to find something good to say about it. Even that ridiculous novel that we had in for that competition. Do you remember?"

"Yes, I remember that," said Lisette, suppressing a giggle.

So did I suddenly, feeling a sense of shame flooding over me. Octopus had adjudicated a novel competition, and one particular entry was so bad we'd all laughed over it.

"No, no," said Dr. Bonnar sharply. "Even Mirren was scathing about that one."

He was right, hence the shame, for I'd been just as cruel as everyone else. It hadn't been like me, but for once, I had put my judgement before my soft nature. Well, that was certainly me put in my place. I tried to ignore it, and not hope Victoria would be the next victim.

I told them all I was going to make a list of all the possible theories. I wrote the black magic theory down first. "Let's not dismiss anything," I said.

Then there was Lisette's theory of a revenge on Patrick, which looked even more ridiculous on paper. The jealousy theory was the most popular, if popular was the right word.

"Haven't you ever heard of Ockham's Razor?" said Dr. Bonnar. "It's a theory, which says the simplest, most straightforward explanation is the most likely. So it's either jealousy from another member or it is Patrick O'Kane."

"Don't forget the so-called poet," Victoria reminded me. I cast my mind back, recalling Petronella's poetry. The stuff she wrote was dire, cluelessly-constructed drivel, yet she thought she was some kind of literary genius. There was no doubt a sense of narcissism in her, but surely no one so utterly dense could execute two murders in cold blood without leaving a shred of evidence.

Still, I wrote down Petronella's name. I refused to write down Patrick's. As I reminded them, D.S Morrish had asked us to think about who might hold a grudge against us.

"Maya Brodie has always borne Octopus a grudge," said Billie.

"Yes, Billie, very astute of you," Dr. Bonnar agreed. "She'd sell her soul to get into Octopus."

I glanced at Billie's face as she reacted to this. He gave her a smile, but she didn't smile back. Her look was one of pure disgust. Why?

"Write Maya's name down," said Victoria. "She once offered the club a large donation, you know. Her husband works in the oil industry, so she's monied." She looked at Billie. "You were there, remember? There was just a lightly-veiled stipulation that it would only be forthcoming when she was made a member of Octopus."

"It's true," Billie agreed. "I'm afraid Victoria was quite harsh with her. Told her bluntly that she would never be a member of Octopus while Victoria was alive." Billie gasped and her hand flew to her mouth. "Those were… her very words."

"I do not suffer fools gladly," said Victoria, turning to the trolley to top up her gin. "Or hacks."

Billie watched me as I jotted down Maya's name.

"It was just a figure of speech," she said, hesitantly. "I mean, would it have made Maya want to murder us?"

I looked around their faces. "Anything else?"

Everyone looked blank.

"I was thinking…" I said. "Talking about that adjudication, do you think it feasible that someone would take such offence at our criticism that they might kill?"

Victoria scoffed and knocked back some gin. "If we're going to cover all the adjudications we've done, and all the harsh criticism, then we may as well settle down for the winter."

"True," said Lisette. "Where do we start? We can be very cutting."

Correction, I thought, Victoria can be very cutting. Everyone else tends to pile in behind her.

"Not necessarily," I said. "I would think the adjudication would have to be quite recent. Octopus has only been around for the past five years. Lisette only joined two years ago."

"Maybe it happened before I joined," pointed out Lisette, optimistically. "That means I might not be in any danger."

"I think we should go back through those competitions, from the latest backwards. We should try and remember the ones we were most scathing about." We would have a job, though. Victoria enjoyed vilifying what she saw as bad writing. There were times when she was like a cat toying with a mortally injured mouse.

"But how would that help?" asked Dr Bonnar. "I mean, all the entries come under a pseudonym."

"Hopefully, Elsa will have a note of the addresses she sent the entries back to."

"If Elsa ever comes back."

"Perhaps we should start with that one adjudication, the novel we all thought was so awful… we were all very cruel about it."

"It was utter tripe," Lisette said, before adding smugly. "Even you thought so."

"I know that. I just think it's worth considering."

"Oh, write it down then, if it keeps you happy," Victoria said. She was becoming slurry, and she was angry that her criticism was now being criticised. "Personally, I think it's nonsense. I mean, if a writer can't take adverse criticism…"

Before I had a chance to write anything, the doorbell rang. I hurried to open it, half hoping, half expecting that it might be Patrick.

It wasn't. It was D.S Morrish, looking ashen. My first thought was Elsa. She'd been found. Alive? Dead?

"Is it Elsa, tell me?"

He shook his head and stepped into the hallway. "No. Though we are increasingly concerned about the whereabouts of Ms Fordyce. Is Patrick Myer here by any chance?"

"No," I said. "I haven't been able to contact him all day. He's not answering his phone."

"Neither have we," he said. "So it would seem another member of Octopus is missing now."

CHAPTER NINE

"Well, Inspector, it seems to me you've found your murderer," Dr Bonnar said with conviction. "See? Ockham's Razor: the simplest explanation is the best."

"I'm a D.S, that's Detective Sergeant," reminded Morrish. "But we can't say that with certainty, not yet."

"On the other hand, he might have disappeared because he's in danger too," I said. Not least, I might have added, from the suspicious minds within Octopus itself.

Victoria saw such little merit in my suggestion that she didn't comment at all, she just laughed, an over-the-top, drunkish sort of laugh. "His stories should have told us more. They were all about death, murder. Tortured stories from a tortured mind."

"I liked him," said Billie softly. "I really did."

"Why, in the past tense?" I asked.

She was startled. "Oh, did I say... oh, I just meant... I still do."

"What's it to you anyway?" Lisette asked me sharply. "Whether we like him or not. Perhaps you know where he is?"

"I don't," I said.

"Perhaps you wouldn't tell us if you did."

In that moment, I saw that Lisette disliked me. Maybe she'd never liked me, or maybe it was because of Patrick. Maybe she didn't like any of us. I supposed deep down that I didn't like her either.

"Perhaps I wouldn't," I answered.

"I hope you don't mean that." Morrish sounded severe.

I stared round at all their faces. "You've practically convicted the man because of his past. So, why would he show up here tonight? And then there's all the media attention. That's probably why he has run off, if he has."

"As I said to Dr Bonnar, I haven't pinned anything on to Mr Myer," Morrish assured me. "But we do have to take his past into account. And he was the last person to see Ms Fordyce that we know of. Running away just makes it look worse."

"There was evil in his eyes." This was Billie, speaking softly with a faraway look on her face. She jumped when she realised everyone was staring at her. "Not my opinion, sorry. It was Vee Kirk's. Don't you remember? Right from the beginning, she said there was evil in his eyes."

Dr Bonnar sat down beside her and put his arm around her. "There, there, Billie."

I watched Billie May shrink back from him, as if she couldn't bear his touch. I glanced at Dr Bonnar's face, expecting him to look hurt, but he didn't he looked as if he could slap her, or worse, as if he hated her. It passed in an instant, so quickly in fact that I wondered if anyone else had spotted it. Indeed, if I'd imagined it in the first place.

"Your little group is losing members fast," D.S Morrish said as everyone was leaving. "Three tentacles in one week."

"Yes, apparently we'll soon have to change our name to Hexapod." I used Lisette's line, before I realised that Hexapod probably didn't apply any more, no matter what it meant. That's what I get for plagiarising.

"Hmm... an insect with six feet," he said, before adding without a glimmer of humour. "Funny."

At the front door, I gave him the list, such as it was, and he studied it. "And this Petronella Green?"

"I don't know, it seems far-fetched. I mean, she was basically a nice lady, though she believed she was more talented than she actually was."

"We'll look into it anyway, although it does seem far-fetched. You never know. You know writers better than I do. Would another writer really kill because you lot criticised their writing?"

He looked dubious. He knew nothing about writers then.

He kicked the toe of his shoe against the doorstep. "For what it's worth, I think you're right. Myer just panicked and run off, because the newspapers discovered his identity. He probably thought we were going to blame it all on him. A man can do that, even if he's perfectly innocent. But we will catch up with him, and it will go worse for him when we do. With the press, the public, and with the police. And you?" He raised an eyebrow at me. "Tell him what I said if he tries to contact you."

"Do you think he might?"

"Yes, he might. I get a sense there's something he hasn't told us, something he's holding back."

I had a feeling Morrish thought I knew too. Another ten seconds and the lamp would be in my face and I'd be grilled. But he didn't get the chance. He was waylaid by my mother, sprinting as fast as her wee legs could carry her up the path, waving her arms wildly. She took the poor man completely by surprise.

"A polis car at my door! What are folk gonnae think? Is my lassie deid?" She caught sight of me then, standing behind him, and crossed herself quickly. "Thank God! Wait, is she being arrested?" By her tone, I thought maybe that was the most shameful of the two fates.

"Tune in next week folks, for another exciting episode!" I burst out, in a phoney American TV accent. I giggled, if only through self-embarrassment.

Mother turned on me. "This isnae a laughing matter. This is dead serious. I know aboot these things."

"She used to clean a lawyer's office," I explained to Morrish.

"You pick up a lot of things in a job like that."

"You do that, paper, rubbish…"

Mother appealed to the policeman. "She cannae take anything serious, that lassie. She'll be the death of me."

James Morrish leaned closer to her. "Not at all, she's a credit to you," he said. "I can see where she gets her intelligence from… and her good looks."

I did one of those double-takes you see on TV. He wasn't mocking her, not at least that I could see. He was genuinely being nice.

Naturally, my mother was nothing less than delighted with the compliment. Her cheeks flushed, and she put on what locals called her pan loaf voice. "If I can help you with any of your enquiries, detective, just ask. Did the lassie invite you in or offer you a cup of tea?"

I hadn't, and she made me apologise for the oversight.

He wouldn't come in, however, even at my mother's insistence. Not many people could stand up to that. Finally, she allowed him to leave, but only after he promised to return soon, unofficially, for what my mother called 'a good sit-doon spread.'

Next morning, I did my duty visit to Vee's husband. He was tall and gaunt and practically bald. His face was set in stern lines, but he didn't seem overly perturbed by his wife's death. Was this austere, uncaring man really the cause of jealous rivalry between Victoria and Vee all those years ago? It hardly seemed possible. I stayed an awkward half hour and drank good sherry from very old crystal glasses, as fragile as poor old Vee always seemed to be. As I left, I bumped into Victoria, arriving in style.

She was wearing an emerald green coat with a multicoloured shawl thrown around her shoulders. After greeting me, her eyes brightened as she looked behind me and saw Mr Kirk standing at the door.

"Donald, how are you, my dear?"

Donald was brighter for seeing her, there was no doubt. His back straightened, and he brushed his single strand of hair across his forehead, though it didn't take long before it fell back around his ear.

"I'm bearing up. How good of you to come." He took her arm as she swept past me and reached him, then both of them stood on the doorstep and smiled on my leaving, as if they were a couple. "It was good of you to come too," Donald said to me, and Victoria seconded this.

"Have you seen the papers?" she went on.

I hadn't. Who even bought newspapers these days apart from my mother, who usually got one every morning, except today, because this was her day off.

"They're full of Patrick's disappearance. If he isn't guilty, he's doing himself no good by going off like this." She turned to Donald. "Vee sensed he was evil, you know. From the very beginning."

"She often said she was psychic, you know," said Donald.

Victoria turned back to me triumphantly. "You can't still trust him, surely!"

Did I? Vee had warned me about Patrick on the very night she'd died. Had he overheard? Had her murder been his revenge? But why with a rope? Why in the manner that she herself had written about? No, that had to be some twisted mind that knew the irony would not be lost on us. A writer. One of us. And yet... Patrick was a writer, and was he not one of us in the end?

I took a drive down by Pier Thirteen. I didn't know why.

Perhaps I was searching for something. It didn't look half as eerie by the light of day. Planks were still strewn across the ground. Patrick was the one who'd saved me. Looking back towards the end of the road, where I saw his car coming from, there was no way in hell he could have been lurking here, stalking me, He wouldn't have had time to run back to pick up his car. In any case, he had every chance while we were alone down here to kill me. Why hadn't he done so then? Hadn't me even given me a gun? I would believe in Patrick. I had to.

I called into the taxi office to see John. Gail, one of our daytime controllers smiled at me as I went in. "You're in the bad books. Why the hell didn't you let us know you were getting a lift off someone else the other night?"

I felt the sick seed of doubt planted in my stomach once more. "What? But Patrick said he called the office. He told you he was going to pick me up instead."

Gail looked puzzled, but not suspicious. "Did he?" She flicked through a notebook. "There's no record of it here. A taxi was sent out for you and you weren't there. We just took it you made your own way home. Och, it'll be that new girl. She's right bad-tempered. She'll have forgot to write it down."

I seized on that. "Yes, that must have been what happened."

"But you know John. When he found out he was worried sick. He ended up phoning your Mum. She said you were already home and in bed."

"Tell him I'm okay, and I'll call him later."

I spent the rest of the day at home, in my room writing. It must have been the stress and anxiety that fired me up. It had given me energy and inclination. I somehow found I had words flowing out of me.

"A born writer should not need any input to write," Victoria always said. "However you feel, you must roll up your sleeves and get working. Talent and Perseverance, that's all you need, and not necessarily in that order."

At the moment though, I was grateful for the energy and inclination. I even ventured to the post office to send off a story, the first one I'd sent out in weeks. I had to suffer the embarrassment of discreet eyes on me, wondering if I were to be the next victim or even a potential murderer.

"Do you think Elsa will turn up safe?" asked our postmistress, June. I was at the head of a long queue and it was pension day, so a whole line of people stopped whispering and listened to my answer.

"I certainly hope so."

"I think she's deid," the woman behind me said with absolute confidence.

"But there's never a murder in her book," came one old man further back in the queue. "She writes these ah… romances? Or was it fantasies?" The significance of the methods of murder had not been lost on the press or the public. Annabel's missing fingers, and Vee's death by rope had not remained a secret. Word had spread far and wide.

"Romantasy," I answered. "Very popular these days."

"Aye," agreed the man drily. "Yon murderer will be struggling tae find a dragon roon here."

Some wag at the back tutted. "They're probably reading her book aloud to her and boring her to death." That had them all laughing. That included me, I'm ashamed to say. No, I wasn't really ashamed. I come from a people who can conjure a joke out of the grimmest, most disastrous situation imaginable. A safety device probably. I was glad of it. I hoped in all honesty that if and when it was my turn to get murdered, they would get a good laugh out of me too. I just hoped it wouldn't be my turn soon.

By the next day, I'd begun to see why Patrick had switched his phone off, because mine was going constantly. Phone calls kept coming and text messages kept pinging in. I was sick of reporters asking for an interview. I was sick of so-called friends ringing to check I was okay, but really just to ask the gory details. And what was with the perverts suddenly sending dick pics? How did all these people even get my number?

The most disturbing call of all came from Maya Brodie. She was yelling so loud, I had to hold the receiver at arm's length.

"I have just been interviewed by the police. I resent this very much! I'm a respectable woman, a lot more respectable than certain other people I could mention. I've never had any dealings with the police in my life."

"Neither have the rest of us..." I began.

"Haven't you? That just shows how much you know, Mirren. Why don't you ask in Octopus just how many have little secrets that they'd rather keep hidden? I'm not one to break a confidence, of course..."

What a lie. She was exactly the type to break a confidence. And her husband was a lawyer. Was that what she was referring to? Had someone from Octopus had dealings with the law that he knew about, and he had told her?

Still, she kept ranting on. "I've never heard anything so ridiculous. As if I of all people could hold a grudge against Octopus!"

"Maya, two people have been murdered. They have to look into every detail, every possibility."

"Well, it's nothing to do with me. I had no part in it. You've all got too big for your boots, that's the problem. That's why you're being picked off, one by one."

Now I was getting angry. "That's a very insensitive thing to say, Maya."

"Is it? I don't care. I'm going to see more about this. Don't think I'm going to let the matter rest there. There's things I can tell about certain people, and I will if I have to. By the way, don't even consider asking me to join your group now, because I'd refuse!"

"The thought hadn't even crossed our minds," I said.

After that, I switched my phone off, though deep down I feared I might miss a call from Patrick. If he called, that is. Perhaps the police had tapped my phone. Could they do that without telling me? They could certainly have me watched without telling me. From the front room window, I could see the car, a man presumably reading a newspaper. His eyes every so often glanced over at the house. Was he there for my protection, or to watch out for Patrick's return? Did anyone else have a cop watching them? I decided to switch my phone on again, ignoring all the pings, and phone Billie, just on the off chance she'd heard something about Elsa. Her phone went to voicemail. No doubt she'd got sick of all the messages and switched her phone off too.

As the hours wore on, I couldn't sit still, or settle myself to anything. Vee Kirk was dead. Somehow, that hadn't really hit me before. That sweet, funny old woman whose grey hair was always hanging out of her many hats. I would miss her. She had always been confident of my success. "You'll make it, no doubt about that," she would always say whenever I complained about my latest rejection.

It would be nice to have a souvenir to remember her by. I would ask Mr Kirk next time I saw him for one of her hatpins, perhaps. She loved her hatpins. Hatpins of every shape and design. Hatpins like I'd never seen before. A giraffe head made out of pearls, a swan's elegant neck encrusted with sparkly gems. They were so interesting in fact that Victoria had written that whole piece about them, and hadn't that caused quite the stooshie between them. I once asked Vee where she got them from. All she said was that it was mostly from the internet, but where? I should have followed that up, as I'd probably never know now, though I could ask Mr Kirk.

It was almost five in the afternoon and it had been dark for a while, when I saw the policeman across the street get out of the car and cross to my door.

"D.S. Morrish has been trying to get in touch with you," he said when I opened the door. "Did you switch off your phone?"

He was young, quite good looking, with one of those arrogant attitudes that some women find so attractive. Well, I do, and I'm a woman. What can I say?

"I was getting too many..." Even before I finished he was nodding his head in understanding.

"It's always the same in a case like this."

"Will I phone D.S Morrish?"

"No. If you'd like to accompany me to the station..."

"That sounds ominous," I said, and he smiled.

"He only wants to talk to you."

"Has anything happened?" Please, God, no. Not another body... Not Elsa... or Patrick.

"Do you think they'd tell me? I'm only the poor bugger sitting in the car..."

"-Watching me," I finished for him. "Why? Protection... or surveillance?"

"Bit of both."

He certainly wasn't going to tell me anyway.

To make things worse, I wasn't taken directly into Morrish's office. Instead, they led me to a side room, an interrogation room. That seemed even more ominous, like I was an actual suspect. I had to sit there alone for fifteen minutes, drumming my fingers on the table top. Isn't that what they did with suspects in the movies? Let them cool their heels in an interrogation room, while watching them from behind one of those one-way glass windows. I glanced around, but this room didn't seem to have anything that would fit as a one-way window. All I knew was that something had definitely happened, but what exactly?

Someone came with tea in a plastic cup. The dregs lay cold and dreary at the bottom before the door opened again and D.S Morrish came in.

"What are you trying to do, sweat some information out of me?" I asked.

That seemed to take him aback. "What?"

"A confession, is that it?"

"Why, have you got something you want to confess?"

"Don't tell me you suspect me?"

"It seems to me everyone in this case has something to confess."

"Has something happened?"

He hesitated. "It's Ms Fordyce."

"Oh God!"

"No, she's alive and well."

My anxiety switched to anger. "Alive! Where the bloody hell has she been all this time? Why worry everyone at a time like this? What does she think she's playing at?"

"That's why I wanted to see you first. You see, she has a story to tell."

"Elsa always has a story to tell," I said. "And that's not because she's a writer. So what is it this time?"

"She claims she ran off... because Patrick Myer tried to rape her."

I almost fell off my seat. "What! And you believe that?"

Morrish gave a small shrug, all the while never removing his eyes from mine. "He was hiding something, I knew that. Perhaps this is what it is."

"What exactly did she say?"

"Ms Fordyce says he took her home that night. He insisted on coming inside the house on the pretext of making sure it was safe… and once he was inside the house…"

I knew what was coming. I just didn't believe it. "And then what? He tried to have his wicked way with her… like the hero of one of her novels. 'Course, she'd have had to ride a dragon with him first… and that's not a euphemism."

"I'd say more like a villain, Muzz Murdoch," said Morrish. "But then, I am hopelessly old fashioned."

"Look, believe me, in Elsa's novels this is exactly what always happens. Her heroes are a bit rapey. It seems to be alright because it's set in a fantasy world. I mean, it's not my cup of tea, but hey…" I stood up, pushing the chair back with a loud scrape, and punched the table. "It's not true! I don't believe it!"

Morrish stood up, pressing his fists down on the table top and confronted me, face to face. "Why would you believe a man like him?" he said. I hadn't heard him sound so forceful before. "You hardly know him. And you know as well as I do that he's hiding something."

The ridiculousness of the situation hit me, the two of us arguing like fishwives, or an old married couple. I began to giggle. He sat back down in his seat, raising his eyebrow in disapproval. "Your mother's right. You don't take anything seriously."

I shook my head. "If you knew Elsa well enough then you'd know. I bet it was she who practically raped him… not the other way about."

"He told you this, did he?" he asked sternly.

"Of course not. He didn't mention it." And why would he have mentioned it, either to me or to anyone? Why would the police believe Patrick, who was in most people's eyes nothing more than an unconvicted murderer? Moreover, why would they believe him over a successful novelist and local celebrity, like Elsa? Why should I, for that matter? Well, I did, and not only because I knew Elsa. "So instead of coming to the police, she decides to run off and hide?"

"She said he began to frighten her. She almost thought he was going to strangle her because she refused... to give in. When he eventually left she thought she'd be safer spending the night in a hotel in case he came back. Next morning, when she heard about Mrs Kirk, she was even more frightened. She was too afraid to come forward."

"Or even phone? Seriously? You, the police? Even her husband?"

"Even her husband, yes," he said. "It wasn't until she read that Mr Myer had disappeared too. Only then did she have the courage to get back in touch, firstly with Mr Fordyce, and then with us."

"Patrick isn't even here to defend himself, or tell his side of the story."

He leaned across the table. "I wonder about you, Muzz Murdoch. I wonder why you have so much faith in him, when all the evidence seems to be stacking up against him. Are you in love with him, by any chance?"

"I hardly know him," I said quickly. "But I do know Elsa. She always has to be the star attraction, the main event."

"This is a murder investigation, a very serious business. I've warned her what could happen to her if she lies, so why should she?"

"Publicity. I mean, she's front-page news now. It's not going to do her any harm, is it?"

"Would you like to see her?"

"I most certainly would," I answered.

James Morrish left the room, and a few minutes later in swanned Elsa, flanked by two female police officers. Her face flushed when she saw me, and she went into a dramatic faint. The two PCs had to prop her up.

"Oh, Mirren, oh Mirren, I am so sorry for giving everyone all this worry. But I've been so frightened." If I hadn't known her so well I might well have been taken in by the red-rimmed eyes and the flushed cheeks. It was totally convincing to the uninitiated, but not to me.

"Elsa, you're a bloody liar!"

CHAPTER TEN

Elsa went weak-kneed in the police officers' grip. They both glared at me, shocked by my apparent lack of sympathy to a friend no doubt, while they sat her down.

"What...exactly do you think I am lying about, Mirren?"

"You know what I'm talking about. Patrick. You know it never happened that way."

"I should know what happened. I was there." I watched as her eyes filled with tears. I wondered if she'd been taking acting lessons from someone. "It was awful."

"You lied to the police. You told them you had a lift home. What you wanted was a chance to get Patrick alone. You practically had his arm up his back forcing him to take you back to your empty house."

She was suddenly screaming at me. "I didn't know! I didn't know he was going to do that! He was like a wild animal! I was afraid, Mirren, Patrick Myer is a murderer. He's the one, I know that now."

"That's a very serious thing to say, when you have absolutely no evidence to support it."

She looked wide-eyed at Morrish, who had appeared at the door, leaning against the door frame with his arms folded and staring expressionless at her. "No evidence, she says. With his past... and..." She looked more sure of herself now. "And then he runs off. Is that the action of an innocent man?"

"It could also be a frightened one," I answered.

"Patrick Myer isn't frightened of anyone. You didn't see him, those wild eyes, it was terrifying."

"No, I didn't, did I?"

"You don't believe a word I'm saying, do you, Mirren?"

I decided honesty was better than anything else on this occasion. "No, I don't, Elsa. And I'll tell you why. You had your eye on Patrick for months. You were desperate for him to take you home that night. I offered, remember. And why should he do that to you? Every female in the club fancied him." At that, I was sure I heard a snort from Morrish, but when I glanced up at him his face was just as expressionless as it had been before. "He could have had his pick. He doesn't have to behave like someone out of one of your books."

"That's what it all comes down to, isn't it? I made it all up. Well, what do you call this then?" She pulled down the neck of her mohair sweater. Her throat was black and blue. It was then too I realised that under the makeup, her face was also bruised and swollen.

"Trying to fight you off, was he?"

It sounded bitchy and cruel. Maybe it was. Both the female police officers took a gasp. Elsa's jaw dropped. It had come out because the bruises had taken me so much by surprise. Why was I defending a man who might be capable of that?

"Oh, you're protecting him. There's always some idiot somewhere that does."

"It still doesn't make him a murderer, Elsa."

"If you'd only seen him when he left me, there was murder in those eyes. Maybe Vee was unlucky. He came across her when he left. He took his anger out on her."

"I don't believe that."

"Well, he's run off, hasn't he? How many times must I say it? Would a man who was telling the truth do that?"

"You ran off too! Would a woman who was telling the truth do that?"

Her face crumpled as if she was about to burst into tears. "I was so afraid, Mirren. You must see that. Even more so when I heard about Vee Kirk. Poor Vee."

It was an excellent finishing line. I felt Elsa had won our little confrontation. She sank into her chair, and one of the police officers brought her a glass of water. As she handed it to Elsa, the police woman glanced up at me coldly. Definitely no prizes for guessing whose side she was on.

D.S Morrish had remained silent the whole time. Deliberate tactic, I was sure. Now at last he spoke. "I'm going to try and keep this from the press for the moment. I'd like to ask you, especially, Ms Fordyce, not to speak to them."

Elsa looked up at him with cow eyes. "The last thing I want to do is talk about it. But what am I going to tell reporters? I'm something of a celebrity. They'll want some kind of explanation."

At the thought of the press, her face brightened visibly. She began rummaging through her Cartier handbag, searching for her make up. That was our Elsa.

Morrish could read her just as well as me. I could tell by the tiniest uplift in the edges of his mouth. "My advice would be, say nothing, it only adds to the mystery. Remember Agatha Christie? She once disappeared, I understand. It didn't do her any harm."

She smiled at him gratefully. "Can I go home now, Inspector. I haven't closed my eyes for two days. I'm exhausted."

Now that I certainly didn't believe.

"I'm a D.S, and your husband's waiting for you in the corridor," he answered.

At the door, Elsa turned to me. She was never content without an exit line. "Just be thankful, Mirren, that he got to Vee before he got to you, or else you might have been his next victim."

I was still thinking about that when James Morrish came back in the door.

"You can't really believe her story," I said at once.

"And why not? She's a respectable woman. Never been in any bother with the police before."

"She's never been involved with a murder before either," I said.

"And how do you explain those marks all over her neck and face?"

"That could have been someone else. Why does it have to be Patrick?"

"Bit of a coincidence, isn't it, if she was attacked by someone else while she was away, don't you think? And why should she lie about him?"

"She's annoyed Patrick didn't fancy her as much as she would have liked him to. Hell hath no fury, and all that..."

"Is there any particular reason you believe Mr Myer? Or is it just..." He left it unfinished for a second. "Intuition?"

I shrugged. "I just believe him. And I do know Elsa for who she is."

"I would remind you that when Mrs DeVere was killed, Patrick was one of the very few people who'd read her play. He was also the one who helped her with her research. When Mrs Kirk was killed, Patrick has no alibi. So, he takes Mrs Fordyce home, and she claims she was attacked by him. She has the marks to prove it. Added to that, he disappears. Everything comes back to Myer, I'm afraid. And from experience, that usually means we're dealing with a guilty man."

And Patrick, sneaking out of the car park the night Annabel was killed... And Patrick turning up at Pier Thirteen. He was right, it all came back to Patrick.

Morrish moved a step closer, speaking under his breath. "There's something you're not telling us too, Mirren Murdoch."

I swallowed. "What makes you think that?"

"Do you think I'm an idiot? Don't you know that I'm trying to solve this? That you can trust me?"

I thought about telling him, I really did. I knew I could trust him. But somehow, with so many things stacking up against Patrick, it seemed like a betrayal. "Well, if you're so sure it's Patrick, now that he's gone the killing will stop, won't it?"

"He hasn't gone. He's just out of sight. That means we can't see him, but he can see us."

"Can't you trace his phone or something?"

"You've been watching too many films," he replied flatly.

"You mean you honestly think... there's going to be more?"

He reached out and gently touched my arm. "I would like you to be very careful, please, Mirren."

I didn't go straight home. I went to Victoria's house instead. No matter what I often thought of her, she was a rock, and I needed a rock to cling to right now.

I loved Victoria's little cottage. It was surrounded by a magnificent garden, where she sat writing in summer, ensconced in her little summer house. The house was full of little nooks and crannies where she crammed books and manuscripts. It seemed the ideal setting for a writer. Her study was undoubtedly my favourite room. The bookcases were stacked with books. There was even a grand piano in the corner. I followed the path up to the French windows. The light was on inside, and I guessed she'd be in there working. I stood outside for the moment, watching her shadow through the warm glow of the floral curtains, drawn shut against the chilly November night, savouring a thousand memories of happy times here.

"You should really lock these doors. Anyone could walk in," I said, letting myself in. She was there, typing away on her laptop,

"I do hate a locked door," she said dismissively. "Anyway, how nice to see you, Mirren. I was just about to stop for tea… or perhaps something stronger."

"Elsa's back," I said, perching on the seat beside her.

She kept typing for a moment. "I know. She phoned me, ridiculous woman. There's a murder and nothing's happening to her, so she makes things happen."

"Didn't she tell you why she went?"

She glanced at me, her fingers resting for a second on the keys. "Patrick? I don't believe that story for a second." She continued typing. She was an unbelievably fast typer, much faster than my pedestrian efforts. "For Elsa to suggest that Patrick Myer was so overcome with thwarted passion for her he strangled poor Vee in retaliation is as ridiculous as one of her plots. Why, he never as much looked interested in her. If he was going to have a fit of passion for anybody I would have thought it would be…"

I waited expectantly for my name to be mentioned.

"Billie," she said.

"Billie?" And yet, why should I have been so surprised? Hadn't I thought so once myself?

"Of course, Billie. There was so much soul in both their writings, didn't you feel it? I thought they were on the same plane. I pushed it a little, I admit. I thought a love affair might help Billie. Her writing, and looking after her sister, was all she had. Anyway, it didn't work out. I did wonder why not. Maybe it was the wrong time. I was sorry about that… I'm not sorry now, though."

"You still believe he's guilty then? But you said about Elsa…"

"I don't believe a word Elsa says, on principle. But… there's too much evidence stacked against him, I'm afraid. I'm a great one for the logical explanation. No matter how much I don't want to believe it. Come along," she said, standing up. "Let's have a gin."

"I'm driving. I'll have tea."

"Ugh, tea then."

I always loved how Victoria served tea. A silver tray, crisply starched napkins, the finest bone china and her own home-made scones. She brought out jam in a fine crystal dish, laying it down gently beside the scones. "Elsa's. do you remember the night she had us all at her house? A champagne buffet, and then the presentation of Octopus jam to each of us. Her little pots of it were left for us on the hall table, looking distinctly like country fare with those pretty little gingham covers. She had them all carefully labelled with our names." She sighed. "It seems so long ago now."

We sat in silence for a while, perhaps thinking along similar lines. It really hadn't been so long ago. Only a few weeks had passed since Annabel's death, when this whole nightmare had begun. Elsa made her special jam for Octopus every year. A pot for each of us, and usually a half dozen, laid aside in a box separately for Mrs Bonnar, who was especially fond of it. My mother was the only person I'd ever come across who didn't like Elsa's jam. "And yon Mrs Bonnar can eat six jars o' it? She must have the constitution of an ox."

Octopus jam, Elsa labelled it. I often wondered what people might think reading the labels.

"I took Vee's jar by mistake that night," Victoria went on. "She refused to believe it was an accident. Thought I'd done it deliberately to annoy her. You know, Mirren, my great regret is... we could have been friends, Vee and I." She shivered, as if dispelling the memory. "Let's talk of other things... Mirren, how is your writing going?"

"Bloody terrible!" My response caught her off guard and she

smiled. "Well, it is. Feels like I'm disappearing off the face of the earth. My emails have dried up. My post consists of bills and nothing else. There was a time there, I don't know, I had calls with people. I had new stories and projects. It all seemed so hopeful, like I was getting somewhere. Now it's nothing, it's like someone's thrown up a brick wall. No one wants to know me. Oh, Victoria, it's so depressing."

Here I was off again. Even I was sick listening to me.

"Have you tried phoning these people you were in touch with?"

"I did. Once. Someone said he would phone back later. He never did."

"Perseverance, Mirren! What am I always telling you? Keep trying."

"Yes, but there comes a point when you need to see these people ghosting you as a no."

Victoria sat looking at me, then stretched her hand across the table and touched mine. "It will come," she said, more reassuring than she could have suspected. "In this business, you have to keep trying, keep plodding on, keep sending, submitting, pitching. The only difference between a published writer and an unpublished writer is that the former refused to give up. You know, every one of us has gone through a bad patch, even me." She said that as if it was the last thing anyone would believe, and I had to smile. "Remind yourself of your successes. Decide what you want to achieve next. Roll up your sleeves and get to work. Does it look like a mountain to climb? Well, yes, that's because it is. Sometimes it takes what the Aussies call 'good hard yakka' to get yourself up it."

She spoke with such conviction, almost vehemence, as if she was daring the fates to deny her. I could have launched myself at her and kissed her.

"You know, Mirren," she went on. "I know you've often felt as if you were in Billie's shadow."

"I've never had a moment's jealousy about Billie," I told her. "I mean, I could never be her kind of writer, and honestly, I'd never want to be."

"I have favoured her..." she mused. "But, it was only because her nature needed that boost, you see. I quite believe Billie May would never have realised her potential if she hadn't come to Port Gowrie writers' group. She seemed unaware of her own potential. I'm sure she'd still be sitting with that first chapter of that manuscript if I hadn't pushed her. Even now, I suspect there's a great danger that she might slip back into her shell. But you... you're different. You're so quick. You'll try different mediums, throw yourself in. You could probably write well in any genre. You never really needed anyone's help, even mine. You would never have sat at my feet, listening to words of wisdom. You argue with me, or, more often giggle. Billie was different. And I do like having people like Billie, and now, Lisette, around me. You, Mirren, don't need a writers' group."

"That's the nicest thing anyone ever said to me." And we were both laughing. "You know that Billie is hurt that you seem to be favouring Lisette?"

"Is she?"

"I wondered why you did that... given Billie still needs you."

"Lisette is a very talented writer. She's going places."

And Billie has already got there, was that it? If so, I understood. I wondered if Billie did.

Victoria was lost in thought, and when she spoke it was as if I wasn't there at all. "Although, sometimes I've wondered... wondered if there's something we don't know..."

"Something we don't know...? I asked.

She jumped as if she just realised I was still there. "Forgive me. Thinking aloud."

As she spoke, I was sure I saw a shadow pass the French

window. I half-expected someone to come in on us and was surprised when no one did. It must have been only the moon passing over a cloud, I decided.

CHAPTER ELEVEN

So we were all gathered together in the Chapel of Rest, at yet another funeral, this time Vee's. Once again, I found myself sitting next to D.S James Morrish.

"Don't say it," I whispered.

"Say what?" he asked.

"We have to stop meeting like this."

"I hope this is the last time," he said, nodding respectfully at the coffin.

Once again, too, Patrick was absent. And Maya Brodie. I thought that was very small-minded of her. But the mourners were far outnumbered by the media representatives who pressed themselves, cameras at the ready and notebooks in hand, against the back wall of the chapel. What were they waiting for, I wondered? For Vee to sit up suddenly in the middle of the hymns and point out her murderer? For Pat O'Kane himself, (for Patrick it must surely be. Every newspaper in the country had already decided that), to leap through a stained-glass window, knife in hand, to pick out his next victim?

Elsa didn't let them down. She'd taken Morrish's advice and was playing up her 'mystery woman' image to the hilt. She arrived in a black Givenchy dress, her face covered by a veil, her eyes covered by black sunglasses. It was a wonder she didn't fall over something on the way. Elsa made her way straight to the front row. Throughout the service, her sobs could be heard drowning out the minister and the organ.

"I thought you told her to stay quiet," I said to Morrish.

"One of her sobs is worth a hundred words," he replied.

Of course, Elsa had to be helped from the chapel, pausing only briefly as she stumbled to her car, parked handily just in front of a phalanx of photographers. Mrs Kirk's husband walked stiffly up the aisle, arm and arm with Victoria. I couldn't help thinking they looked more like a couple going back up the aisle after a wedding rather than a funeral.

"Come up with any ideas?" Morrish asked me as we walked back to my car.

"Isn't that your job?"

"All help gratefully appreciated," he said.

"I think it was some passing lorry driver, totally barking mad, who's since left the area and will never return. How's that?"

"Is it fairy stories you write?"

"That bad, eh?"

"Anyway, I hope you don't intend going out in that taxi again."

"And how am I supposed to earn a living? You tell me."

He leaned an elbow on the roof of my car and spoke softly. "Mirren, this is dangerous, you know that? Ask your boss if you can work in the control office until we've caught whoever's responsible."

"And how long will that take? Sitting in an office makes me stir crazy."

"Surely you sit in an office to write?" he asked, puzzled.

"That's different. Anyway, I'll tell you what I'll do. I'll take my mother out as a minder. You've met my mother. No one would dare attack me with her in the vicinity."

He didn't show even the glimmer of a smile. "This isn't a joke, it's deadly serious."

"I know it is, and I appreciate your concern. But honestly, I'll take care. I'll take one of Octopus out with me."

"What makes you think it isn't one of them? You'd be sitting in a car on your own with a potential murderer."

"It could just as easily be me."

He paused for a moment, casting narrowed eyes around the departing congregation. "I know it isn't you."

"How can you be so sure?"

"How can you be so sure it isn't Patrick Myer?"

He walked off before I could ask him what he meant by that. But whatever it was, he lifted my spirits tremendously.

"Mirren, we've been invited back to Donald's." it was Victoria at my elbow. Her eyes followed my gaze after James Morrish. She made a tutting noise in her throat. "You can do better than that, Mirren. A policeman?"

"You've got the wrong idea, Victoria."

She raised an eyebrow. "I think it might be you who has the wrong idea." Then, with a sigh, she added. "Well, are you coming?"

"Of course I am. Anyone need a lift?"

I could see Billie disappear into her own little red Fiat. Elsa's lavish Mercedes was already gliding down the drive. Lisette was by her own car, hoping, I suspected, to give Victoria a lift, but Victoria dismissed her.

"No need, I'm travelling back with Donald."

I watched Lisette for her reaction as Victoria stepped past her, pushing reporters out of her with all the gentility of a gorilla. Lisette was obviously not pleased to be overlooked like this. She looked too, more than a little embarrassed. Victoria had forgotten to tell her that her services would not be required.

She was still het up about it when we reached Donald's house.

Caterers had been brought in and had laid out a lavish buffet on a table along one wall, lending even more to the atmosphere of a wedding celebration rather than a funeral. White-aproned servers hovered around ready to top up our drinks. There was no one else here, as it turned out, but the survivors of Octopus. That's what it was increasingly feeling like we were now: survivors. Vee never had any children, and the rest of her family all lived abroad.

"Why do that?" Lisette was snapping. "I was hanging around there like a knotless thread. She told me earlier she'd need a lift, so I waited. And then, off she goes with hardly a word."

"Never mind, Lisette," I comforted her. "You'll get a story out of today, for sure."

"You bet I will," she went on. "I'm not going to waste a minute of this. This is first rate stuff. I might write a crime novel, you know."

Billie caught the end of this as we joined her at the buffet table. "I don't know how you can look at it like that, Lisette. Haven't you forgot Vee was our friend? I just want everything back the way it was."

"Writers can't afford to ignore any experience. You above all should know that."

I think, for once, Lisette was actually giving someone a compliment, though Billie didn't look on it like that. "You mean, I should write about life with my sister... a comic novel perhaps?"

"Sounds more like the basis for an inspiring family saga, but it's a good idea. It would be like therapy." Lisette sounded so light and frivolous. I wondered if she had any real feelings. For the first time, Billie looked like she was on the verge of anger. "What!"

I pulled Lisette away before anything more could be said. "How many feet can you get in that mouth of yours, Lisette?"

"I don't know, I just like to see people's reactions when confronted with truth. Sometimes those reactions can be surprising, not what you expected at all." She glanced over at Billie, lowering her voice. "I mean, have you ever considered the possibility that she was relieved by her sister's death?"

"Maybe deep down, she was. But she'd feel guilty about it. Is that so hard to understand?"

Lisette shrugged and popped a mini sausage roll into her mouth. "She's so hung up about the whole thing still. And something else..." She lowered her voice still further. "I can't help but wonder why she can't stand Dr Bonnar anymore."

I'd wondered that too, and I'd wondered if anyone else had noticed. But I would never have told that to Lisette.

"Does he know something about her... or does she know something about him?"

She glanced around suspiciously. "I'm doing a little investigating of my own, Mirren. Can you think what a story it would be if I solved these murders? It's too good a chance to miss."

Oh God, she was going to do a Miss Marple on us now.

"I can see why crime fiction appeals to you."

"Well, if you're prepared to think the worst of people and their motives, it seems you are a born crime writer."

"Well, that's certainly you... always trying to see the other person's point of view, especially if it's psychopathic."

Just at that, Victoria hovered into view and beckoned to her to join them. I thought Lisette might give her the middle finger, but instead she hurried over to catch the latest pearls of wisdom, and I ambled back to Billie.

"How's the new book going?" I asked. As far as I knew, it had been coming along very slowly. She hadn't produced anything since the first novel.

"It was coming along, until about three weeks ago."

Three weeks ago, when Annabel was killed.

"I understand," I said. "it's enough to drive anyone's muse underground. I can't get down to any writing myself... not that that's any great loss to humankind."

"But when you write, you write so fast... I can't do that. I write slow. I write and re-write and tinker until..."

"Until it's perfect and they put you forward for the Booker Prize."

She smiled. "Not quite."

"I just put a jumble of words together and hope for the best."

She abruptly changed the subject. "Does the Inspector still think it's Patrick?"

It took me so much by surprise I was momentarily lost for words.

She went on, "I don't want it to be him, Mirren. I liked him."

For once, I took Lisette's advice. I wanted to see Billie's reaction. "From what I hear, you liked him a lot... and he liked you."

She blushed and looked away. "Who told you that?"

"So what happened?"

You can tell when someone is nervous. They begin to breathe heavily and, in Billie's case, little beads of sweat appeared on her upper lip.

I touched her arm. "Why did nothing come of it?"

"I said I liked him. I didn't say I trusted him."

"You mean, you think..."

She shook her head. "Silly, really. It was all Victoria's idea. She thinks she can run everyone's life. Tell them how to act, how to feel. I had my sister on my mind. I couldn't be doing with a man in my life." I could see her watching Lisette standing at Victoria's side, listening to her with rapt attention. "She thought a love affair would do me the world of good. But Mirren, I'm not used to men any more. I was a carer for years, I had no room for them. And certainly not for men like Patrick. I was a bundle of nerves every time I met him. I felt he was always watching me. Poor Victoria, I think I must have let her down badly."

"She thinks the world of you. Surely you must know that," I said. Billie was still watching Lisette. "She took up with Lisette because Lisette can do with her help. You don't need her. There's nothing you can learn from Victoria."

"But you see, I didn't want to stop learning. I liked things the way they were. Octopus, and our meetings, I enjoyed all that."

Victoria had been right. Quiet Billie May would have been content to just sit at her feet, hiding her own talent, stifling it, afraid of challenge or change. Well, someone was changing things, that was for sure, giving her no choice but to move forward. She'd already been interviewed on TV and the sales of her book had apparently spiked since the news came out about killings in our little writers' group. It was now in the top ten in the Sunday Times bestseller list. One newspaper speculated that the death of the loved one in Billie's first book had almost marked her out as the first victim, although nothing more of that theory had come from James Morrish. But even the mere chance of it had raised the book up in the public consciousness and sent sales flying.

"That's all in the past, Billie. Frankly, I think Octopus is finished," I said, sadly.

She looked at me as if I'd said something she hadn't even considered. "Surely not."

"Surely yes, Billie. Someone's out to destroy it."

Dr Bonnar came across the room then, smiling and heading in our direction. Billie showed signs of definite panic. She began to move away, but I held her back. "You don't trust him either.

Why?"

"No, I don't," she managed to say, but then she was off just as Dr Bonnar reached us.

His eyes followed her across the room, annoyance in them, and maybe a glimmer of something more. Honestly, I never thought that Octopus had so much hidden under the surface.

"What have you done to Billie, Dr Bonnar?"

His annoyance was replaced by white-faced alarm. "What? What has she been telling you?"

"I don't know. What would she tell me?"

He still gazed after her. "She couldn't tell you anything... I've done my best to make it up to her, the little fool."

I stood there, shocked, as he brushed past me and hurried over to Victoria's charmed circle. Make what up to her, I wondered? They all had secrets, I'd just never noticed before. And I had hinted that I knew them all. In the circumstances, that was probably not the wisest of moves.

"Come and join us, Mirren," called Victoria. "You look as if you're not enjoying yourself."

I almost burst out laughing. As it was, I had to bite my lips to keep from telling Victoria that we were at a funeral, so actually I wasn't supposed to be enjoying myself anyway.

Vee's husband, Donald, might not have minded. He seemed to be enjoying playing the host. I almost expected him to ask if we were having a nice time. I sauntered over to where they stood. I took his apparent good humour as a cue.

"I know this is probably the wrong time to ask, Donald, and I feel a bit awkward," I said. "But I would so like a small memento of Vee."

"But of course, Mirren. Was there anything in particular you would like?"

"Well, if you wouldn't mind, I'd love one of her famous hatpins. It's what I always associate Vee with. I'd really treasure it."

He wasn't in the least offended by my request, which was a relief. Indeed, he seemed delighted. "She would have loved you to have one. With us having no children, so much will end up in some antique shop when I pass on. I'll go and get you a hatpin now. Was there any particular one?"

"Well, I've always loved the swan's head pin."

He patted my hand. "I'll be back in a minute."

Lisette butted in. "Hey, do you think he'd give one to me?" Lisette was never one to miss a freebie.

Billie looked horrified by all this. "Imagine asking for her hatpin!"

"Why, do you think it's dead expensive?"

"I must say, I think it's all very insensitive of you, Mirren."

Lisette ignored her. "If she's getting one, then I think I should get one too. I knew Vee just as well as she did."

"I knew her better than any of you," came Elsa. Who else? "I think I should get a hatpin also."

Donald hurried back to us with Vee's open jewellery box in his hand. "Do you know, it's funny, but I can't find it." He proffered the box full of hatpins for our inspection. There was the giraffe's head, and the quill pen with agate. "Would any of these do instead?"

"Any of them would be lovely," I assured him. "But, it's funny the swan's head isn't there. Is this where she always kept them?"

Elsa sniffed. "My God, Mirren. Wouldn't any of them do just as well?"

I ignored that, as something came to my mind. "Of course, perhaps that's the one she was wearing when she… oh." I shrugged. "The police probably still have it. Listen any one will do, any time, I'm just so grateful." By now my cheeks were beginning to flush. I was beginning to feel I was being quite insensitive, especially with all the tutting that was going on around me.

Donald Kirk looked vague, then puzzled. "But I've had Vee's belongings returned to me. And do you know, Mirren." He stared at me. "It's just occurred to me that there wasn't a hatpin among them."

At my insistence we called D.S Morrish immediately. It seemed to me that an important piece of evidence was missing.

Victoria was annoyed at me for spoiling the funeral for everyone. "Are you sure that was the hatpin she was wearing, Mirren? We could be getting the police involved for nothing."

"I'm not sure. But if it didn't come back with her clothes and it isn't in the house, then where is it? She always wore one. Can you remember which one she was wearing that night?"

Victoria hated to admit there was anything she didn't know. "How am I supposed to remember a thing like that? I had better things to do than stare at people."

I looked around the rest of them. "Anyone else?"

They all shook their heads. I looked at Dr Bonnar. "Didn't you notice, Doctor? You were the last person to speak to Vee at the club."

His face went red. "Of course I can't remember. I don't notice things like hatpins."

"What did she want to speak to you about anyway?" asked Billie, who couldn't bring herself to look at him directly.

His face, it seemed to me, grew even redder. "Nothing important. Some silly committee business."

"This has nothing to do with the missing hatpin," Victoria

said, snapping the conversation back to the relevant subject. I was sure I saw relief in Dr Bonnar's face.

"Here we are all not noticing stuff," I said. "And we call ourselves writers."

I closed my eyes and tried to recall that last night at the club. Vee had spoken to me, warning me about Patrick. Now... which hatpin had she been wearing? "Ah, of course!" hadn't it almost flown off and impaled someone? "See, I remember." I sounded superior, and I didn't care. "It was the swan's head, definitely."

If Victoria was peeved, D.S Morrish when he arrived was positively annoyed. "Now why on earth did no one mention a hatpin before all this?"

"Well, how were we to know it didn't come back with her belongings," sniffed Victoria.

Donald began to apologise. "It's my fault. I simply didn't think. I don't think I really looked."

"Could it still be lying at the scene of the m... at Laburnum Grove?" I asked.

"Hardly likely," Morrish replied. "The forensic team are pretty thorough. Although, now we'll have to go over it all again."

A new slant on a needle in a haystack; a hatpin on a side street.

"Perhaps, that's why Vee was killed," said Billie eagerly as I was driving her home. "It certainly looked valuable. Her death might be totally unconnected with Annabel's."

I instantly thought of Dr Bonnar's Okham's Razor theory, that the simplest explanation is almost the most likely. "Wishful thinking. Although I can't think why her murderer would take the hatpin. I mean, it's evidence. If he or she still has it, that alone could convict them."

"My sister wasn't cremated you know," came Billie, once again abruptly changing the subject.

I took my eyes off the road to look at her. "What are you talking about, Billie?"

"They could exhume her body." There was a little sob in her voice. "Do you think I should let them, if they ask? It might stop all this speculation."

"Have they asked?"

"No. the Inspector said they would need a lot more hard evidence before they would consider it."

"Then don't think about it, Billie."

"Mirren, if I thought... if I thought..." I watched her fists clench and unclench on her lap. "If I thought anyone..." I reached out and covered her hand with mine.

"I'm sure no one did."

"Let's change the subject," Billie pleaded, even though she was the one who brought her sister up. "It's all right for you. You're going back to your cheery mother. I have to spend the night in that mausoleum."

"Why don't you sell it?" I'd often wondered why she kept it on, with so many memories of her sister's suffering. It was as if she read my thoughts.

"The unhappy memories were only at the end. We had so many good memories there." She smiled at some private memory. It was only then I realised that to Billie she had been a sister and friend for most of her life, a vibrant person with personality and character, while to me, she had been a pathetic soul trapped in a tortuous existence in a useless body. She could barely even move, just a hand, and her eyes. And the look in those eyes had always disturbed me. I was always glad to get away.

I halted outside Billie's large Victorian villa with its sombre ivy-covered walls.

"Wait, why don't you come home with me tonight? I could

do with the company. That cheery mother of mine is on night shift."

She opened the car door with a sigh. I hadn't expected her to say yes anyway. "What's the point in putting it off? I've got to come back some time."

She was about to shut the door when I asked, "Are you ready now? To tell me what Dr Bonnar did to make you dislike him?"

Even as I said it, I could see by her eyes that it was more than dislike. It was hate, disgust, and perhaps more than anything else, fear.

"No, not today. I'd rather not talk about it." She smiled, then added. "It has nothing to do with all of this." But she said that as if she was trying to convince herself.

As I drove off, I tried to remember when I had first noticed the change in Billie's attitude to the doctor. She used to sit beside him at meetings. She used to laugh with him. He had been much impressed by her talent. I thought carefully. Billie had missed so many meetings during her sister's final illness, and while she was in hospital, Dr Bonnar had been in constant attendance. Billie had seemed grateful at the time for that. Then something had changed. Even before her sister's death. We had grown worried about Billie's intense devotion to her sister. She spent night after night in the hospital, lying on a cot in her sister's room, becoming almost paranoid about the medicines they were giving her. Terrified to let anyone be in the room alone with her. And quite suddenly, Dr Bonnar had stopped attending. He had told us, and we'd believed him, that her illness was far too advanced for any medical help. There was nothing more he could do. At the time, we were all more worried about Billie to even question that. After her sister's death, it had taken her a long time to come to terms with her loss. And it was then, yes, after that, when she finally came back to Octopus meetings, that the antagonism had become obvious. Did Billie blame him in some way for her sister's death? Was that it? Why hadn't I thought about it before? So caught up in my own problems to care about other people's.

"Well, and how did Mrs Kirk's funeral go?" My mother asked me, as if she was wondering how I'd enjoyed a late-night disco.

"Oh, it was wonderful, a lovely day out."

"Now, you know what I mean, lassie. Did you mind and tell her man I was that sorry I couldnae make it to pay my respects."

"Of course I did."

"No' that he'll mourn her for long," she went on. "See yon Victoria, she'll snap him up. You wait and see. Poor Mrs Kirk will hardly be cold in the ground before they two are marching up the aisle."

I thought of them as I'd seen them today, marching, just as she predicted, up the aisle of the Chapel of Rest. I felt honour bound however to stick up for my friend. "They're a bit too old for that sort of thing."

"Ha! You're never too old for that sort of thing."

This, coming from my mother, shocked me no end. "Mother, you devil."

She laughed. "Well, you think you young ones invented it."

I was laughing as I hung my coat in the hall. One thing about my mother, she brightened my life considerably.

I waited until my mother went off to her nightshift before I sat down and, with a deep breath and a nervous flutter in my belly, switched on my phone for the first time since the funeral. It began to ping almost immediately. Texts, e-mails, missed calls. I scrolled through, skipping over the messages from reporters. Then, almost when I'd given up and switched the thing off again, was a call from Patrick. I phoned him right away.

He sounded far away, his soft, lilting voice almost a whisper. "I'm so sorry, Mirren, running off the way I did."

"But why, Patrick? You only made it look worse for yourself."

"You mean with Elsa?" The story, of course, in spite of all Elsa's protestations to the contrary, had somehow leaked to the press. "You can't believe that, Mirren!"

"Tell me what did happen, then."

I heard his low sigh before he began. "When I took her home that night, she insisted that I come in with her. I'm not a fool, Mirren. I knew what she had in mind. You think women are the only ones to suffer from sexual harassment?" There was almost a smile in his voice when he said that. "I had no choice but to go in with her. She was alone, claimed she was terrified. What else could I do? Ach, Mirren, it was embarrassing. The way she flung herself at me. I hope I never have to fight off a passionate woman again. I think she was upset I didn't accept the gift she was offering me. Herself, that is. She made it sound as if she was giving it to me on a plate." Oh dear, now that did sound like Elsa. "In fact, she was more than upset. She used some choice language too. I never thought a romantic novelist would even know some of those words. She was bloody mad."

"Mad enough to lie?" I asked.

"Mad enough to kill." He winced as soon as he said that. "Ach, you know what I mean, Mirren. She was mad."

"But why didn't you tell me this that night? You know I wondered what had kept you."

"How could I tell you? I thought about it, that's why I drove around for so long. But I thought she would probably have regretted what she'd done in the morning. Telling you seemed like an awful betrayal. Although, if I'd known what she was going to do, to be quite honest I'd probably have sold my story to the press."

"But... the marks on her neck, Patrick. The bruises..."

"I had nothing to do with that, Mirren. I swear to you. I never touched her. The most I did was to hold her by the wrists. You've got to believe me."

"I do believe you." And I did, I couldn't help myself. "But the police don't. They're naturally going to take the word of a fine upstanding novelist like Elsa before they believe you. If only you hadn't run off. She'd never have dared come up with that story if you'd been here."

"I couldn't stay. I was... I still am the prime suspect. Elsa disappears, I'm the last one to see her. Two women are murdered. They were closing in. I told you, Mirren, I couldn't bear being in a cell again. I'd rather die first."

I wished suddenly that he was so close I could wrap him in my arms. Goodness, feeling like this didn't half make you think soppy.

"Where are you, Patrick?" If I'd known, I would have flown to him, and I don't care how that sounds.

"Better you don't know. I just wanted you to know, I didn't do what Elsa said. I'm innocent."

I knew then that he'd only come back to me once all this was solved. Maybe I could do a Miss Marple, like Lisette, and solve the case myself to get him back.

"Oh Patrick, you will be careful, won't you?"

"It's you that has to be careful. You won't drive those taxis any more, will you?" That was a harder thing to promise. As scared as I was that night down by the pier, the taxi was my livelihood. "Of course I won't."

"I care about you, Mirren. More than I can say."

And before I could tell him just much I cared about him, he was gone. I called his name down the line as if I could reconnect us by sheer will power. Finally, I slumped down on the floor and cried.

CHAPTER TWELVE

For three weeks, nothing happened and life seemed to settle down again to some semblance of normality. Meetings of the Port Gowrie Writers Group resumed with Maya Brodie leading the ant-Octopus faction. Maya insisted vociferously that she had not forgotten her threat. She was as determined as any murderer to destroy Octopus.

No one had seen or heard from Elsa. The first thing I tried to do after Patrick's call was visit her, but the house was closed up, although I was assured by James – yes, it was James now – that the police knew exactly where she was.

"She wanted away to work on her latest book," he told me.

"Based on her real-life experiences with Patrick Myer. It's probably the only first-hand experience she's ever had."

"Now, that doesn't sound like you, Mirren."

After three weeks, however, I told him she should have returned. It never takes her that long normally to finish a book.

James called in on me often, keeping me abreast of the details of the case. The hatpin could not be found. Forensics had turned up nothing. They still had no clues to the identity of the killer. He also wanted to know if I'd had any word from Patrick. I told him I hadn't. He didn't believe me. And always after he asked me and had got the same answer, he would leave, slamming the door behind him. I couldn't escape the feeling that there was more than professional frustration in that. He liked me. I had to admit, I liked him too.

But, as for Patrick Myer, that was more like love.

After three weeks, Elsa turned up again, all starry-eyed brightness, waving her new manuscript before her... and the nightmare began again.

I visited Elsa on the morning after her return. Her husband, Mike, let me in to their lovely home set high on the hills overlooking the Port.

Elsa saw at once that I wasn't here on a social call. She kept up the pretence that I was beautifully, at least until her husband had left us alone. As she smiled at him, I noticed that he didn't smile back. There was a definite strain in the relationship. "Will you bring us some sherry, darling? Dry, Mirren?"

As soon as he'd left, I turned on her. "Don't you think this has gone on long enough, Elsa? Don't you think it's time you cleared Patrick's name?"

"Oh, I see, is that what this is all about? Well, my story won't change. It happens to be the truth."

"The hell it is. And I'm going to prove it."

"Are you indeed? You're such a fool, Mirren. Be grateful he left you when he did. Remember those marks on my neck. Do you really think I could have made them myself?"

I knew she couldn't have, but I still refused to believe Patrick was to blame. Maybe Elsa had another lover. Maybe that's who she'd gone off with for those three days.

She saw the doubt flash through my mind, and saw me doubting Patrick again. She smiled. "Anyway, don't think for a minute Patrick was interested in you either. There was only ever one woman in Octopus who interested him."

"Either? Elsa, does that mean he wasn't interested in you... EITHER?"

Her cheeks flushed as she realised her slip. "It was Billie he wanted!" She almost screamed. "It was Billie he was after, from the beginning. But Billie had the measure of him. She knew about his hidden violence. Suspected long ago that he had a secret."

"And Billie confided all this to you?"

"Yes, she did. And if you don't believe me, ask her."

"Do you hate him so much for preferring Billie that you'd lie like this about him? Isn't he in enough trouble?"

"I think you should leave, Mirren. This conversation is beginning to bore me." She swivelled away from me and began to drum her fingers on top of the mantelpiece.

"Oh, for God's sake, Elsa. Have you always got to talk like a character in one of your books?"

She swung round to face me, her face flaming. "That's it, isn't it? Always bringing my writing down. Well, I hate to tell you, but my books sell. I could pick my publisher now. And I'm earning more from my writing than Billie ever will." She paused, ready to strike. "And I'm doing a lot better than you. When was the last time you earned anything from your writing, Mirren Murdoch? I think you've peaked. It's all downhill from now on. But me... my moment of glory is just beginning."

That shot home, as she knew it would. And in a way I didn't blame her. What right had I to make a fool of her for her writing? She sold. People wanted to buy her books. I didn't, and no one ever had the chance to read any of mine.

I caught myself on. Why did I always have to be so understanding.

Mike was heading to the living room with two dry sherries in his hands as I left. "Oh, you're going already? Did you fall out?" he asked, nodding in his wife's direction.

"Just a little."

"You know, Mirren," he said. "It's a terrible thing to say, but it's as if with these murders she's come alive. She's bursting with some kind of demonic energy. Does that sound silly?" It did actually, though I didn't tell him that. He went on, "It's all going to her head, all the publicity. She's changed so much. I hardly recognise her. She's been a different person since all this began… Sometimes, it actually frightens me."

"Mike," I asked, in a whisper. "Do you believe Patrick Myer assaulted her?"

I so wanted him to say 'no'. He didn't. In fact, he grew quite agitated in her defence. "Of course he did. Why, who else do you think could have done that to her?"

I left Elsa's house feeling dejected, depressed and dirty. I had gone there to confront her. Instead, she'd confronted me with a side of myself that I didn't like. So much for Mirren Murdoch, amateur detective. I was useless as a writer, useless as a detective, and useless at just about everything.

It was Patrick, in spirit at least, who pulled me out of my mood. His face, across the table, his voice telling me… "Give it up then. Stop writing."

By the time I reached home I was smiling.

Never.

Victoria arranged a meeting of Octopus to celebrate Elsa's return. I went, but with only one thought in mind. I was going to suggest disbanding the group. Who ever heard of an Octopus surviving with only six tentacles? I knew Victoria would protest. I didn't care. I wanted it finished.

I rang the bell when I arrived but no one answered. After standing for a couple of minutes, I began to make my way round the house. Victoria so often left her French doors unlocked, and as I suspected she had done so tonight. She was always being told how dangerous it was, especially now with a murderer on the loose.

The room was warmly lit by a couple of lamps at each side of the fireplace, and except for the gentle ticking of one of the clocks the house was in silence.

"Victoria?" I didn't expect an answer. Somehow you know when a house is empty. I moved from the study into the hall, and then into the kitchen. A buffet table was laid out for us, a salad half-prepared on the worktop. The room had all the appearance of being left in a hurry. Yes, there was a half-full glass of gin and tonic by the kitchen sink. I took the liberty of pouring myself one, then made myself comfortable in Victoria's front room. I had no doubt that she'd be back soon. Victoria was always the perfect hostess.

I was leafing through one of Victoria's local history books when I heard a car draw to a halt in the drive outside. I peered through the curtains, expecting to see Victoria herself, regally alighting from a taxi. It wasn't, it was Elsa, wearing sunglasses and clad in Gucci. I opened the door to her and she swept past me, almost like I wasn't there.

"I don't know where Victoria is. She seems to have left in a hurry."

"I'm sure she'll be back. She was so looking forward to tonight." Elsa dropped her jacket from around her shoulders, and I was just in time to let it slip through my fingers and fall on the floor, where I let it lie.

"At least we can have a drink before the others come." She poured herself a glass of red wine. "It was so nice of Victoria to arrange this, wasn't it? Ah, champagne." Elsa lifted a dripping champagne bottle from an ice bucket that was sitting on the sideboard, assuring me that it was a very good year. "I was brought up on good wines."

I could hear my mother's voice in my head, saying: 'Aye, *Blue Nun*, probably.' I didn't repeat it, but I did giggle. Fortunately, Elsa didn't notice.

"I wonder what she's celebrating," I said.

"We're celebrating the fact that it's over. It's been three weeks now, and Victoria believes it is finished. So do I." She looked at me straight in the eye, and said with confidence, "Patrick's gone now, you see."

"For Christ's sake!" I snapped.

"Oh, I forgot. You'd rather have him back, murdering us all in our beds... or don't you still think him guilty of anything?"

She turned away theatrically. I bit my lip, if only to stop myself bursting out in giggles. She really was too much.

The doorbell rang, and Elsa looked at me expectantly. I tugged an imaginary forelock in her direction before getting up.

I opened the door to find Dr Bonnar and Billie arriving at the same time. The doctor looked stern, and Billie was flushed and nervous. I got the distinct impression they'd exchanged words.

"Can I use the bathroom?" Billie asked at once.

"Go ahead," I shrugged, not that it was my house anyway. As soon as she was gone I turned to the doctor. "What on earth is going on?"

He looked genuinely angry as he replied. "Stupid girl! First, she refuses a lift from me, and then... she runs off, makes me look very suspicious, like I'm trying to abduct her. I mean, right in the middle of a busy street with everyone looking."

"Why wouldn't she take a lift from you, Doctor?" I asked, as if I knew already. His face flushed and he couldn't meet my eyes.

"She's a very foolish girl," he said, and turned away.

"Well, it all better be forgotten when she comes back," said Elsa, at the doorway. "This is a celebration. Octopus lives on, no matter what. As soon as Lisette and Victoria arrive, we'll open the champagne. You can do the honours, Doctor." Elsa was talking as if she was the hostess. "By the way, have you seen Lisette's new story? She's been waiting for this one to come out."

She tossed a magazine in my direction. "A triumph! How does she think up twists like that?"

I glanced at the story, with Lisette's name printed in big letters. I recalled the plot from when she'd first read it to us. The heroine, to everyone's surprise, takes a dive from the top of a skyscraper in New York, the double twist at the end being that she was the murderer all along. It was a great example of what they called the 'unreliable narrator' story.

I suddenly wished Lisette and Victoria would hurry up and make their appearances. "I'll ring her." I picked up my phone and tried Victoria's number. It rang out and went to voicemail.

"No answer?" said Dr Bonnar.

I shook my head. "I ought to tell you that I'm not coming back to Octopus." I said it as much to change the subject as much as anything else.

If I'd hit Elsa with a brick she couldn't have looked more stunned. "You, of all people can say that, Mirren. Because of this? But that's defeatism. And I, for one, will have none of it."

"And neither will I." it was Billie, framed in the doorway, speaking as defiantly as Elsa. She looked more beautiful than I could ever remember. Sometimes you couldn't see the beauty in her, she retreated so far inside herself that it looked insignificant… but not now. "We can't let whoever is doing these things beat us. We can't let them destroy Octopus."

Elsa held out her arms to her. "Darling, if only Victoria could hear you now."

"Where on earth is she anyway?" Dr Bonnar put in. "Invites us here and isn't even at home."

"It isn't like her," said Billie.

"Maybe she had a call and had to rush off somewhere," I said, thinking of the half-prepared salad and the half glass of gin and tonic by the kitchen sink. She would have definitely sunk that.

"You'd think she would leave a message."

"I'll see if she has," Billie said, and went off in the direction of the kitchen, although I was sure I would have noticed one myself. She came back a moment later and told us with a shrug that there was nothing.

"Maybe she and Lisette had something to do together," Billie said, trying not to sound peeved.

I rang Victoria a second time. Yet again, it went to voicemail. I left a message. We waited for twenty minutes, though not very patiently, while the ice melted in the bucket. Finally, I decided to ring Lisette.

"She must be on her way. There's no answer."

"Well, surely they must be together at least," said Elsa. "Maybe they went to the pub to start their celebration early." She added an almost hysterical laugh at the end.

A moment later, the doorbell rang, and we all breathed a sigh of relief. Elsa went off to open the door, saying with a wave of her hand, "You can open the bottle now, dear doctor!"

The champagne cork popped just as she came back into the room. Behind her, not Lisette, not Victoria, was James Morrish, together with a uniformed constable.

James's face was grim. "I am afraid you have nothing to celebrate this evening."

I stood up, my heart jumping in my chest. "Lisette."

Billie clung to Elsa. "Is it Victoria?"

D.S Morrish looked around us, from one face to the other, before he answered. He was watching for our reactions to his next words. "I'm afraid it's both of them," he said at last.

"Both of them!" We all said the same thing. How foolish we must have sounded.

"It may be that one was waiting for the other. Muzz Bonvieux for Muzz Ashe, or the other way about. Muzz Ashe was found on the top floor of the multi-storey car par in the town. Muzz Bonvieux was lying directly below her. Five floors below her."

"She was pushed over," Elsa gasped. "Just like in her story."

"What story?" James asked. I handed him the magazine. He skimmed through the story quickly.

"Does this mean... Is Victoria the..."

"We don't know what happened yet. It looks as if they met, there was a struggle and Muzz Bonvieux was pushed over the wall. But we don't know whether Muzz Ashe pushed her and Muzz Bonvieux managed to kill her before she went over or..."

"It must mean Victoria is the murderer," Elsa said with conviction. "Lisette dies exactly as in her story, but not before dealing a fatal blow to the murderer: Victoria." Yet she still looked as if she could hardly believe it. Neither could I.

"That must be right," Billie agreed. "It would be too much of a coincidence otherwise."

"Perhaps," said James slowly. "Except for one thing."

"What... one thing?" Dr Bonnar asked.

"The way Miss Ashe was killed."

"How... how...?" Billie's question sounded more like a wail.

He looked around us, watching for our reactions again. "Let's just say we've found Mrs Kirk's missing hatpin. It was in Miss Ashe's neck."

I had to jump to catch Billie before she fell. Unfortunately, no one caught Elsa. She slumped to the floor with a thud. I looked up at James Morrish. "That was a nice way to break the news, I must say. Could you not have sat us down?"

"I had to see their reaction."

"Oh, and were you satisfied>"

"My God, I can't believe they're both dead. I simply can't believe it." Dr Bonnar was helping Elsa to her feet.

"Oh, did I give that impression, Doctor. I'm sorry. Muzz Ashe is dead, yes. But not Muzz Bonvieux. She's still alive, but only just."

CHAPTER THIRTEEN

Elsa let out a sob. Dr Bonnar sat down suddenly, knocking over the bottle of champagne onto Victoria's thick piled cream carpet. No one moved to pick it up. Billie had gone chalk white, and I dipped my handkerchief in the ice bucket and held it out to her head.

"What makes you so sure Lisette was pushed?" I asked.

"Her car was parked on the top floor of the car park. There are signs of quite a struggle. The way she clawed at the wall. Her fingers... were broken so she would let go." He was deliberately trying to shock us.

Dr Bonnar hid his face in his hands. "God... no..." was all he said.

"Poor Lisette," came Elsa, theatrically. "She so wanted to be the narrator in this drama, not one of its victims."

"Oh knock it off, Elsa," I snapped. "This is real life. Lisette could die."

"At the moment, she's hanging on to life dearly," James assured me gently.

"Good for her," I said. "It's a pity we can't have that champagne after all. We could drink to Lisette."

"Wait, doesn't that mean the murderer could be scratched, bruised at least?" asked Billie.

"Not necessarily," James answered. "Her struggle came after she went over. She clawed the wall, not her attacker."

Somehow that made it sound even worse.

"Can we see her?" Billie asked.

James shook his head firmly. "No visitors. Not until she's out of danger, or regains consciousness."

"I demand that we have police protection," Elsa said, blinking back tears. "Hasn't enough happened to justify that?"

"You will. In fact, from now on you will each have a police officer accompany you everywhere." He looked pointedly at Elsa. "And I don't want anyone making up some feeble excuse to get rid of them."

"I'm a doctor. I can't have a policeman hanging around me all the time," said Dr Bonnar.

"He won't be sitting in with you when you're examining patients, if that's what you're worried about. Anyway, there will be plenty of policemen in the hospital."

"I want to go to the hospital. I want to see her," sobbed Billie.

"You can't, Miss May. Her parents are the only people who are allowed anywhere near her."

"You forget, Billie," said Dr Bonnar. "Lisette will almost certainly be able to identify her attacker. Am I right, Inspector?"

"Well, yes, we certainly hope so, Doctor."

"I don't like this sitting around waiting for someone to kill me," said Billie through her tears. "Can't we do something?"

"Let us deal with it."

Billie had begun to shake beside me. I grabbed her as she was about to keel over again. "Is there any brandy?"

"It's alright, Mirren. I wouldn't take the stuff."

"Billie lives alone," I said to James. "Don't you think it would be better if she moved in with me?"

He nodded in approval, but the idea of moving in with me

seemed to alarm Billie even more than the brandy. "No, I can't. I have so much to do. My book... and you've seen the machine I work on." Billie had once shown me her study. She liked to use her sister's ancient word processor for her writing. A chunky, yellowing, relic, it used an ancient operating system – MS DOS – and it had no internet access, which she said was a plus, because the internet just distracted her. I could imagine my mother's face on seeing us lug that contraption into our house.

Billie went on, "I have a deadline, and I'm not nearly finished. I just want to stay where I am. I'll be careful, I promise."

"We can arrange a female PC to stay with you."

"No, thanks. I don't like strangers."

"You're all in real danger," James reminded us. "You have to think about who could hate you this much."

"The list we gave you, didn't it help?"

"Not much. We checked out that woman, Petronella Green. The one you blackballed." He glanced at me with distaste, as if he was ashamed of me being party to such a thing. "She lives in Kent now. She's quite elderly, has a lot of mobility issues, and spends her time tending her garden. So, we can discount her. By the way, her poetry got published."

I could almost hear Victoria dismiss that piece of news. "In a real book?" She would absolutely have said it if she'd been here. She'll never be here again, I reminded myself sadly. I only wished there was somebody who could hold me up if I wanted to faint.

"Maya Brodie, well, much as she seems to hold a grudge against you... Did you know that she's been complaining about you lot with that solicitor husband in tow?" That seemed to amuse James. It might have amused me too, if I could just push away the picture of Lisette clinging to the balcony of a multi-storey car park while someone bashed and broke her fingers to prise her loose.

Not Victoria. Surely not Victoria. It wasn't possible.

"Anyway," he went on. "We don't think Maya Brodie is murderer material. Certainly not this type of murder. Not the furtive, planning out cold-blooded type of murder. Because this was all carefully planned."

He looked around us all. "Lisette was due to come here, she always comes early, I understand. She met someone in the car park, either by accident or assignation."

"Victoria?" I asked.

"Have you any reason for saying that?" he asked.

"When I arrived here it looked as if Victoria had left in a hurry. As if she'd just taken a call while preparing the salad in the kitchen. You can see for yourself. Perhaps that call had come from Lisette."

"We're assuming she had a call..." Billie said. "Couldn't she just as easily have made one?"

"To meet Lisette. Does that mean you think Victoria was the murderer?" asked James.

Billie looked shocked. "No, of course not!"

"It must have been one of them," said Elsa. "Thank goodness, at least we know now."

"And what about Patrick?" I asked. "Was he their willing accomplice?"

"Patrick! Patrick! Patrick! Is that all you ever think about?"

Now it was my turn to blush.

"Perhaps Patrick killed both of them. Perhaps he killed them all," said the doctor.

"You forget, Doctor," James reminded them softly. "One of them is still alive."

"Does this mean it's all over? That you have your murderer?" asked Billie.

"We'd like to hope so, if Muzz Bonvieux recovers, but we will have to wait and see about that." He looked around us. "I'm afraid I'll have to know all your movements during the past few hours."

"You can't possibly suspect any of us," Elsa said haughtily. "It's over. Lisette or Victoria must have been to blame."

"But which one, and how will you ever find out the truth? You can't let one take the blame when they've only ever been a victim." And I thought of Patrick, always blamed for a murder he had been tried for and found not quite guilty of.

James Morrish seemed to read my thoughts. "We'll find out the truth. Statistically, we usually do."

"Well, I have an alibi. I was with my wife." Dr Bonnar looked pleased with himself.

"You stopped to give me a lift in the middle of town. Not too far from that car park. And you were alone." Billie sounded pleased to be able to point an accusing finger at him.

"I was dropping my wife off." He looked around us. "She was going to her craft class." He glared at Billie. "And you? You were as near to it as I was. And where was your car tonight?"

"Everyone knows I don't always use my car. I prefer to walk. You know that Mirren."

"Well, I wasn't anywhere near there. I was typing in my workroom," said Elsa. "Mike can verify that."

"Did he see you, Elsa, or only hear you?" I asked. "If he only heard you clicky-clacking on your keyboard then that's an old trick. Recordings, they've been done to death."

"And what about you, Mirren?" she responded angrily. "Seems to me you didn't get on with Lisette at all. She was a bit too successful for your liking. Well, where were you tonight?"

If truth be told, I didn't have an answer to that. I certainly had no alibi to speak of. My mother was working all day, and I'd been alone in an empty house before making my way to Victoria's.

It was Billie who came to my rescue. "Oh, this is nonsense. I can't believe it either, but it has to be true. Either Lisette killed Victoria and Victoria pushed her over the wall, or Victoria pushed Lisette over the wall, but not before Lisette managed to stick that hatpin in her. That has to be what happened, even though none of us can believe it."

"But I can't believe that either, Billie," I told her. "It's too much of a coincidence that Lisette was pushed over a wall exactly as in her story. And Victoria, stabbed with a hatpin, one of the hatpins she wrote an article about." And I knew by their silence, they all agreed with me.

"But how could someone overpower both of them?" Billie's question came out as a sob.

"Perhaps they didn't have to." I thought about it. "Perhaps the call Victoria received was to lure her to the car park." I looked at James. "Her phone should tell us."

"We haven't found their phones yet," he said. "It may be the killer took them."

"What about their phone records at the phone company?"

"We do check these things, Mirren, and we will."

"But we can easily check if she went by taxi?"

He nodded.

I went on, "Lisette always arrives early at Victoria's. So what about this? She drives up just in time to see Victoria driving off. Lisette already told me she was doing her Miss Marple on this. So, curious, she follows the taxi. Arrives too late to save Victoria, but in just enough time to see who the murderer is. There's a struggle and Lisette goes over the wall, but not without a fight." I could imagine that fight too, Lisette, small and lithe, struggling for her life, but not strong. Not strong enough.

"That means you do think it was a coincidence her going over the wall," said Dr Bonnar.

"Good thinking, Doctor." Because of course he was right. This murderer wouldn't leave anything as important as the method of murder to coincidence. That was part of the plan. "In that case, Lisette must have been summoned there too."

"If we can find their phones, then we'll check."

"Perhaps she watched, saw Victoria die. Or, perhaps she went over first, and Victoria saw that happen." I could feel my voice breaking now. Another moment and I'd be in tears. I looked at James. There was a reassuring smile in his eyes. He wanted me to go on. I blinked back the tears. "No. This was all carefully planned. It had to be."

"Then it's Patrick!" There was a definite dramatic sob in Elsa's voice. "This is all my fault! It's me he's after. Can't you see that?"

"We don't see that at all, Elsa," I replied.

"I've told the truth about Patrick. This is his vengeance. Poor Lisette. Poor, darling Victoria. It's all my fault."

At that moment I cheerfully wished it HAD been Elsa who'd been pushed over the balcony.

"No one can blame Patrick for this, surely," Billie said softly. "He must be miles away by now."

James took a while to answer. "I'm afraid that's where you're wrong. We've had reports of Patrick Myer being sighted in Port Gowrie in the past two days."

I returned home, alone. A patrol car followed discreetly behind and remained outside my house all night. I couldn't sleep. Victoria dead. I hadn't realised how much I cared about the woman until now. I knew that as soon as I was in my house I'd cry, and I did. All that life, all that intelligence, gone. I remembered the last time I'd come to her cottage. She had said all the things I needed to hear. I had a mother, of course, but Victoria felt like my writing mother, and now I'd lost her.

Someone else had heard me cry, I was sure of it now. That hadn't been a cloud passing the moon. That had been someone, listening at the window outside. But who? Maybe my policeman come to check?

And Lisette, fighting for her life. How could anyone have done that to her? I refused to imagine that it was Patrick. Yet what did I really know of him? Nothing. Annabel had died, and I'd seen him sneaking out of the car park. Vee Kirk had died, and then he'd disappeared. Elsa swore he attacked her. Now he'd been spotted in the town, at the same time that Victoria had been killed and Lisette pushed over a multi-storey balcony. The evidence was piling up against him. Was I a fool, resolutely believing in his innocence?

What did I know after all of any of Octopus? Billie was afraid of Dr Bonnar. Why? Or, was it Dr Bonnar who was afraid of Billie? Who made those marks on Elsa's neck if it wasn't Patrick? And what had made Victoria rush off like that? A call from someone? Or had she indeed been calling someone else? I tried to imagine Lisette lying in wait for her on the top storey of the car park. Lisette, with Vee's swan head hat pin in her hand, ready to strike. Or Lisette, confronting Victoria with her guilt. Lisette, the petite detective. Or, the petite murderer. Which one? No, it had to be someone else. Some outsider. It all came back to Patrick.

Even my mother at breakfast looked frightened. It was hard to tell. I'd never seen her frightened before.

"Now, that's you finished wi' these taxis. That's my final word. And as for that writing group, you get shot of that. There's somebody oot to get every one of ye. I couldnae care less about the rest of them, but I don't want it to be you."

I promised her I'd take care, and even went to the extent of asking my friendly neighbourhood bodyguard outside if I could ride with her down to the station.

Morrish didn't seem surprised to see me.

"How is Lisette?" was my first question.

"No change. But I have to tell you... the doctors don't hold out much hope. She's in a very bad way."

I began to cry. I took poor James so much by surprise he stepped back, as if it was catching. "Sorry," I sobbed. "What's happening, James? Who's doing these things?"

"You don't think it might have been Lisette, or Muzz Ashe?"

"No, I can't believe that. What happened to Lisette is worse than killing, worse than death... If Lisette lies like that forever. I mean, God knows we had our issues, but..." Fiery, adventurous, ambitious Lisette. I still didn't know whether to pity her or hate her.

James put a comforting hand on my shoulder. I leaned against him and clung round his waist. What I really wanted was to sit on his knee, but I didn't think that would be allowed, certainly not in his office. When I looked up, his cheeks were red. He was embarrassed enough already. "I don't really have an alibi either," I told him. "My mother was out long before I left the house." I felt my eyes sting with tears again, but I sniffed them back. I wasn't comfortable crying in public. "It has to be an outsider, or someone with a grudge against us."

"Yet someone who knows all your movements."

"But what motive do you think we all have?"

"Elsa might resent the way you disclaim her talent, though I'm not sure it's much of a motive for murder."

I giggled, and he furrowed his brow at me. God, he did not know writers at all.

"Elsa has enough faith in her talents to dismiss any of us completely."

"Dr Bonnar, now I've been reading some of his blog posts. Did you know he has a blog?"

I nodded. I had to confess I hadn't read it. James went on, "He has some weird notions. Some very right-wing ideas. He seems to believe in survival of the fittest. Perhaps he thinks none of you are fit to live."

I giggled again. I'd certainly picked up on some of Dr Bonnar's ideas during our conversations, and I didn't like them.

"And then there's this…" James fished in his drawer and brought out a copy of Dr Bonnar's novel, *PanzerKommander,* dropping it onto his desk with his thumb and forefinger, as if dumping a soiled newspaper in the bin. "Does it not strike you as strange that a man like him can write a story like that, where the main characters are all so … nasty? I mean, they're Nazis."

"What, you mean, how does he get into a character's head, and make you believe in it? That's kind of the whole point." Whoever your characters were, bad or good, as Victoria often pointed out, you needed to put yourself in their shoes. Empathy was the biggest tool in a writer's toolbox. "As much as his book was definitely not my bag, he did well, I thought. I mean, you really felt you were on the Russian front in a freezing tank."

"Do you not wonder where this stuff comes from in a person like Dr Bonnar's head, and what else might be in there?"

While the jury was out on Dr Bonnar for his views, I felt I had to defend him as a fellow writer. For me, the fact that something like his book could come out of such a grey, ordinary-looking man from the west of Scotland was, in its own small way, a thing of wonder. "You might ask Stephen King the same question. Or the guy that wrote Hannibal Lecter. Or Clive Barker, my God! And what about William Shakespeare? Have you ever seen *Titus Andronicus*?"

He nodded. "A fair point. Billie… now she could have gone loopy after her sister's death."

"She retreated inside herself, that's all."

"Muzz Ashe… all the other deaths could be a cover up for just one. Mrs Kirk's. She wanted her out of the way so she could get her lover back."

Another giggle, which turned into something of a fit. The man must be thinking I'm an idiot. "She waited a long time to do it."

"Perhaps she saw time running out. This was her last chance."

"But Vee was out of the way, so why Lisette?"

"Lisette's been nosing around, doing her, as you say, Muzz Marple thing. Getting right up my nose actually." He looked suddenly like a put out little boy. "Perhaps she got too close. Perhaps she found something out. Perhaps she made the arrangement to meet Victoria."

"Stupid place to arrange to meet a murderer, is it not? The deserted top storey of a car park, at that time?"

"Perhaps she didn't know then that Victoria was the murderer. Perhaps she thought she was confiding in someone she could trust."

"Lisette could have pretended she knew too much. She was a good one for that. Just to see people's reactions. Maybe this time she just picked the wrong person."

"Do you think it's over, James?" I asked him before I left.

Typically, he answered with another question. "Do you?"

That evening, I decided to go to Billie's. A police car was sat outside.

"She's not long back. She was at the library," the police officer told me as I passed.

I walked up the drive to her house, and found her front door ajar. That was odd.

I pushed it wider. "Billie?"

I hated this house. There had always been this musty smell of death and disease inside. It permeated the air, even now.

"Billie?" There was no answer. I flicked a switch but Billie's ancient lighting refused to come on. Damn her. She had no competence whatsoever for the essentials of life. I doubted if she even knew how to change a fuse. I was sure I heard a sound, muffled, somewhere in the shadows. I was suddenly afraid. Where was Billie?

There was a police officer just down the drive. Why didn't I shout on her? Because I was stupid, that's why.

There, the sound again.

"Billie, is that you?"

There must be a lamp somewhere. I remembered a big old-fashioned lamp somewhere underneath the stairs. I began feeling my way towards it.

And my feet touched against something soft... something human.

A low moan. I held my breath and reached across to switch on the lamp. The 40-watt bulb hardly lit the hall, but it was enough for me to see Billie, lying practically unconscious at the foot of the stairs.

CHAPTER FOURTEEN

Billie was rushed to hospital. I travelled in the ambulance with her, sure every minute that she was dead. Her breathing seemed so shallow. Porters took her from me at the door of the accident and emergency unit and rushed her inside. I was left standing, not quite knowing what to do, like the proverbial knotless thread. Finally, I wandered inside the building and sat in a long corridor beside a drunk with a bandaged head.

Lisette, and now Billie. But she'd just arrived back, and a police officer was watching her every move. How could they have let this happen? Had she caught someone inside her house? Had they been waiting for her when she'd come in from the library? Whoever attacked her must still have been in the vicinity when I got there. This time, I hoped, they would have better luck catching him.

I was so wrapped up in my thoughts I didn't hear D.S Morrish's hurried steps along the corridor.

"Are you alright?"

"It's not me, it's Billie."

"She's going to be fine. You wait and see."

That didn't reassure me. "We're being taken out, one by one. This hospital won't be big enough for the casualties."

He ruffled my hair gently. It was such an unexpectedly affectionate gesture that I almost began to cry again. Almost, but not quite. He slipped an arm around my shoulder as he sat by my side. "Tell me exactly what happened."

I told him. "I suppose Patrick will get the blame for this too."

"It's a possibility. We've got to keep everything open. Surely you can understand that?"

"Maybe it was an accident. She might just have fallen downstairs."

"Perhaps," he said, and we both watched my hand trembling. "Would you like a cup of tea?"

Only a man like James Morrish would suggest a cup of tea instead of something stronger to steady the nerves. I nodded. "Yes, please."

He got up and went to the vending machine. I knew a police officer should be with me at all times. I was glad it was James.

He brought the tea back in a foam cup. It was vile. "Would you accompany me back to Billie's house?" he asked.

"I'd rather stay here and see how Billie is. She'll need someone." If there was anyone, among us all, who needed someone, it was Billie. And yet, there were so many questions buzzing in my head.

"There's nothing you can do here. Come on. It won't take long."

At Billie's house, the police presence was very discreet. There were a couple of cars in the driveway, and some officers searching in the bushes.

Inside was a different story. Policemen and forensics officers buzzed around in every room, and though every 40-watt light in the house was on, the place still looked dank and gloomy.

"The big light in the hall isn't working, so there's a good chance Billie just fell," I said. "I mean, it's funny how that top step disappears in the dark."

He didn't look at me. His eyes were scanning the hall. "You say the front door was open. Now why would she leave it open?"

"She might have meant to shut it later. She was laden with library books, remember." I looked around. "But where are the books?"

There was not a sign of them. On a table, on the floor, or in the hall. Nor had they been scattered around her still figure when she fell. "Why didn't she leave the books on the hall table?" I wondered.

"Because she carried them straight upstairs," he said.

"Or perhaps something made her go upstairs straight away, taking the books with her. Maybe she heard something, someone. Maybe the front door was already open when she got here."

"So why didn't she just go and get the police officer who was sitting at the bottom of the drive?"

"Maybe she's a bit like me." I'd done exactly the same thing – or rather, failed to do exactly the same thing – when I'd come into the house before. "Besides, you have to know Billie to understand. She doesn't like to bother anyone. And this house doesn't frighten her the way you'd imagine it would. It scares the sh…" I coughed, and changed the word I'd been about to use. I didn't want to shock James. "… the pants off me. But Billie, this is where she's comfortable."

"So where does the noise come from?" he asked.

My gaze rose with the stairs. "If she fell downstairs, she must have been upstairs." I began climbing, with James beside me. "She heard something, and decided to go up to investigate."

"She doesn't seem the intrepid type."

"I told you, she doesn't like bothering anyone."

We reached the top of the stairs. "And where from here?" he asked.

"Find her library books," I said.

Billie's bedroom was stark. A few family pictures surrounded her bed, and the bed was made neatly. There were no books.

Next door was her sister's room, which was even starker, like a mausoleum. The blinds were pulled low. Her old wheelchair sat by the bed. Billie had once asked me to find out if anyone could use it. I had forgotten to do that, and the sight of it made me feel guilty. This room gave me the shivers.

"This one is Billie's study." The door was already slightly ajar. Here was the only room in the house that seemed alive to me. Even now, quiet and still, it breathed. Billie's ancient MS DOS word processor was sitting there. It was switched on, its pale grey light flickering, awaiting Billie's magical words. Her reviews, of which there were many to be proud of, were all pinned on a cork board on the wall. And she always said she didn't care what critics said. Liar! The cover of her book was pinned up there too, her smiling, beautiful face in a box on the back flap. On the desk, the only untidy things were her floppy discs, which she saved her work onto, scattered around haphazardly. And there, too, in a neat pile, were her library books.

"Whoever it was couldn't have been in here," I said. "She would have seen him as soon as she reached the door. She wouldn't have walked right in and laid her books down."

"Why on earth didn't she put on a light?"

"Maybe in here she didn't have to. The word processor gave her light enough." A thought struck me. "Wait a minute. I take it none of your men would have switched on the word processor?"

"Certainly not. Billie must have done that herself..." He called one of the men to verify this, and he did.

"Now maybe," I said thoughtfully. "Billie was one of those people who leave their computer on when they pop out. I never would. Everything is saved, backed up and switched off." I'd learnt that from past experience, when I once lost an entire day's work after leaving my computer on for a few hours, with a document unsaved. The thing crashed when I was out, and I could never seem to get the words back. "The thing is, I'm not sure exactly how she works on this ancient word processor. I assumed she had to save everything to discs. With that in mind, I'd imagine she was like me, religiously saving every paragraph as she goes. But what if she came back and heard someone moving about up here... she comes upstairs, finds the word processor switched on... but why? Can I put one of the discs in the machine?"

James shook his head. "Not until they've all been fingerprinted."

"Do you think she was pushed, James?"

He shook his head. "We won't know that until she comes round."

"So, it isn't over yet."

"She's still alive, like Lisette. That's two mistakes the killer made. We'll get to him, don't worry."

"Or her."

He took this as a defence of Patrick. Maybe it was.

"All he has to do is turn up and tell his side of the story."

"Why should he think you'd believe him?"

It was the next morning before Billie came round and could speak. I was by her bedside when she did, along with one of the doctors, James and a police officer.

Lisette was to be allowed no visitors. Even the location of her room was kept a mystery. I'd been given a strange look when I asked, and the nurse I did ask told a police officer, who in turn told James.

"It's much better you don't know," he warned me.

"Are you seriously considering me as a suspect?"

"Any survivors are suspect, and that includes Lisette."

Billie cracked open her eyes and we all held our breath, waiting for her to speak. Had she seen someone? Could she solve the whole mystery? She looked around the room, as if finding it difficult to focus. She'd broken her nose and an ankle, but apart from that, she hadn't been badly hurt.

Slowly, her memory returned. "Mirren…" she tried to smile, but found it hurt too much. "Oh, Mirren…"

Tears began to stream down her face. I stroked her hand. "It's alright. You're not badly hurt, you'll be fine."

She began to shake her head, very slowly. "No… no…"

"You will, you'll see."

The doctor bent forward, feeling her pulse, her head.

"Can you tell us what happened, Muzz May?" James Morrish asked in his highland lilt.

Billie's eyes shifted to him.

"Did you see anyone?" he repeated.

"There was no one there… I didn't see anyone…" Her gaze shifted back to me as she spoke.

I squeezed her hand. "You must tell him." For I had a feeling she was lying.

"No… no one… there was no one." I wanted to believe her. Why didn't I? She looked at me. "Honest, Mirren, I fell. I wasn't pushed." Yet I still felt she was holding something back. "Oh, Mirren." She grabbed my hand and held it so tightly it hurt. "Mirren… I can't believe anyone could be so cruel…"

She was sobbing now, and the doctor bent forward again, anxious she shouldn't be too disturbed.

I leaned forward to catch her words. "My book, Mirren. My book…"

"You'll get it finished. I'll help you."

She was clinging to my sleeve now. "You don't understand." Her voice was broken, and she was pulling me so close to her mouth it was almost touching my ear. "It's gone... the whole thing... wiped out. I came back and every disc had been wiped clean. Every copy I made, obliterated. They've destroyed my book."

CHAPTER FIFTEEN

The doctor had to sedate Billie, she grew so agitated and only when she was calm and sleeping again did I leave her and follow James into the corridor.

"I want to go back to the house. I want to see."

And yet, I knew what she said must be true. The way the discs had been scattered around, it was so unlike the scrupulous Billie. There was panic. Billie trying desperately to see if any of her blood-sweated book remained. It was different perhaps, for those of us that worked on modern laptops. My main copy of anything I wrote was always on my desktop. I always saved it every night to a USB, which I kept separately. Every week I would e-mail the latest version to myself, and then there was the cloud, and so on. She used her sister's ancient MS DOS word processor, where everything was held on floppy discs and there was no access to the internet.

How could anyone hate her so much? Or Annabel? Or poor Vee? Or Victoria and Lisette? Any of us. "It has to be someone who knew her," I said absently, as if I was talking to myself. "Someone who knew how she worked, who knew she used that old word processor and where she kept her floppy discs. Someone who knew wiping those discs would be worse than death for Billie."

"Will you be able to tell if those discs have been wiped?"

I nodded. "I think so, it's not hard. I should have guessed, really, when I saw them scattered there. She's always so neat with her work. Everything is in order and in little boxes, ically built for the purpose."

or Billie, every word struggled for life, pushing their way out f her. Delivering a book was like going through labour. She'd often told me so herself. She worried about every sentence, every paragraph. No wonder it took her so long to write her books. To lose all she had written so far, that would kill her.

We went back to Billie's house, where I went through each disc, every one of them numbered, chapter by chapter, and then two copies. All of them were blank, empty, destroyed. "This is what she found when she came back. Her word processor switched on, her book wiped. No wonder she ran..." I looked up at James, feeling Billie's desperate sense of panic and despair. "You know, I think she might just have fallen in her panic. Whoever did this had no need to push her down the stairs to finish the job. They've killed her by doing this, just as sure as they killed the others. Billie sweats blood over her books, and this one... she's been sweating on it most of all. Poor, poor Billie..." I sunk my head in my hands.

"That means it might still have been Lisette or Victoria. One of them could have done it when Billie came into town, just before meeting the other. Chances are she didn't come in here when she returned from Muzz Ashe's house. Perhaps all of yesterday too. The word processor could have been switched on from the night before, could it not?"

I was already shaking my head. "Victoria would never do such a thing. Despite all her flaws, no, never. She loved Billie's writing." James was looking at me as if I was some strange curiosity. He just didn't understand writers. "And anyway... why not switch off the word processor when they finished, unless they wanted it discovered right away. No, James, I can't believe that. And she's hiding something..."

"Aha... You saw it too?"

"Oh yes... but why... or is it someone she's protecting?"

"Have you checked your own laptop lately?"

For the first time that day I laughed. "That would be no great tragedy if they wiped mine, as I'm sure the killer knows. They'd probably be doing the world a favour. End up being awarded a Nobel prize for literature."

"You talk yourself down too much," he said.

"I know." But I was nervous, frightened. There was someone out there who knew all our secrets, and knew how to hurt us most. That's what frightened me more than anything. "Victoria couldn't have done this, I know that. Surely, even Lisette..."

"Someone's got to be doing it. And it's got to be someone you know."

I knew the someone he was referring to was Patrick.

"I always did go for the underdog. I always wonder if the police have really got the right man."

"Just promise me one thing. If he contacts you, get in touch with me. Don't take the chance. He might be dangerous."

"Of course I won't."

But did I really believe that?

Newspapers were having a field day. Port Gowrie had always been a sleepy little port town, and had never been famous. Now it was besieged by press and television. Us Octopus members were already fearful for our lives. Those of us who remained could hardly step out of our front door without being set upon by reporters and photographers. Dr Bonnar was angry about the intrusion into his life. He tried as best as he could to carry on with his duties at the hospital, but it must have been difficult. He tried his best to carry on with his duties at the hospital, but it must have been difficult. He resented too anyone even talking to his beloved wife.

"I'm so worried about her, Mirren. This whole business is

depressing her," he told me one day at the hospital.

I didn't like to remind him that it was killing the rest of us.

Elsa, on the other hand, absolutely gloried in the publicity. She'd already been offered a new book deal. I knew the story already; a fantasy Ruritanian kingdom with dragons, a darkly handsome anti-hero from a noble family, besotted by a beautiful woman (Elsa's alter ego).

I met Elsa at the hospital. We'd both come furtively to escape the hordes of journalists. Me by a back route, Elsa by the front door, of course. I was surprised to find her in the room set aside for us, because up until then she hadn't visited. She hadn't even called about either Billie or Lisette. Yet, here she was complete with a tray of fruit.

"Hello, Mirren," she said stiffly. She had never retracted her story about Patrick. There was even less likelihood now that she would. "Do you think we might be allowed in to see either of them?"

"We can see Lisette through the door, but we're not actually allowed in the room." I had already met with Dr Bonnar there, staring silently through the glass panel at the still figure hooked up to tubes and drips. "Billie has been allowed visitors from the start though," I said pointedly.

"I didn't think she'd be kept in. Is she badly hurt?"

"It was James's idea. The more of us he has under one roof the better he can protect us." I had a notion myself then to hospitalize one more. Billie hadn't been badly hurt in a physical sense, but emotionally and mentally she was suffering badly, and I was growing increasingly worried for her.

"Does Billie know who did it?"

I thought she did. Or at least she knew more than she was telling. Perhaps she was trying to protect someone, or perhaps she was only trying to protect herself. I shook my head. "She says there was no one there."

"And her book wiped out too? How could anyone be so cruel? I tell you, Mirren, that would kill me."

She walked right into it every time. "Come on now, Elsa, you could knock another one out in six weeks. No hardship to you." I'd never learn to keep my mouth shut.

"Of course, you think one of my books would be no loss. Thank God the public and my editors believe differently."

I almost apologised, but it doesn't come easy with Elsa. "You're doing well out of all this."

"Not deliberately, I can tell you. I can't help it if I'm hot property all of a sudden."

"Lucky you."

"Luck has nothing to do with it," she said viciously. "Talent. That's what it takes. Why, they've already sold the film rights to the new books, and I haven't even started writing them yet."

"That does take talent," I said.

"I wonder about you, Mirren," she said, scrutinising me closely. "If they're looking for someone with a motive, they could look no further than you. Everyone in Octopus is doing better than you. Do you resent that? Your biting sarcasm certainly suggests you do."

"Be serious, Elsa."

"Oh, I am. Nothing much has happened to you, has it? I intend to keep my distance from you from now on."

"That suits me fine." I was biting my tongue, trying to hold onto my temper. "But there's just one thing you seem to forget. I thought we already had our murderer: Patrick. The man who tried to rape you, or had you forgotten him? Or do you know something we don't?"

A moment later, we were led in to see Billie. We were both still fuming and keeping well away from each other.

If anything, Billie looked worse with every passing day. Her black eyes were edged with yellow. Her face was paler than usual. She tried to smile.

"Thanks so much for coming."

"You're sure you didn't see who did it?" said Elsa.

She glanced at Elsa and lowered her eyes. "No."

"That's a pity. Who would do such a thing? Your whole book."

Elsa sounded extremely cheerful about the whole thing.

"She's alive, isn't that enough?" I reminded her.

She shrugged that off with a wave of her hand. "That book meant everything to Billie, didn't it dear?"

"She'll just have to write it again. It's doable."

Billie began to cry softly, shaking her head. "No, I can't, I can't..."

"Yes, you can." Though in my heart I doubted it too. I suppose all of us in Octopus knew how much that second book meant to her. She'd poured her soul into it. Yet it had been almost complete, the long-awaited sequel to her first magnificent novel.

I touched her hand. "Please don't get upset. They'll throw us out again. Look, I brought you some fruit."

Elsa narrowed her eyes and pressed forward her own cellophane-covered tray. "So have I."

Hers, of course, contained mangoes, kiwi fruit, dates and even avocadoes. They made my oranges, grapes and bananas look pathetic by comparison. We laid both trays side by side on the bedside table like sacrificial offerings.

"How's Lisette?" murmured Billie.

"Still on the danger list... but she's still holding on," I said.

"I'm going up to see her after this," Elsa said, as if she was doing something for charity.

"If you meet Dr Bonnar up there, tell him he'll have to leave through the mortuary if he wants to avoid the press."

Billie touched my hand. "Has she regained consciousness?"

Before I could answer, Elsa replied cheerfully. "They doubt she ever will."

Billie gasped.

"You really should be in the diplomatic corps, Elsa," I said, shaking my head. I leaned closer to Billie. "Now you're sure you weren't pushed? You can tell me."

She couldn't hold my gaze. If Elsa hadn't been there, I would have made her tell me what she was hiding.

"She doesn't have to say," Elsa said. "We all know who it is she's protecting. You're the only one with any doubts."

And for once, I couldn't say anything. Me, stuck for words, and with Elsa of all people.

I glanced at Billie and found her watching me. Had she seen Patrick? And if she had, then why was she trying to protect him?

"Tell me Lisette's going to be alright," Billie croaked.

Once again, before I could answer Elsa jumped in with both feet. "If she ever wakes up, which is doubtful, they say she'll be paralyzed from the neck down."

I couldn't believe she had said it. The doctors had hinted at it as a possibility, but they wouldn't know until Lisette fully regained consciousness. But for Elsa to tell Billie, almost as if she was imparting some exciting gossip, it was tactless and cruel.

Panic, and something else I couldn't for the moment fathom, appeared in Billie's eyes. "Is that true, Mirren?"

"They can't tell, not yet. So there's no need to worry." I shot Elsa a venomous glance.

"She had to know some time. People are stronger than you think, especially we writers." She said it in a way that did not include me. "She'd be better off dead, anyway, if you ask me," she added softly, as if hoping Billie wasn't listening. "Someone like Lisette would rather be dead than be left like that."

Those words stayed with me for a long time after Elsa had zoomed off, police escort and all.

She would rather be dead. So would Billie. The worst thing in the world had happened to them, had been done to them. What vengeance would that be for someone? And why? Had we found the killer already? Or was there more to come? And even if we had... what was the motive? The police had looked into so many things. They had completely checked out the list I had given James.

Yet, hadn't I left something out of that list? The adjudication, yes. It hadn't been added. And I never told James about it. Perhaps I should have.

James wasn't there when I went to the station, but they were already getting to know me quite well, and I was led into a side room to await his arrival. As I waited, I practised exactly what I would say to him, trying to remember everything that had been said that night when we had adjudicated the manuscripts. It began to sound quite silly when I repeated it, even to myself. Would anyone kill for such a paltry reason?

When I began to talk, I was sure he was going to laugh in my face. I could imagine it well. James, sitting across from me, his face stony and unsmiling. "You know Octopus were often asked to give adjudications? Sometimes, for example, we adjudicated competitions run by other writing groups."

He would nod.

"I always tried as much as possible to be positive, to make my criticisms constructive. Some of the others weren't so good at doing that. Victoria set the pace. She always said that criticism that isn't true and to the point isn't helpful. You're better to be harsh, firm and honest, no matter how it hurts."

"And could she take this kind of criticism herself?"

I would laugh at that. "Oh, Victoria had an easy answer to that. She didn't believe any adverse criticism. Anyone who criticised her work didn't understand the deeper implications of her writing… and she is good, you know."

She was good, I reminded myself sadly.

It grew dark in the waiting room, and as I switched on the desk top lamp, shadows seemed to leap from nowhere.

"Well, what if one of our adjudications was so cruel, so offensive, that it sent someone teetering over the edge into madness. Someone reading our remarks could not take it. Perhaps this was their last chance to make it as a writer, and we told them to give it up. These murders are their revenge."

It sounded crazy, even to me. How could I possibly explain it to James?

Suddenly, Imaginary James was back. He was right in front of me, trying to get my attention. "Mirren?" That's the worst thing about me, when I conjure up a dream, I find it hard to get rid of it.

"You can remember an adjudication like that, can you?"

I was ashamed at the memory. "Yes, it was a novel competition. We were sent three chapters and a synopsis. There were twelve entries from all over the country. They all wrote under pseudonyms. That's how we do things. But Elsa would have had to send the manuscripts back to the writers. She'd probably have stamped addressed envelopes enclosed. We do our adjudications the old-fashioned way, by paper. No e-mails. For an adjudication, the whole point is to get back a full criticism of your manuscript. Anyway, we all read each of the entries, and then met one night in Annabel's house to discuss them.

"I remember, we discussed them all and gave each our criticism… all except for one. None of us would talk of it, until the very end. Then it was Annabel who broke the silence." She'd been the first to speak that night, and the first to die. "I remember she held it up by her fingertips, like she thought she would catch something from it. 'What do you think of this one?' she'd asked. Then she started to giggle. I have to admit, I laughed too, but then, that's what I do. It was such a load of pretentious drivel. Someone was trying hard to be deep and meaningful and making a complete ars… I mean, fool of themselves in the process."

"And you all felt the same about this entry?"

I thought back. "Yes, I think we all did. Some of us more than others. Billie is quiet and never cruel, but even she laughed. 'I didn't like to say anything,' she told me, 'Not until I knew what the rest of you thought.' Vee Kirk usually disagreed with anything Victoria said, but that night they giggled like soul sisters. Annabel read parts of it out that were really awful… and, it shames me to say it, we had such a laugh."

Imaginary James tutted and I looked up at him from under my eyes. "Och, Mirren, you never did."

"I did. I know, it's awful."

Oh no, it would be too shameful to tell him this.

'Who on earth told this person they could be a writer?' laughed Annabel. 'Take up another hobby, like embroidery or window cleaning.' Annabel insisted on that being put into the criticism. Then Victoria added. 'Unless they're going to write romantasy.' Elsa nearly had a stand-up fight with her about that. She was like a lioness defending her young.

"You see what I mean about writing meaning so much?" I was trying to convince James, but his face remained as impassive as ever. "No matter how successful Elsa becomes, she always feels like she has to prove herself, and that's because of people like Victoria, and their attitude."

And mine, it had to be said. I resolved then and there I would apologise to Elsa.

"And what did the rest of you say?"

"I did try and be constructive, but I ended up making jokes about it as usual. Lisette, she'd only just joined Octopus, so she wasn't saying too much, but I remember she did make one remark. 'Perhaps you'd like me to resign so this writer can join your hallowed ranks.' Everyone thought that was hilarious. Billie and I just looked at one another."

"And that was written down too?"

"Not in so many words. Actually, Lisette said too that if she had written this, she would tear it up and think again. She didn't actually suggest giving it up altogether. But then, Lisette wouldn't. Give up, I mean. She's a fighter."

"You sound as if you approve."

"I do," I said, even surprising myself. Approve of Lisette? Yes, I suppose I did. Surely, even now, inside that inert form, fiery and lively Lisette was still struggling to fight another day.

"As for Dr Bonnar, he was all for recording all the criticisms. He said the writer should have asked someone to read it before they sent it into a competition, then they would have been spared the embarrassment."

"And Ms Fordyce?"

"Oh, she put down screeds. How the writing lacked clarity and sense. The characters were wooden, their motivations vague and conflicting, and the plot a cliché in every sense. Ha, Elsa, complaining about cliches. Cliches are the key ingredients in her books. Ack... there I was again, dissing her writing. I would need to break the habit.

"And who sent off the criticisms?"

"Elsa, as secretary, would do that. She typed them up and sent them off." I could picture him looking at me quietly. "And you think this writer might have been so enraged when they read your criticisms that they, he or she decided to eliminate you, one by one?"

"They'd have to be a little mad already, I suppose."

And he'd be beginning to look at me as if I was a little mad. I was trying to get him to say, "Mirren, I think you're on to something." Instead, his face creased into a smile, then suddenly, he was laughing, so loud the door opened and someone came in to investigate.

"Mirren, are you talking to yourself?"

James, the laughing, imaginary one, vanished into the ether. James, the real one, came in the door, looking puzzled and very much flesh and blood.

"Of course not," I snapped, in a 'as if I would do such a thing' sort of tone.

"You wanted to see me?"

I hesitated, considering whether to tell him or not. I thought about the imaginary interview I'd just gone through. He would only laugh. I was sure of it now. No, I'd need to give my theory a bit more substance before I brought it to him, or indeed anyone. "Do I need an excuse?"

His face brightened. "No. I'm flattered. You've nothing to tell me?"

I could feel myself blushing. "No, nothing."

"Good."

I stood up. "Suppose I'd better go. I didn't mean to wait this long. My police escort will be wondering what's keeping me."

"How would you like a new police escort tonight?"

"What do you mean, D.S Morrish?"

"I mean, we could go for a meal. I'm just about finished here for the night."

"Is this… like a date?"

He narrowed his eyes at me. "I don't know… is it?"

CHAPTER SIXTEEN

James Morrish was good company. As I always suspected, he liked good, plain, honest fare. He wasn't interested in Chinese or Indian. Instead, without consulting me, he took me straight to the Thistle Hotel in the west end of Port Gowrie, where he ordered a large steak, (rare), with no trimmings and no fancy sauces. It summed the man up, and I meant that as a compliment.

He seldom smiled, even on this sort-of-date, though it could also have been a sort-of-interrogation.

"And why haven't you ever married, Mirren Murdoch?"

"I was engaged once, James Morrish," I told him. "When I was nineteen and he was twenty. We had set a date, booked a hotel…" I paused and smiled. "This hotel, actually. I didn't know how to break it off. I don't even know when I realised I just didn't want to get married, but I just couldn't go through with it."

"Have you ever regretted that?"

And I could say, without hesitation, that I never had.

"And what about you, James? Haven't you ever tied the knot?"

He sat thoughtfully for a minute, playing with a tall glass of water in front of him. "I was married."

That took me by surprise. "I had no idea."

"She died. Five years ago. Cancer."

"Oh, I'm so sorry."

He gave a soft shrug. "Long time ago now."

I wanted to ask him more, but the time wasn't right.

The evening passed too quickly, and when it was over he took me right to my front door. "Is your mother on night shift tonight?"

I said yes.

"Are you sure you'll be alright? I don't like the idea of you being alone in the house."

If any other man had made that remark, I would have expected him to then suggest coming in with me, 'just to check'. But not James Morrish. He was wholesome with a capital W. Worse luck.

"I could get a female PC to stay the night with you."

"You'll do no such thing." I said it more sharply than I intended. But honestly, had the man no sexual intent on me at all? "My poor mother would be the next casualty if she came in and found a stranger... even a woman, sleeping on her couch."

"I suppose you're right," he said, sensibly as always. "I should come in and check the house."

"No, don't bother." I only said it because I knew checking the house was exactly what he had in mind.

He was more than a little puzzled by my change of attitude. "I thought we had rather a nice evening."

"Oh, we did, yes..." Then I added more softly. "Aye, we did."

He shuffled his feet. "I'd better not come in anyway... it might not look too good." He nodded to the gate where my watchdog sat in the police car, discreetly not watching us. But even in the dim light from the street lamp I was sure I could distinguish a little curl of amusement in his face.

"So that's it?" I said.

"So that's what?"

"Our date. Over, finished. You're going home?"

"Why?" It seemed to me, though I couldn't be sure, that an

eyebrow was lifted at this point. "What did you have in mind?"

I didn't really know what it was I had in mind, but I wasn't going to let on to him. "Don't you even want to…" The hesitation, so unlike me.

James took a strategic step back at this point, and that was probably what decided me. I did something I've never done in my life before. It was all James Morrish's fault. He'd brought out the beast in me.

I threw my arms around his neck and kissed him. I took him so much by surprise that he took another of those strategic steps back, and I almost fell on top of him. He grabbed me by the waist to steady me, and by that time he'd really got the hang of this kissing thing. He was rather good at it… for a policeman.

Finally, he let me go… or was it me who let him go?

"Mirren Murdoch…"

"James Morrish…"

He glanced down the path, and his officer was trying hard to study the evening paper. How he could read in that light was anyone's guess.

"You shouldn't have done that."

"Why, didn't you like it?"

He smiled very slowly in response. "You be careful now."

He waited until I'd put the key in the lock and went inside the house. As he walked down the path, I heard him begin to whistle. Then he stopped himself before anyone made the mistake of thinking he was happy. It was only as I stood in the dark hallway I realised he hadn't said anything about seeing me again. Maybe my spontaneous show of affection had been a bit too spontaneous for him.

As I walked through to the kitchen, I slipped off my jacket and hung it on the banister. I stopped in mid stride. Had that been a noise upstairs? My mother? No, my mother always clattered about noisily, even when she came in at five in the morning, and every light in the house would be on if it was her.

There it was again. A soft footstep coming down the stairs. My imagination?

No!

A creak now, the third step from the bottom. I ran for the door, ready to scream. Not for the back door. Thank God my brain still worked. The back door would be locked, and outside of it was a long, dark garden. At the front there was an unlocked door, and a policeman at the end of the drive. Safety. He would hear my scream.

Funny, but screaming just doesn't come naturally, even in a situation like that. Panting for breath, all that came out was a little sob. I reached for the handle, not even glancing at the stairs where there were too many shadows.

Suddenly, a hand clamped over my mouth. I was pulled back from the door, from safety. Pulled further into the house, into the shadows. I struggled and kicked for all I was worth. I wasn't going down without a fight. Was this how it had been for Annabel, and Vee, and Lisette and Victoria? I was afraid. No, I was terrified.

A mouth, warm, close to my ear, whispering. "Mirren, please, shhh. It's me."

The voice was Patrick's. Against all common sense, as soon as I heard I stopped struggling.

His grip relaxed and he pulled me closer against him. "Mirren, Mirren…" and his murmurings became kisses. He turned me to him and his lips found mine. I kissed him for a long time. Not the way I had kissed James Morrish, mischievously and with more than a little devilment. I kissed Patrick with a passion I never knew I had.

He held me so tight it was painful. If he could have drawn me inside him I think he would have.

"Patrick," I asked at last. "What are you doing here? It's dangerous."

"I had to see you... before I go."

"Go? Where?"

"Anywhere. Anywhere a man with a Not Proven verdict can hide."

"But you can't just leave. You have to stay, to clear yourself."

"And what if I can't? The evidence all stacks against me. I told you, they'll never put me in a cell again, Mirren. Never." His voice held as much passion as his kisses. "As long as you don't believe it was me."

"I can't believe it was anyone I care about."

"And you care about me?" He was kissing me again. How could I not care? "You have to believe me, Mirren. I'm innocent."

"I must," I said. "Or I wouldn't be with you like this. I'd be screaming my head off. There's a policeman outside, you know."

"I heard. What's going on between you and him?" He sounded jealous. He had an awful cheek, but it pleased me anyway. "You were kissing him too."

"Just a friendly one. He's a nice man. You can trust him, Patrick."

"He's a cop, and I bet he thinks I'm guilty."

What could I say to that? "The murders aside, he'll want to question you about Elsa."

"I know. Elsa lied. I never touched her. And I heard Billie is in hospital?"

I told him about the fall on the stairs, and her book being wiped.

"I never did that. I never wiped her book. Didn't she have copies?"

"They got wiped too."

"Didn't she e-mail it to herself at least?"

I had to explain to him about her ancient word processor. "Billie never said a word against you, though I'm not sure she's telling us everything. What can she be hiding?"

He was shaking his head. "Find out why she's so afraid of Bonnar, Mirren, will you? You didn't think she was protecting me, did you?"

I hesitated too long. I felt him withdrawing from me. "You did," he said, disappointed.

"You seemed the only one she would want to protect. She likes you."

This time it was Patrick who hesitated. "Does she? When I first came to the club, I thought so. I liked her too. Or, her writing at least. But she soon made it quite clear she wasn't interested in me. She would hardly talk to me after a while."

"You made her nervous. You frightened her." I was sorry as soon as I said it. I hadn't meant it to sound like an accusation.

"I'm better away. I can't bear it if you begin to distrust me too."

I pulled him closer. "I don't. I don't."

And he was kissing me again, and I never wanted him to stop. "Don't go, Patrick."

"No, I must, Oh, Mirren."

"I don't want you to go, Patrick. Please stay."

"You think I want to leave? But I must."

Now, when I had found something I had always been searching for, it was to be snatched away from me. I couldn't bear it.

"Let me stay with you tonight, Mirren."

And already he was making it impossible for me to refuse, with his hands, his lips, with his caresses. Pulling me tighter, closer. Murmuring his love, his desire, his passion for me. I could have written the script myself it was so exactly what I wanted to hear.

Patrick stayed.

He had gone from me even before my mother came clattering in at five o'clock in the morning. He left nothing but the smell of him, and a note I'd treasure.

'I love you, Mirren,' it read. 'And I'll be back when I can clear the charges against me. I swear I murdered NO ONE.' 'No one' was written with such force, such passion, that he'd gone straight through the paper.

Such force, such passion. That was how he made love too. I had never known it could be like that. A bungled attempt at nineteen with my then fiancé had left me with the distinct feeling it wasn't all it was cracked up to be. A feeling my mother always assured me was the right one. Now, after last night, I knew different. I lay awake, clutching the note, going over every sensation, every wonderful second, feeling – I liked to think - just like Scarlett O'Hara after that night with Rhett Butler, a little enigmatic smile playing about my lips. Finally, I drifted off to a contented sleep again.

My mother must have gone straight to bed, for she was asleep when I eventually got up. Just as well. I'm sure she would have guessed I'd had a man the night before. Mothers can always tell, especially mine. She can detect fornication as if she used radar.

I had breakfast and left the house, smiling cheerfully at my watchdog and greeting him with a jaunty good morning. He smiled. I'm sure he thought James Morrish must be responsible for my good humour.

James Morrish, I'd all but forgotten him.

I'd taken over the dayshift in the taxis and was kept busy all day. It was unusual to be so busy in mild weather in Port Gowrie, but then of course, by now, I was notorious. To travel in my taxi was as close as any would come, or want to, to a murder. I was past caring about the nosy stares, the subtle innuendos, or even the typically west of Scotland directness. "Right noo, tell us all aboot these murders."

Anyway, dayshift was never as lucrative as nightshift by the docks, and with no money coming in from my writing I needed every fare I could get. And today, after that last wonderful night, nothing could get me down.

James was waiting for me by my front door when I came home from day shift.

I blushed to my roots when I saw him. He smiled, that slow smile of his, thinking, I supposed, that my embarrassment was entirely due to my kisses last night. If only he knew. I was imagining him in the room with us last night, watching, seeing everything, knowing now.

"I'm glad to see you're doing the dayshift at least," he said.

I edged past him to open the door, not daring to look him in the eye. "I have to work."

"It's time you got yourself a proper job."

"Writing is a proper job, it's just nobody's employing me now, remember?"

He followed me inside the house, not waiting to be asked. "I didn't want to ring the bell in case I woke your mother."

I looked up at the time. Four o'clock. "She'll be up and about by this time. Sure, she hardly sleeps anyway."

I switched on the kettle. "Coffee?"

His brow furrowed in disapproval. "Tea. I've never understood this predilection of the Scots for coffee. It's a very American idea. The Yanks brought it over with them."

"Surely tea is very English."

"Not the way I make it."

I sat down. "Okay. You make it then."

He did too. Tea, a la James Morrish. Very strong, very dark, very sugary. Tea that you could melt your spoon in. I enjoyed it.

"So why are you here? Lisette, has anything happened?"

"No, she's still unconscious. I wanted to ask you something about Maya Brodie."

"Maya? What?"

"Did she ever hint to you that someone in Octopus was involved in a police matter?"

That phone call, so long ago now. "She did, as a matter of fact. I didn't really take any heed. My God, someone hasn't gone and murdered her too, have they?"

He ignored that. "Did you have any idea what she was talking about?"

"Elsa, drunk driving, by any chance? Victoria, sued for libel?"

"More serious than that, I'm afraid," he said, and I was suddenly serious too.

"What?"

"This must go no further than you. Maya Brodie is in very serious trouble for leaking this information, but... Dr Bonnar, it seems, is being sued for malpractice. He's been accused of administering a lethal injection to a terminally ill patient."

"Oh God," I gasped.

"She said she'd told you long ago, Mirren. That's why I'm telling you now. It may have nothing to do with these murders."

"Then again, it might," I said, and I told him about Billie's sister.

"You think he might have killed her?"

"Billie might suspect that he has. She was so terrified to let anyone be alone with her sister, and suddenly Dr Bonnar wasn't there with them anymore. It all seems to fit, and yet... why kill Octopus, one by one? What has one to do with the other?"

"We'll be questioning Dr Bonnar. I'll have to ask him about Billie's sister too."

I sighed. "I thought it was over, James. I so wanted it to be over."

"I'm afraid it is far from over."

A few moments later, he was gone, and I was glad I hadn't mentioned the adjudication. That theory seemed even more ludicrous to me now. However, I still called Elsa and asked her to look out all the information about it. She reluctantly agreed, telling me she kept records of everything. She was always a very efficient secretary. I told her I'd be over in half an hour.

Elsa hardly glanced at me when she opened her ornate front door. She looked every inch the successful novelist, with a silk scarf swathed around her neck, an emerald green dress flowing around her, and matching silver earring glinting through her hair.

"Sorry if I'm disturbing your work, Elsa."

"It's quite alright. I've already written four thousand words, which was my target for today. Nothing gets in the way of my daily word target."

"What would you do if the news said an asteroid was going to hit and we had four minutes to live?"

She gave a wry smile. "Why, I could crack out another thousand words in that time. In here..."

I followed meekly, and was led into Elsa's inner sanctum, a bright spacious study looking out onto her beautiful walled garden. The patio doors were closed now against the circling darkness. Sofas, squashy and comfortable, lined the walls. In one corner, her desk was littered with manuscripts and books. She went over to it, pulled open a drawer and lifted out a file.

"You remember it?"

CHAPTER
SEVENTEEN

I was still standing there when Lisette's mother appeared. She looked drawn after her weeks of vigil at her daughter's bedside. She stopped by me and looked into the room to Lisette and Billie.

"It's an ill wind, true enough," she said. "There's my Lisette lying in there. We still don't know how she'll be, or if she will ever wake up, and there's Billie, just taking over. She knows what she's doing, you know. Taking care of her sister for so long. She's been a huge help. It's as if a huge weight has been lifted from my shoulders." She sounded relieved too. Happy, almost. I suppose I could understand that.

Billie looked up then and gave me a wide smile. A kind of smile I hadn't seen in her for a long time. She pulled her hand from Lisette's with reluctance and wheeled herself over to us. "She hasn't moved, not one bit, but I've been talking to her constantly. You see, she might hear, somewhere deep inside. It's important she knows someone's there. Someone who cares."

Mrs Bonvieux clutched at Billie's hand. "Oh, dear. You've been so good. Now off you go and enjoy your visit with Mirren. I'll sit with her now."

I wheeled Billie back down to her own room. All around us were the signs of an approaching Christmas. Decorations were being hung in wards, tinsel entwined in bed frames, and muted carols played on loudspeakers.

"Is there really no change in her at all?" I asked as we waited for the lift.

She shook her head. I couldn't see her face, but I could hear the emotion in her voice when she answered me. "Don't expect miracles, Mirren. They don't happen."

As soon as we reached her room I changed the subject. "I suppose you'll want to catch up on all the news."

"About what?" she asked, looking puzzled. Had Billie forgot how she and Lisette had come to be here, wrapped in the cocoon-like security of the hospital? "Oh, that... I suppose if nothing else happens they'll decide it must have been Victoria."

"Or Lisette," I whispered. The idea seemed to surprise her. "They can't rule anything out."

She shrugged. "Well, surely even if she is guilty, she's suffering enough, isn't she?"

There was no use talking to Billie. She was no longer interested. I decided not to bore her with the details. Certainly not to tell her about Dr Bonnar, for the moment. Billie had enough to go through.

"I must say, I am surprised though, that they've allowed Lisette visitors."

"Oh, there's a police officer present constantly," Billie told me.

"So they said."

"Besides, she needs someone there, someone to hold her hand and talk to her. You just never know how much is getting through. I'm glad I'm so close, I can pop up any time." She seemed glad to change the subject back to Lisette.

I left when her agent and her publisher both arrived. They'd shared a ride through from Edinburgh, and converged on Billie as soon as they got inside the room. Did she have a paper copy of her book? Could she rewrite it? How long would it take?

To all these questions and more, Billie's replies were vague. Her mind, I could tell, was elsewhere. Down a long, polished corridor in a room with Lisette… and her sister.

I was on a mission. First, I phoned the office and told them I'd do the nightshift tonight instead of the dayshift.

"Are you sure?" John asked.

"Of course I'm sure. I'll see you tonight." I didn't think James Morrish would be too pleased with me, not to mention my mother, but they weren't the boss of me.

Then I drove all the way to Glasgow to the tiny sub post office in Pollockshields in Glasgow, where Elsa had returned the elusive manuscript.

The sign above the door proclaimed 'The Happy Service'.

"A manuscript? A manilla envelope? A4?" The young woman turned up her nose as she flicked through a large notepad. "When was this?"

I told her the dates, and she gave a wearisome groan as she flicked further back in the notebook. I was keeping her from doing something important, like licking stamps.

"It was picked up," she said at last.

"Can you tell me who picked it up?"

Her already sour face turned an even greener shade of sour. "How am I supposed to remember that?"

I didn't think she was much older than I was, but her face made her look much older. I wondered what on earth had turned her into such a misery.

I leaned towards her over the counter. "This is 'The Happy Service' post office, is it not?"

"It is."

"Seems to me you're contravening the Trades Descriptions Act."

"What's going on here, Chelsea?" Another sour-faced woman appeared from the back, an older version of Chelsea. Her mother, it looked like.

"Ah, you must be Mrs Happy Service herself, I presume?"

I suddenly felt an affinity with Chelsea. Mothers can do strange things to you.

"Is there a problem?" She pushed her daughter to one side and drew herself up a full five foot three of threatening cobra.

"I'm just enquiring about a package that was sent here post restante." I went back over the details again.

Chelsea tutted and rolled her eyes at the older woman. "As if we're supposed to remember someone picking up a parcel that long ago."

"Actually, I do remember," said the woman. That was poor Chelsea put in her place. I knew that feeling. "I remember because the woman was a half-wit."

"She?"

"Yes, the woman who came in to collect it. Spoke as if she had a mouthful of cheese. And then finished off with a *Merci*, as if she was French or something. Big, skinny woman, looked like a horse."

Annabel.

I was so stunned I just stood there, staring. A queue of angry pensioners was building up behind me. One woman with a zimmer began to swear. A toothless man was waving his walking stick. "Get a move on there at the front," he growled.

"I don't suppose you remember just when this was?" I smiled at last.

"I can," she said, as if I'd just insulted her by challenging her memory. "It was... let me see..." Her finger ran along the line in the notebook. "It was a Tuesday morning. We shut early on a

Tuesday. October the 8th."

Tuesday October 8th, the day Annabel had been murdered.

Eureka.

I began the drive back to Port Gowrie but had difficulty concentrating on the road. I had to pull into a drive thru and order a double espresso. This had been where it all began, and I had been right. It was all connected up to this manuscript. I stopped in a layby for a long time, sipping my coffee and collecting my jumbled thoughts together.

Why had Annabel picked up the envelope? She had been the first victim. Had she known who'd written it? My mind flicked over the events of her last day. She'd been seen giving Patrick a manila envelope. The significance of that wasn't lost on me. He'd said it was her play, and she was giving it to him for his opinion. Someone had phoned her too. Her last words to her husband had been, 'Something strange is going on.' She'd been upset and worried. Why? Because she'd discovered that the manuscript she had collected had belonged to someone we knew.

Could it be that someone in Octopus knew who had submitted that manuscript? Elsa, trying to write that serious novel for once? Dr Bonnar's beloved wife, wanting to try her hand at writing. Friends of Victoria, or Billie, or Vee that we knew nothing about. All I knew was everything started with that manuscript. And could those criticisms infuriate someone enough to kill? To take us out, one by one. The thought was absurd, and yet... one by one, we were being murdered.

It was dark by the time I got back. Dark, wet and miserable, a typical December evening. At least, by now I had collected my thoughts. I went straight to the police station, sure that I had something to tell James Morrish.

Instead, he had something to tell me.

I knew by the flurry of activity in the incident room that

something had happened. James was in his shirt sleeves and motioned me to sit down till he'd finished his phone call.

"Not another..." I began, a chill seeping into my spine.

He was nodding before I even finished.

"Who?" Even as I asked, I realised that I had little or no alibi. I had been at a small sub post office in the forenoon. I made quite a show of being there. That could look like establishing an alibi. But on the way back I'd sat in a lonely lay by. For how long? Long enough, I thought, for someone to ask why I hadn't been back in Port Gowrie hours ago.

James laid down his mobile and looked at me. "It was Dr Bonnar's wife."

That stunned me. "What! But she's not in Octopus. She's not even in the writers group."

"I know."

"The killer must have meant to kill Dr Bonnar. It doesn't make sense otherwise."

"Oh no, the killer meant to kill Mrs Bonnar, alright."

"How do you know?" I asked.

"Mrs Bonnar was poisoned. The poison was in her breakfast jam. She only opened a fresh jar this morning. It's been in the house for months. Dr Bonnar never takes jam, and the jam was made especially for Mrs Bonnar... by Elsa Fordyce."

I still went ahead and did my nightshift. I couldn't stay off again, not just because of another murder. They were, after all, becoming commonplace.

Poor Mrs Bonnar poisoned! Her death, lying in wait on the shelf in the cupboard. There seemed neither rhyme nor reason in the murder. Elsa, ruining a good pot of jam with poison? I couldn't see that at all. And Victoria, or Lisette could still be the killer, poisoning that jam jar months ago.

I drove fares in a dream. So much that one man ended up in the opposite part of town from the one he'd requested. He was so drunk he didn't even notice. He got out, paid his fare and disappeared into the night. He even gave me a tip. I was half way back before I realised what I'd done. Then I spent another fifteen minutes going back and circling the area to try and track him down. I never did. God knows where he went to.

I gave up at four in the morning, phoning in my apologies to John, who'd taken over the control for the night. He understood. In fact, he was relieved. He thought I was mad going out in the first place. Word of Mrs Bonnar's death had already got around, though it wasn't yet on the news or in the papers.

At home, my mother was waiting for me, sitting by the fire wrapped up in her dressing gown with her face pinched into an uncharacteristic frown.

"Whit's this I hear?" She snapped before I even got my coat off. "Mrs Bonnar deid noo as well? Is that right enough?"

I slumped down. "Right enough."

"Oh my God!" She paused only for a split second. "And where the hell have you been? I've been worried out of my skull."

"Nightsh…" I didn't even get the whole word out before she exploded.

"Nightshift! Night-bloody-shift?" She jumped to her feet. "You've lost your mind. Well that's the last. You're getting yourself a proper job, d'ye hear me?"

Hear her? She was practically bursting my eardrums with it. But maybe she was right. Maybe I'd need to look at something else.

It wasn't long before my phone went.

"Who's that at this time?" growled my mother.

I answered it. It was Elsa, sobbing.

"Oh Mirren, my jam… my jam."

"Oh Christ!" came mother. "Not Barbara Cartland with dragons again!"

I told Elsa I'd be up at hers shortly, after a shower and some breakfast.

Elsa opened the door to me, looking distraught. Her hair, which was normally so neat, was wild and unruly, and her panda eyes showed she'd been in tears.

"Oh, God, my jam!"

The way she was going on about jam was enough to send me into a giggling fit, which I struggled to suppress. I followed her inside to her study. "I was at the police station all last night, answering questions." Her hand flew to her brow theatrically. Overacting came so naturally to her now that it couldn't be called overacting any more. "I didn't put any poison in there. No one's going to blame me for this. Someone's jealous of my success and wants to ruin it." The idea suddenly made her look squarely and accusingly at me. "I've thought this whole thing through. I know who the murderer is."

"You do?"

"Yes, you, Mirren Murdoch! It has to be you. You're jealous of me. You always have been. Especially now. I heard you talking to Victoria, pouring out your heart and soul."

"Aha!" So, I had seen someone outside Victoria's curtains that night… Elsa. "Yes, and Victoria's dead too."

"Don't go blaming me for that!"

"What about Patrick? Are you bored blaming him now too?"

"You wanted him and couldn't get him. It was Billie he wanted. Only a fool couldn't see it. The way he followed her. But she wouldn't have anything to do with him. He wanted me too. Wanted my body."

I couldn't hold the giggles in any longer. He wanted her body. "Oh, come on, Elsa, act your age!"

"Act my age? Don't talk to me like that. I'll kill you!" she snarled. She was becoming hysterical, her carefully cultured voice and manners dissolving fast.

Me trying not to giggle was too much for her. "Bitch!" Suddenly she lunged at me. She grabbed me by the hair and snarled. Funny how you return to your roots in a fight. Elsa pulled me from the chair, and suddenly we were rolling on the floor. It all seemed so ridiculous. I couldn't suppress the giggling, until, that is, I felt Elsa's nails scrape down my face. I yelped with pain, then pulled my fist back and landed one on the side of her head. I came from just as tough a neighbourhood as she, and I hadn't forgotten it so quickly. I rolled on top of her, my fist ready to punch her square on the face, breaking that petite, stuck-up nose of hers. Suddenly something hit me on the side of the head. Elsa's face became two, and I fell sideways off her. She'd only gone and walloped me with her latest book, in hardback too. As soon as I hit the floor she was upon me, her book raised, ready to bring it down on my head, all 392 pages of it. I kept thinking that the last thing I was ever going to see was a glossy, black and white photo of Elsa -looking a bit like Audrey Hepburn from Breakfast at Tiffany's - smiling down at me from the back cover.

"Mrs Fordyce, put the book down!" I'd never been so glad to see James Morrish. Both of him.

Elsa slumped back against the sofa, exhausted. "You've... come to arrest me?"

"Only if Muzz Murdoch makes a complaint against you."

"But she started it!"

This remark almost made me launch myself at her again. "That's a bloody lie! You jumped on me, called me a bitch! You know you did."

"There's your murderess!" She pointed an accusing, theatrical finger at me.

"Sit down, Mrs Fordyce, calm yourself. I only want to ask you some more questions." I had to admit, James's commanding voice was quite commanding. Even I calmed down.

Elsa pushed herself up onto the sofa, dabbing at her eye with a lace-trimmed handkerchief. She sniffed. "I did not put poison in that jam, you must believe me!"

"Then can you think of how it might have got there?"

"You gave it to Dr Bonnar the night we were all here at your house," I put in. "The jars were all left on the kitchen table for us to pick up on the way out."

"Yes," Elsa agreed. "That's right, any one of us could have touched them."

"All of it for Mrs Bonnar?" asked James.

"There were six jars for her, and a jar each for the rest of Octopus."

"So, you all received a jar of jam?"

"Yes."

He nodded. "The poison was only in one jar. It seems to me that any one of you could have put it in there."

"Yes, any one of them," Elsa admitted, eagerly shoving blame on to the rest of us.

"So, would Dr Bonnar have lifted the jars at random?"

"No," Elsa said at once, remembering. "He was the last to leave that night. I remember distinctly. There were only six jars left on the table. I put them in a box for him."

"No, Elsa, you're mistaken," I said, and she glared at me as if she could gladly kill me. "You already had all our jars carefully labelled with our names. Mrs Bonnar's jam was boxed and ready on the table separately."

Her face flushed. She said, quickly, "Oh, of course, yes. I

remember now. I really did forget, Inspector."

"And it was all labelled the same, you say?"

"Yes."

"But it would have been simple for any one of us to go out into the kitchen, take the top off one of the jars, put in the poison and reseal it. No one would have noticed."

Elsa was absolutely delighted at this. "Yes, of course."

"Do you realise, James…" I pointedly didn't call him 'Inspector', not least because he might remind me again that he was a Detective Sergeant, not Inspector. I also wanted to show off to Elsa. "If the jam was poisoned all that time ago, then this thing has been planned long before Annabel was murdered."

"That has occurred to me."

"And if only one jar was poisoned, a jar specifically labelled by name, then the intended victim was undoubtedly Mrs Bonnar."

He nodded.

I waited until we were leaving until I asked him about the malpractice case against the doctor.

"It's a private prosecution," he answered. "He says he won't discuss it without his lawyer present, and at the moment, with his grief, that's not happening. He does maintain that it's all an unfortunate mistake."

"Poor Dr Bonnar," I said. "His beloved wife. The thing he loved more dearly than anything else in the world."

James was nodding. "Yet again, the murderer hitting where it hurts the most."

I have to go and see him. He'll be devastated."

"Well, you won't find him at home. He insisted on going into the hospital. Says he'd go crazy if he can't work on through this."

CHAPTER EIGHTEEN

Dr Bonnar's wife had loved her annual supply of Elsa's jam. I'd seen her spoon it liberally on her toast, on hot muffins, on pancakes and scones. So, it seems, had her murderer. And what did that mean? Was it one of us?

But why? Because of a manuscript torn to ribbons by Octopus? After all, we had all suffered, except perhaps myself. As for Elsa, she'd only benefitted from all the publicity. Sales of her books had soared, and she'd won a new book deal along with film rights, and all for something that hadn't even been written yet. Although that was last week, it might well have been half-finished by now. Elsa, who'd gone missing for three whole days, and had come back covered in bruises, as if she'd been in a fight. Patrick had been to blame for that, she still insisted. But what if... what if Vee had been responsible for the bruises, as she fought for her life. Elsa was strong enough to kill her. Hadn't I just witnessed it? She was strong enough to overpower me, although she needed a volume of her own book to do it. Elsa could have gone off knowing she had no explanation for those bruises, until the revelation of Patrick's true identity had allowed her to furnish the police with a new and very satisfactory suspect. And Elsa listening outside Victoria's window. Why had she done that, and what was she listening for, apart from my confessions? Victoria... wondering about something... if there was something we didn't know. What had she been talking about? Had Elsa thought she was talking about her? Had she silenced Victoria to stop her from finding out? Finding out what? It was Elsa's jam too that had been poisoned.

An awful lot of things, it appeared to me, came right back to Elsa.

But Elsa, a murderer? It sounded too absurd to be true.

At the hospital, I found Dr Bonnar in the corridor outside the mortuary. Even here, and looking ridiculously incongruous, someone had draped tinsel over the sign proclaiming, 'Pathology'.

The doctor looked like he hadn't slept in days.

"I'm so sorry. If there's anything I can do…"

He sank down on one of the uncomfortable-looking plastic chairs in the corridor. "I… don't understand. Why her, Mirren? What had she ever done? She wasn't even allowed to attend any of our meetings. The only link she had with us was over me. I mean, I once wrote an article for a medical journal about poisons, but then, why not poison me? Why her?"

I clutched his hand. "You know, for a while there we thought that Billie's sister had been a victim. Remember in her book, how the heroine has to come to terms with the loss of someone dear? And you know how that loss affected Billie. Just the same way that this is affecting you. Maybe you're still right. It might be an idea to get the body exhumed."

He pulled his hand from mine. Here I was doing a Lisette again, confronting someone with the truth just to see their reaction. Dr Bonnar's reaction frightened me.

He looked stunned, more than alarmed. "Do the police think they are connected? Have they said anything to you?" He turned round, gripping my shoulders tightly, so tight it was painful.

"Let me go, Doctor. No, they said nothing. Have they said anything to you?"

His face whitened. His eyes stared around, searching for an answer… or for a question. I was suddenly afraid of Dr Bonnar. I wished that I wasn't alone here with him. "Tell me the truth, Mirren. Have they said anything to you? You're very cosy with that young inspector. Do you know something… something about my wife's death?"

Suddenly two nurses came round the corner. We both heard them, their happy chatter echoing down the corridor. Both of us looked up at them, and as they came closer his grip on me relaxed. His eyes, strange, demented eyes, turned on me. "My wife's dead. I don't care about anyone else, do you hear me? Anybody else." He was on his feet, hurrying away from me.

I sat there for a while, staring at the cold walls, painted the colour of school custard. Dr Bonnar had for the first time ever scared me, in a way I'd never been scared before. Except perhaps that night on Pier Thirteen. Finally, I went along to see Lisette.

Not surprisingly, Billie was there with her, along with an ever-present police officer.

"She fluttered her eyelashes, Mirren. That's an excellent sign." Billie was flushed and happy-looking. I should have been pleased for her, but I wasn't. I didn't want her to start living through Lisette, as she had once lived through her sister. And that's exactly what she was beginning to do. What was it they called it, replacement therapy? I didn't think that's what Billie needed at all.

"You must be due getting out of here."

"Couple of days, they said, but I'll be here anyway."

"You'll have to start on that book again."

She looked at me as if I'd reminded her of something painful. "I can't think of that." She turned her eyes to Lisette with affection. "I promised Miss Bonvieux that I'd help with Lisette when she gets home."

"You have your own life, Billie. Come with me." I spoke like a stern older sister. Billie said nothing as I wheeled her out of the room. She only turned to have one last look at Lisette, as if wondering whether it was safe to leave her.

"Are you giving me an intervention, Mirren? Is that what it is?"

"Yes, I am. You can't take care of Lisette. You took care of your sister for all those years. You've done your bit. Now you have to live your own life. You have to write."

She was shaking her head. "It's not the way you think, honestly. I just want to help. I know how to nurse someone like Lisette. I know how to talk to them." Her eyes filled with tears. "I'm… stagnant, Mirren. If I do this, my writing will flow again, the way it did. I just know it. I'm not going to get paranoid about it, I promise you. I just… I need someone to need me."

She sounded sane and sensible, and I felt foolish. What right had I to interfere, after all? Was I conducting my own life, and my own writing, as well?

"You and Patrick, what happened?" My change of subject took her by surprise. "Why did you stop seeing him?"

"Patrick was too…" she searched for the right word. "There were undercurrents to him I couldn't fathom. He… frightened me."

"Well, he's not responsible for all this. At least we know that now."

"We do?"

It was then I realised, with shock, that Billie didn't even know about Dr Bonnar's wife. No one had told her. I waited until we were back in her room before I spoke. Her face paled and she sank back. I thought for a moment she was going to faint.

"Mrs Bonnar?" She looked puzzled.

"I know. I don't know why. She wasn't a member of Octopus. But if the killer wants to hurt us where it hurts most… Lisette's vitality, your book… and now… Dr Bonnar's wife. The poor man, he's devastated. He adored her."

To my astonishment, Billie smiled, but it fled in almost a second, guiltily. "Did he?"

"You know he did."

"Maybe he just appeared to."

"How can you say that, Billie? You know he adored her."

She shrugged and looked out the window. "If you say so. Have you seen him?"

"Yes, I was talking to him only a minute ago." I thought about telling her how he'd frightened me, but decided against it. "He wants to continue working."

Her eyes went wide. "You mean, he's here? At the hospital? Oh, God!" She looked as if she was about to faint again.

"Billie, what's wrong? Tell me?"

She was trying to get out of her chair, frightening me so much I almost called the doctor, but as I moved away from her she tugged at my sleeve. "Close the door," she said softly.

I did, and for a moment neither of us spoke. The wind rustled in the trees outside, and somewhere down in the car park someone was having an argument. Voices were raised, car doors slammed, an engine revved up. Still, Billie didn't speak. She stared into space, into some memory that pained her.

"You always wondered why I disliked Dr Bonnar."

I sat beside her, holding her hand. "I used to think he was fond of you, and you of him."

"He was, I suppose... maybe he still is. I don't know." She looked at me suddenly, fear in her eyes. "You mustn't let him near Lisette. Promise me."

"Why... you don't think it could be... Dr Bonnar?"

Her fingers gripped tightly round mine. "Promise me."

"I promise. But no one is let near her, you know that."

"I am."

"You've never been alone with her. They wouldn't allow that."

"He's not the man we all think he is... thought he was, rather." There was a long pause, quiet in the still of the hospital. "Dr Bonnar wanted to kill my sister."

So, I'd been right.

"It happens all the time, he told me. A very simple little injection, no one would ever know. It would free her, he said, free me... as if I wanted to be free of her. I loved her. It would be a blessing, he told me. To my sister, to me. I told him then that if he ever came near my sister, I'd kill him."

And she'd never left her sister, right enough. And we all thought she was becoming paranoid. All the time, she'd been protecting her. From one of us, one of Octopus. Billie began to cry softly, and I put my arms around her and held her, feeling her head rest on my shoulder. "I had to tell you. I've never told anyone before. It was during her last illness. I prayed so much for her to live. I was here night and day, and he came every day, and I was so grateful to him. Until that day... He said she'd be better off dead. She was suffering and so was I. And he could do it, and no one would be any the wiser. He'd done it before, so he said. That's when I warned him off. But I was terrified he would anyway. I wouldn't leave her side after that. Night and day I stayed with her. I know everyone thought I was going mad, but I couldn't risk him doing anything that might harm her."

How could I forget it either? How worried we all were by Billie's intense devotion, not letting any of us near her. It was unhealthy, we all decided. Including, I remembered, Dr Bonnar. Not unhealthy at all, I saw now. Understandable. Poor Billie.

She went on, "He doesn't think a life is worth living unless it is worthwhile, so he said. You see, you mustn't let him anywhere near Lisette. Promise me?"

"I promise. We'll both protect her, Billie."

I left when Billie had settled down and was calm. I went along to the station to see James Morrish. He hadn't asked me for another date, but I suppose with little things like a serial killer on the loose he had other things on his mind.

Every time he looked at me, I was reminded of my night with Patrick. I felt my face go bright red. I'm sure he thought I was thinking of something much more innocent.

"I'm just leaving," he said as I went into his office. "Going to the hospital."

"I've just come from there. I saw Dr Bonnar and Billie." I told him everything that happened.

"So that's why she's so frightened of him. I wonder..."

"You're wondering whether he's guilty or not? Strong enough to strangle Vee Kirk, or push Lisette over a parapet. I would never have thought so. The thought would never have crossed my mind... but today... that look in his eyes. James, it frightened me. But kill his wife? He adored her."

"Did he?"

"That's exactly what Billie said. What do you all know that I don't?"

"What you see isn't always the truth. The obvious sometimes hides a secret. For instance, Mrs Bonnar's death leaves Dr Bonnar a very wealthy man. He had a hefty insurance out on her, and she had quite a bit of money on her own."

I had to sit down. Dr Bonnar. I had always thought of him as the archetypal gentleman. A gentle man. Now I didn't know what to think. I considered some of his extreme opinions. And then there was his book, *PanzerKommander*, about a Nazi tank commander on the Russian front. Empathy was one thing, but I'd always wondered where on earth that came from. James was right. You don't always see the truth.

I left the station and began driving home, but my mind refused to stay on the road. It kept drawing me back to the long corridors of the hospital. Lisette, in a bed, unconscious and vulnerable. Lisette, who had seen her attacker. And Dr Bonnar, staring in the glass panel of her door, day after day. I turned the car round and began heading back to the hospital.

It was dark when I got there, with a smirr of rain falling, soaking into everything. Normally, I loved nights like this. The streetlamps shrouded in misty rain. People hurrying to and fro under umbrellas. But not tonight. There was something eerie, ominous about the rain tonight. I splashed up the stairs and shook myself dry in the foyer. The Christmas tree in the atrium was brightly lit and decorated. Presents for the children in hospital over Christmas were gathered underneath.

The receptionist looked up, recognised me and smiled. "Where can I find Dr Bonnar right now?"

Her face creased into sympathetic lines. "Poor man. Orthopaedics. G3."

I waited for the lift, half considering whether to rush upstairs or not. Why was I in such a hurry. Yet, I was.

I was half way through the door marked 'Stairs' when the lift doors slid open. I just made it before they closed again.

There was no sign of Dr Bonnar on G3. No one could tell me where he might be. My first thought was for Lisette. She'll be okay, I reassured myself, hurrying down the stairs to her floor. There's always a police officer with her. Yet, I'd seen too many movies where the susceptible victim, seemingly amply protected, had been struck down. This time I was ahead, some intuition deep inside warning me, telling me something was about to happen and there was no time to lose.

In her room, Lisette lay still, her breathing controlled and normal. The female officer on duty stood up as I entered the room, looking surprised. "Anything wrong?"

"I was just about to ask you the same thing," I said. "Has anyone been here?"

She shook her head.

Maybe I'd been wrong, and yet... my body's warning system hadn't stopped ringing its alarm bells.

"Who is it you're looking for?" The nurse asked, coming into the room carrying a little covered tray.

"Dr Bonnar, where is he?"

"The last time I saw him he was heading for Miss May's room."

Billie! It struck me at once that she was even more vulnerable than Lisette. Billie wasn't as well guarded. Billie after all had no important information to impart... or had she? Had she seen someone that day, and held her tongue to protect herself? Could she tell us even more about Dr Bonnar and her sister?"

Billie's room was two floors down, and even before I pushed open the half-glass door, I knew I had been right to worry. Both of them lay there, still. I didn't know who to run to first. Billie, half in and half out of the bed, or Dr Bonnar, who was prostrate on the floor.

I ran to Billie, sure that she was dead.

I jabbed the emergency button above her head, then shook her roughly with my hands. "Billie! Billie!"

I glanced down at the doctor, who was face down, and gasped as I saw the hypodermic needle sticking out of his neck.

Within seconds, the room was filled with doctors and nurses, and, oh thank God, with James Morrish.

As soon as I saw him I began to shout. "She's dead, James. I was too late." As if in reply, Billie gave a soft moan. I clutched at her, but she was whisked away from me by the efficient hands of the nurses. Others moved Dr Bonnat's limp body out of the room.

James put his arm around my shoulder. "Come on. There's nothing you can do here just now."

He sat me down in the corridor, watching me as the tears

rolled down my face. Another officer appeared, placing a steaming hot cup of tea into my trembling hands. "You see, you can cry," said James.

"What made you think I couldn't?" I snapped.

He wasn't annoyed. He took my hand in his and held it. "You pretend you're so tough and cynical, always with the funny remarks. But really, you're a wee softie inside."

"Not soft... just scared." I almost added, 'shitless', but even in these dramatic circumstances, I didn't think James would have approved. So I held my tongue. God, what a daft expression. There I was off again, barely serious for a split second. "I'm scared," I repeated.

At that moment, a nurse came hurrying from Billie's room. "She's trying to say something. I think you'd better come."

I followed after James, though I wasn't sure the invitation extended to me.

However, it was on me that Billie's eyes fixed as soon as I'd entered the room. She stretched out her hand to me, her pale eyes awash with tears. I ran to her and held her tight.

"I hope..." her voice was no more than a whisper. I had to strain to catch her words. "I hope... I killed him."

I glanced at James, standing there impassively, saying nothing. "Tell me..." Billie breathed the words out with difficulty. "Tell me he's dead."

I looked again at James. He nodded. "He's dead, Muzz May."

She sank back on her pillows and relaxed her grip on my hand. It was a moment before she spoke again. "I had to, Mirren. I knew he came to kill me, could see it in his eyes. Kill me, like he killed the others. I was almost sure, you know... I didn't want to say. Might have been wrong. When I found my book gone, I was sure it was him. I didn't fall downstairs at all, you know..."

I leaned closer. "I know. You were pushed."

"No." She bit her lip, as if she was ashamed of the confession she was about to make. "I deliberately tripped down the stairs. I had to be here. It was the only way to protect Lisette. I had to watch him. Then, when you told me about his wife... I knew. Mirren, it was all a front. He didn't love his wife, not really. He just wanted her life insurance. He wanted to kill Lisette too, the way he wanted to kill my sister." Suddenly, she was writhing about in a panic again. "Is Lisette really safe now?"

"You're both safe now," I assured her. "You're both safe."

"Good."

"He tried to kill you too, Billie."

"He didn't have to," she murmured, turning her face to the wall. "I was already dead."

Billie slept. James and I had a coffee in a room nearby.

"So it was Dr Bonnar after all? But why?" I asked.

"To cover up one murder, perhaps."

"All those people, just to cover up one murder? No."

"It has happened before. Blood will have blood, as they say. Murder is easy after you've done it once."

"In that case, the manuscript would have had nothing to do with it. It was a proverbial red herring. Quite appropriate in this case."

He looked at me blankly.

"Octopus? Red herring? Very fishy." He still looked blank. "Never mind," I said. "Annabel picks up the manuscript and then dies that same day. No, it's too much of a coincidence for me."

He nodded. "For me too."

"If only that manuscript was still there. There might be a clue in it."

"Perhaps we'll find out when Dr Bonnar comes round."

I looked at him. "What? You mean, he isn't dead after all?"

"I thought it better to let Billie think that he was."

"Good thinking. Don't tell her any different, not yet. She's so afraid for Lisette. It'll only set her back if she starts worrying about her again."

CHAPTER NINETEEN

I was back at the hospital first thing in the morning. Fortunately, word of the events of the night before hadn't got out. I was glad of that. Lisette was still in danger, and if Billie knew Dr Bonnar was still alive, then who knows what effect it might have on her recovery. Billie's mind was so connected up with Lisette's condition at the moment, to such an extent that I wondered how one could survive without the other.

Outside Lisette's room, her mother and her father were waiting for me. For once, they were smiling as they stood up to greet me. "She is conscious. She has come round," said her father.

"She has opened her eyes. Conscious, but that is all," her mother babbled excitedly. "But this might be even better, Mirren. The doctor says there is an operation. An operation that might bring her back to normal. Oh, Mirren."

Mrs Bonvieux hugged me. Her husband stood by, beaming, looking like he'd like to do the same. If only they knew that Lisette's cure lay in the hands of my dear mother. She'd almost set the church on fire with the number of candles she'd put up for such a miracle. When I told her the news she'd undoubtedly take the credit herself, due to her close association with St Jude.

"I'm so happy," the woman went on. "I must tell Billie. She has been so caring."

"Do you think we could go along to her room and tell her?" asked Lisette's father.

"I don't see why not," I answered. "If she's awake, I think it's a very good idea. It will help her no end. Can I go in and see

Lisette?"

They were waiting at the lift as I entered their daughter's room. The police officer smiled, then went back to her book. I stood by the bedside.

Lisette looked more like herself today. The only tubes attached to her now were in her arm. Her face looked peaceful, almost serene. It had been so long since I'd seen that somewhat arrogant expression of hers there, or heard her nippy voice. Once, I'd resented Lisette. I could see that in myself now. I'd disliked her even. I was equally sure the feeling was mutual. Now, I longed to have the old Lisette back again, with her fire and her zest and her ambition.

Now there was a hope she could come back. I was going to stick to that. I took her hand and squeezed it, but her eyes remained expressionless. As if her body was a shell and there was nothing inside. I had only been there minutes when suddenly Billie burst in. For once, she was minus the wheelchair.

"Is it true? An operation? She'll be alright?"

"If it's successful. If it's possible. But look at her, Billie. I can't believe there's anything happening inside there."

I looked back at Lisette's face and knew at once that I was wrong. Her eyes had begun to follow Billie as she moved towards the bed. And I knew then that somewhere deep inside, Lisette had heard every word of Billie's. I recognised the look in her eyes. I'd seen it before in Billie's sister. Dogged devotion, dependence. I don't know what. It was the last thing I wanted to see. I'd had enough of Lisette listening to Billie's assurances that she would take care of her. Now she had to fight for herself.

"Lisette, if you can here me, please listen." Still, she didn't take her eyes off Billie. "You're going to get better. You're going to write great stories. Do you hear me?" I was demanding her attention. I sounded like my mother on a bad day. "How can you write lying there? You've got to get up. You've got to get going." I leaned in front of her, blocking her view of Billie. "Now listen to me!" Only now did Lisette's eyes move to me.

Outside, I had to help Billie back to her room. "You didn't have to raise your voice like that, Mirren."

"I did though. I had to make her listen. For her sake, and for yours. You can't live your life through her. Now that it's all over, we've got to get back to our own lives. Normality. We have to put the past behind us."

In her room, I looked out of Billie's window, just in time to catch a glimpse of Elsa arriving in her Merc, accompanied by a squad of photographers and reporters. "Oh, heavens. Here comes Elsa. I'd forgotten all about her. She'll be delighted to know she's not a suspect anymore."

"Elsa, a suspect?" said Billie with a sniff.

"Yes. I was amazed quite frankly, that she wasn't one of the first victims."

"But why… she was kind, eventually."

"Yes, that's probably what saved her."

"I don't really want to see her, Mirren."

"Of course you don't." I began to help her into bed. "I'll meet her down in the atrium and deflect her."

Elsa was holding a photo call at the reception desk when I got there. In her red and white Dolce and Gabbana dress, trimmed with white fur, and her high black leather boots, she bore a marked resemblance to Santa Claus, minus the beard of course. When she saw me she didn't smile.

"Where's that Inspector Morrish? I was told he was here," she demanded.

"I haven't seen him. Why, what's wrong?"

"I'll tell you what's wrong, Mirren. If I'm not a suspect, I think I should be informed of the fact. What happened here last night? Is it true Dr Bonnar is the murderer? Why wasn't I told?"

The surrounding reporters were scribbling furiously.

"Shut up, Elsa!"

"And why should I shut up?" She cast her eye imperiously around the encircling reporters crowding into the atrium. "Are you taking note of this? I have to shut up. I've to keep my mouth shut and take the rap."

Well, that was it. I burst out in giggles. "Taking the rap, Elsa? What are you writing now, cop thrillers?"

"Oh, always ready to make a fool of me, aren't you, Mirren? Well, the public is behind me, isn't that right? I'm seen as the victim. The real victim."

It was disgusting, after so many deaths, horrible deaths at that, to see Elsa make such a spectacle of herself. Because that's all it was, a show. She wanted to become a 'cause célèbre'. She wasn't glad that we'd caught the murderer. She was disappointed. It would take away from her own publicity. These murders had brought her nothing but good luck. Why then, could she not have been the murderer? That I could have accepted. Or even one of the victims. I could have accepted that even easier. Because finally, she'd been kind, as Billie had pointed out. Not wanting to hurt. Inside, there was some softness. She had been vociferous as the rest of us during that stormy adjudication. Her softening had come later, and no one had known of it.

No one.

Elsa was still posing, and I stopped suddenly, shaking.

Christ! No one had known of it... it had been written into the adjudication later. The manuscript had been sent off, then collected by Annabel. So how had Billie known? I hadn't told her.

I thought no further, but turned and ran for the stairs. Behind me, I heard Elsa's voice ring out in shock.

"Don't you DARE walk away from me!"

I began to run, and bumped into James heading in the direction of Elsa's commotion.

"What's wrong, Mirren?" He gripped my shoulders. "What is it?"

All I said was, "How did Billie know what Elsa wrote?" Then I was hurrying past him. A lift opened and I got in, jabbing the buttons furiously. "Come ON!"

I reached Billie's room. The blinds were drawn and it was quite dark, but she was there, bending over the bedside cabinet.

"Billie!"

She stood up and turned into the light, and only now did I see that it wasn't Billie at all. It was the police officer who had been with Lisette. Her smile faded as an anxious James Morrish appeared at my shoulder.

"She sent me to fetch her slipper." The officer held up a fluffy pink slipper. "It's alright, sir, Mrs Bonvieux is there too. I'd never have left them alone."

I ran from the room. Over my shoulder, I said to James. "I bet her mother isn't there now. She's been sent for coffee, or for a nurse, or for you. Anything."

And all the while I ran, my mind was racing over so many things. Billie in a car following Vee. Billie managing to get admitted to hospital just after Lisette. How better to keep an eye on her? Billie with Dr Bonnar slumped on the floor of her room. My God, she even admitted to all of these things... done deliberately, and still I hadn't suspected her.

Billie May. Who knew what hatpin Vee Kirk had been wearing the night she was killed? "Imagine asking for that one," she'd said. I thought she meant because it was expensive. She hadn't. She knew Donald Kirk didn't have it. She had it, keeping it close, intending it for Victoria.

Billie, who hadn't been worried about Dr Bonnar's visits to Lisette in the beginning. It was only when she thought he was dead and a possible suspect. Only when she could blame him for her crimes.

We burst into Lisette's room together, James and I, and there she was, Billie May, holding a pillow over Lisette's face.

She looked up at us, neither surprise or guilt on her face. "You're too late," she said, triumphantly. "Lisette is dead, and it's all your fault, Mirren."

James darted around the side of the bed, but even before he'd reached her, I noticed Lisette's fingers begin to twitch. Then her head began to writhe under the pillow.

Lisette was fighting for her life.

I dived for the bed, just as James made a lunge for Billie, tackling her like a scrum half and pulling her to the ground. I yanked the pillow away from Lisette's face and saw life, real, fighting life in those eyes again.

Billie fought like a tiger. I couldn't help James, though he was getting scratched and punched and his hair was being pulled out by the roots. I was afraid to leave Lisette. I felt as protective as a mother towards her. I wasn't going to let Billie near again. All I could do was scream. Scream for someone to come and help us.

So, who was the first person to appear at the doorway?

No one but Elsa, all fur and leather. She flew into the room like an avenging Father Christmas. The photographers and reporters crammed in behind her. She grabbed James by the collar and pulled him away from Billie. Then, with one resounding punch, she knocked Billie out cold. A camera flashed triumphantly, capturing the moment for posterity.

Billie slumped to the ground. James was sitting on the floor, looking like he didn't know what hit him. I almost expected Elsa to blow on her knuckles.

"I didn't realise she was so strong," said James, regarding Billie's unconscious form.

"She lifted and laid her sister for years, James. Of course she was strong. Strong enough to kill Annabel. To strangle Vee."

The room began to fill up with police, jostling with medical staff and reporters. Somewhere I heard Lisette's mother's voice. "What's happening?"

James got to his feet. "Get these people out of here," he ordered. "Get these reporters out of here." I admired the authority in that voice more then than I ever had before.

Elsa swanned out, flanked by an adoring press, already whispering in her ear, asking if her story could be exclusively theirs. Adrenalin was still flowing in her. She glowed, smiling as if she'd just finished the final take of a movie. Shock and realisation might set in later. James let her go, but motioned to one of the officers to stay with her.

"She doesn't even realise," I said. "That Billie was the guilty one."

"I have to say, Mirren," he said, adjusting his tie. "I didn't think you were the kind of woman who'd stand by and not help when you saw me being battered to death."

"And I didn't think you'd be the kind of man who'd be beaten by a woman."

Lisette's mother came and replaced my hand with hers on her daughter's skin. She smiled at me gratefully. For now, she wasn't interested in who the murderer was, or even how close Lisette had come once more. All she knew was that Lisette had come through. I smiled back at her and followed James out of the room.

In the corridor, Billie was just coming round. She looked up at me, focussing her eyes. For the first time, I saw the real Billie. The one I'd never known. Vicious, cold and deadly. This was the Billie that Annabel had seen before she died, and Vee, and Lisette and Victoria.

"Why, Billie? Just tell me why?"

"You already guessed. The manuscript." She stood up. She was in handcuffs already. "It was my sister's. Do you know how much effort she put into writing that. Every word typed out on the word processor with her one working finger, every single key stroke a Herculean effort. And what did you all do? You humiliated her. You shamed her. You were all so cruel. I hated you then. Hated you, for what you did to her. One word of encouragement was all she needed. One simple word, and you couldn't even do that."

I was ashamed. I understood, well, almost. "We didn't deserve this, Billie, to be horribly murdered one by one."

"Didn't you? I thought you did. I thought it quite appropriate that you should all die in the manner of your own choosing. Then her final illness, and Dr Bonnar compounded his crime by offering to kill her for me. Kill her! That was when I finally decided. None of you deserved to live. I planned to kill you all."

Dr Bonnar's offer, then, had been the final straw. Dr Bonnar. How could such a gentleman suggest such a thing. "Then Dr Bonnar didn't try and kill you, back in the room with the syringe?"

She gave an ugly smile. "Yes, he did. He guessed you see, that I had killed his beloved wife... tit for tat, so to speak. I believe it was something you said that made him realise it was me. He came to give me the same injection he'd planned for my sister."

"But you told me he didn't love..." I tutted. What a fool I still was, still listening to her words. I had been right about Dr Bonnar's devotion to his wife after all. I was glad of that. That appearance had been true enough.

'Appearances can be helluva deceivin" my mother had told

me. She was right. I took far too many things for granted. Like the look in Lisette's eyes when she watched Billie move around her room. That look hadn't been devotion, or dependence. For Lisette had seen her attacker, and that attacker had been Billie. No, that look was one of fear.

And yet... hadn't I seen the same look in Billie's sister's eyes once? That same look of fear? If Billie's devotion to her sister was a sham, then why was she so afraid that Dr Bonnar might give her a lethal injection? Why had she been so desperate for her sister to stay alive?

And that was how everything fell into place for me. How could I have been such a fool all this time?

"Of course you didn't want your sister to die, Billie. But not because you loved her... no. You didn't want your sister to die because it was your sister who wrote the books, wasn't it? Not you."

The look in Billie's eyes was enough to assure me that I was right. "You must have panicked when she finally did begin to die. She'd only just begun the next book. No wonder you wanted her to live so much. You would have done anything to keep her alive. That's why the books took so long. That's why no one ever saw your work, except for that first chapter when you first joined the club. And no one was at your house that day, when I found you at the foot of the stairs. No one wiped your book, because there was no book to wipe, except perhaps..." Her eyes narrowed at me, hate in them. "Except the manuscript you sent to Octopus. You tried your hand at writing because you knew she would die. You hoped we'd see some of her greatness in it. And it was all such pretentious drivel!" I paused for breath. "How could you do that to your own sister, Billie?"

She began to scream at me like a demon. "And why shouldn't I? I had to cook for her, and clean for her, and lift her and wash her. Didn't I deserve anything?"

"But you would have shared in her success."

"Why should I have to share anything? I deserved it all. I was considered a great writer. I got shortlisted. I was a success. I was somebody at last."

I shook my head. "You didn't deserve any of it. She was the writer, not you. She was your sister!"

"I deserved it. I deserved it all. I told her so."

What a misery that poor wretch's life must have been with someone as warped as Billie. And yet, shouldn't we have guessed. We should have known.

"And when did you poison the jam?" asked James.

She turned to answer him as if he'd forgotten he was there. "Oh. That was easy. The night we were all at Elsa's. I slipped out to the bathroom, and simply took the top off, and then when I finished, I replaced it. I was in no hurry. Mrs Bonnar might have been the first victim, or the last. It didn't matter to me." She grinned. Had I once thought her beautiful? "I wonder how he feels now, getting a taste of his own medicine?" She laughed at her own black joke.

"And Annabel?" I asked. "You sent her for the manuscript deliberately."

"Of course. I told her to check the contents, but not to actually look at the manuscript. I knew nosy old Annabel couldn't resist having a look. Oh, she was upset. And puzzled too. She didn't know what to think. So I told her to meet me in the halls early and I would explain everything. And I did. Explicitly."

"How could you have done that to her?"

"She thought up the method herself," she answered. "I'd say it gave her a rare compliment." She was enjoying herself now, remembering the power she had over us. "And you were all so confused. My manuscript had been written by a fool... but the fool was leading you all on a merry dance. It was rather fun, actually."

"Fun. Billie, how can you say that? You murdered Victoria? I thought you loved her."

"I might have. She might even have lasted longer, if she hadn't begun to suspect. Not that I was a murderer, but something, in Victoria's opinion, that was much worse… that I wasn't a writer. She was beginning to ask awkward questions. She had to go, you must see that. Lisette tried to save her, did you know that? Brave little Lisette." She sneered at the memory. "You were almost right in your scenario, Mirren. I told Victoria I was sure I knew who the killer was, said I had to speak to her somewhere quiet. Said I'd found Vee's hatpin. I asked Lisette the same thing, but told her to be there five minutes earlier. I told her to hide in the shadows, as I was sure I knew the identity of the killer. Fooling her was easy. When Victoria turned up, she insisted on taking the matter in hand. Said she would handle everything. She asked me to give her the hatpin. So, I did, right in the neck. That was when Lisette screamed. I think she realised then who the real murderer was… Well, you know how quick she is. She rushed at me, but I'm stronger than she is. Over she went, very elegantly, I must say… except she just wouldn't let go."

"So you broke her fingers."

"Well, she had to fall, Mirren. Her story said so."

"Then you come out of the car park and bump into Dr Bonnar."

She shrugged. "That was an unfortunate coincidence. When I refused his offer of a lift, I actually had blood on my hands. But no one suspected. I'd already shown I disliked the doctor."

"And you deliberately fell down the stairs that day?"

"Yes. Threw myself down. I worked out everything so you'd think I'd come in, heard someone and hurried up to my study. Even to everything being in a neat pile, except my discs. Scattered, as if I'd panicked. It was so simple to fool you into thinking I was hiding something. I was, but not what you thought."

"You really are an accomplished liar, Billie. You make us realise you're lying, but for all the wrong reasons, so you end up looking more innocent than ever."

She took that as a compliment.

"But you could really have hurt yourself falling down those stairs," I said.

"I didn't even intend to break anything. I simply wanted to get into hospital with Lisette."

"To finish the job?"

That suggestion seemed to surprise her. I honestly believe she had forgotten her original intention had been to kill Lisette. "Yes, you did intend to kill her," I went on. "At least, at first you did. But then you discovered that Lisette might be left helpless for life. Like your sister. I thought it was compassion. It wasn't. You'd already worked out that if you could claim your sister's book as your own, why couldn't you do the same with Lisette's? She was actually safe, until she showed signs of life. Until there was an operation that could save her."

"That was all your fault." She spoke with such conviction, I almost believed it. "Whispering in her ear. Telling her she'd be well. It was your fault she had to die."

And she believed that, I'm sure.

She was mad. She had to be.

"And Patrick?"

"I had no idea who he was. But it did work out quite well, didn't it? He looked so guilty all the time. Anyway, he deserved it too."

"Why? What had he ever done to you?"

"He came to the house to visit me, and then he would sit with my sister. He was the only one I knew who ever did that, who ever wanted to spend any time with her. And I knew there was some rapport between them that I couldn't understand. He was beginning to guess. I couldn't risk that..."

"And what about me? Was that you on Pier Thirteen that night?"

"Of course it was," she grinned. "But I wouldn't have killed you, not then. I just wanted to frighten you. I was leaving you till last, Mirren. I liked you, I really did. No, Elsa was supposed to be the next one… I mean, she was almost the very first one to die, even before Annabel. But then I read her criticisms, and they weren't so bad as all the others, I decided to give her a stay of execution."

She lifted her head high, and reminded me then of Victoria. "It's really all your fault, all of you in Octopus. I just wanted to be one of you. I just wanted everything to stay the same. It was you lot who changed things, not me."

She was led away, looking rather contemptuous of us all.

I called after her, making sure I was heard right down the corridor. "Billie!" She turned to me, as did many others. "What's your sister's name?"

"Caroline May," she sneered.

"Caroline May." And now I smiled. "True Octopus member, and…" I said, pointedly, "*Writer.*"

Billie's smile vanished. Her defiance too, as she was hauled down the corridor towards her fate.

"I'm going to do it too," I told James. "Poor Caroline, she didn't have much in her life. Billie stole her writing away from her. I'm going to make sure she gets it back, that she's remembered for what she was, a damned good writer."

EPILOGUE

Three weeks into the new year, I perched myself on a bench down at the waterfront, only a short distance from the red sandstone community centre where the writers group held their meetings.

The air was cold, and the water was glassy. An icy mist was creeping up the river, but for now I could still see the hills on the other side, topped with snow.

The publicity had died down a bit, which I was glad about, though the story of Caroline May had taken the literary world by storm. The books were all being reprinted with her name, not Billie's. The publishers had sold foreign rights all over the globe, and movie rights too. It was a shame that Caroline May would never know her success.

I couldn't stop thinking of her, that pitiful woman, who'd been trapped in a limp, broken body with no one to help or understand her, writing all those beautiful words, forming sentences, paragraphs and chapters, even though she must have known she would never get the credit. But she did it anyway. Why? Because, like me, she was a writer, and she had to write.

As for Billie, she was dead. Committed suicide in her cell. I didn't think she would ever have stood trial anyway. She was mad. Had to be.

Empathy was an important tool in a writer's tool box, hadn't Victoria always said? And I had tried, over the last few weeks, to put myself in Billie's shoes and imagine things from her perspective. I tried to feel sorry for her, remembering the Billie that I once knew, that I once thought was my friend. But I couldn't do any of these things. The truth was that the Billie I thought I knew never really existed.

I'd since found out that Billie had been sabotaging my writing behind my back. No wonder I'd been going through a lean patch. At some point, I'd told her the name of the producer I'd been working with with at the BBC, so she began sending him abusive emails, purportedly from me, threatening to take my ideas elsewhere if they didn't hurry up and commission me. Same for an agent I'd been in touch with about my novel idea, and the editor at the short story magazine who'd published my first two. Now all the strange silences made sense. I'd been blacklisted. It only came to light because one of them, the producer, saw me on the news and put two and two together. He phoned me, and that's when it all came to light. Fortunately, it meant that I was soon able to sort it all out. Things were moving again. So, it turned out that I had been a victim too. I just hadn't realised.

As for Elsa, she had triumphed out of this whole affair. Perhaps she deserved to. She'd been kind in the end, as Billie said, and more thoughtful than the rest of us. Being kind had saved her, till next time she annoys someone, anyway. I heard that her husband, Mike, left her after a violent row. So violent, apparently, that both she and him ended up with bruises. It made me wonder about the allegation she made about Patrick, which she still hadn't retracted. What if the bruises on Elsa's face and throat, that she said were caused by Patrick, had actually been caused by Mike? What would have happened if Mike had come back to find she'd tried to seduce Patrick while he was away? Perhaps they'd had a violent row, and then Elsa had concocted the story about Patrick without his knowledge. He would have had no option but to go along with it. That threw the rest of her story about Patrick into the realm of fantasy, a bit like one of her books, especially after Billie's guilt was established.

Last I heard she Elsa on her way to Hollywood and was working on adapting one of her books as a screenplay. Maybe she would never come back. Who knows? It was over between me and her anyway. She'd lied about Patrick, and didn't even have the guts to take it back.

As for Patrick himself, I'd only heard from him once. He phoned from Marseilles. We'd caught the murderer, so I begged him to come back. He refused.

"I will come back one day, Mirren, but it'll be when my name is fully in the clear and everyone can look me in the eye without wondering whether I am a murderer, or a rapist – especially you."

"That's cruel," I told him. "I always believed in you."

"But there were moments when you were afraid, when, even just for a second, you doubted me."

And there were, I couldn't deny that.

So, Patrick was gone, and God knows if or when I would ever see him again, though before he rang off, he swore his undying, unending passionate love for me.

Dr Bonnar was being charged with malpractice. He was a different man now, a haunted, chastened man, who now said that even if his beloved wife had been totally incapacitated, he would never have destroyed her life. Perhaps it had made him reconsider some of his views. He could hardly bear his life without her now.

A car drew up behind me. The door opened and James Morrish got out, carrying two takeaway cups. He strolled across the ice-flecked grass.

"Latte, as requested," he said, sitting down next to me.

"Thanks, James." I sat there, toasting my hands on the radiated warmth from the coffee cup, while out on the river a white ship cut slowly through the glassy water, heading out to sea.

"I hear Muzz Bonvieux is doing well," said James after a while. "The operation was a success."

"Yes." Though there would be a long recovery ahead. Up to a year, they said. "Last time I went to visit her she got on my wick. That's a sure sign she's getting better." Lisette was more annoyed than anything, that she'd slept through most of the drama. She was determined to make up for it, though. She wanted a piece of Elsa's success, not to mention Caroline May's. "She's competitive, is Lisette." Casting my mind back to the fight with Billie over Lisette's bed, I couldn't believe I actually felt fiercely protective towards her. She certainly never showed any gratitude.

"Are you still driving the taxis?" he asked.

"I'm giving it up, don't worry." It was time to finally accept what my mother, and James Morrish, and even John, my boss, who was short of taxi drivers, were all telling me.

"What will you do?" he asked.

"I don't know," I said. It felt like something new was beckoning me. I needed a change. Octopus was finished, after all. Billie had destroyed it, or maybe we'd done it ourselves. I was still President of the writers' group, but for how long? Part of me wanted to put the whole thing behind me. I would always be a writer, but the writers' group held too many bad memories now.

"I know the owner at the Thistle Hotel. He's looking for a duty manager. I could mention your name?" he said.

"That's where all the police hang out," I answered. "Are you looking to keep an eye on me, D.S. James Morrish?"

"Hardly," he said. "I'll be in Glasgow from now on. And it's D.I. Morrish now."

"Oh, Detective *Inspector*, a promotion?" At least now, he wouldn't have to correct people when they called him Inspector instead of Sergeant.

He nodded, drained his cup and got up. "Well, I'd best get back."

James started towards the car. I called after him. "My mother wants you to come for dinner on Thursday night."

He regarded me with narrowed eyes. "I don't think that would be very professional, do you?"

"I'm no longer a suspect, so I don't know, do you?"

"Always with the questions, Mary Mirren Murdoch."

Always.

He nodded, got into his car and drove off. I stared out at the water, thinking of lost souls and lost friendships, as the white ship vanished into the icy mist.

The End

MIRREN MURDOCH
WILL RETURN IN...

'DEATH MAY SOON
CALL YOU'

ABOUT THE AUTHOR

Jennet Clyde

Jennet Clyde is from Greenock, Scotland. Previously, she was an award-winning children's author. Now she has turned her hand to murder.

Printed in Great Britain
by Amazon